Dave Kijowski

outskirts
press

To my wife Claire,
For her patience reading the drafts.
For her support and encouragement.

CHAPTER 1

Alex set down the small ship–a pinpoint landing on the newly established Moon base main transfer port.

Alex Kijek had done it, he had proven the Earth-bound skeptics wrong. A big smile crossed his face as he shut the systems down.

Alex Kijek commed the tower, "Tower 3, fusion shut down complete, engine shut down complete, buffer diffused. All safe."

He heard static from the tower then: "Thanks, Captain, checking verification, hold it. Ok, all checks complete. Welcome home, Captain,"

"Ok, thanks, now get me out of this thing," said Alex. "I got people waiting on me."

"OK, they are on their way. One moment please, the boss has something to say."

Oh, great, now the speeches were starting while he was still cramped in a little blister pack.

"Daddy! Daddy! Are you there? This is Tommy, I love you, Daddy, come get us, Mommy is here too. Hurry, come now, we are waiting right here."

"Tommy, my favorite astronaut, I just landed, be there in a minute, and..."

"Mommy wants to talk, can you hear, Daddy, where are you?"

Alex just relaxed with a big smile on his face and rested back into the pilot's seat.

Laura, "Hello Mr. Spaceman, love you, they are going to be taking us down to the tunnel. Tommy is really excited. He has something for you; he's been working on on it for a while."

Alex, "Love you, Laura. I will have you both in my arms in a few minutes, looks like they've pulled me in and are working on the hatch."

Alex could hear the rattling and clanging sounds of the bolts being removed. It would be moments now.

The dull light from the hatch flooded the small cockpit as the tech pulled off the cover. Alex unfastened his belt and flipped off his helmet as he was pulled out by the strong arms of a figure in military uniform. It was General Holmes, probably his closest friend and his current commander. He was primarily responsible for the Moon base propulsion research and gave 100% backing to Alex's test flight despite all the skeptics on Earth.

Holmes pulled Alex out of the pilot's seat into a big hug, "Congratulations, Alex, You did it! You're the man!"

Holmes kept his arm over Alex's shoulder, "Man, oh man! Am I glad to see you, you broke all the records. You're a Superhero now, like in the old days."

Alex couldn't hold back the grin. "I am glad to be on solid ground again. Come on Commander, there is nothing heroic about it, it was all just a matter of enough food and water, so give me a break. Now where is my son and Laura?"

"They are down at the door, the doctors want to give you a quick check, and then everyone is waiting for you. Tommy has the girls to keep him company and Teresa is with Laura."

"Doctors? They are checking me right now? Why do I need to see them?"

Holmes said, "Its protocol, dude."

Alex groaned. "Let's get it done,"

They both stepped into the elevator and rode down to zero level.

As they walked out, there was Doctor Severin and his crew waiting. They quickly formed up around him.

Holmes grinned. "Look at the camera and say Space,"

Alex did as he said. "How about Ass instead."

Holmes just laughed, and moved away as the doctor's crew crowded up to shake Alex's hand.

At that moment, Alex heard, "Daddy, Daddy, here we are over here—over here."

The high-pitched yell of his 5-year-old was very clear and Alex turned immediately, excusing himself from the group of admirers.

He could see Tommy and his wife Laura rushing toward him, Tommy carrying a very large shiny plate of some kind. As they came together, Alex took a knee to hug his young son as he ran into his arms.

"Daddy! Daddy! Here is your hero medal, me and Mommy made it! We love you! Put it on, Daddy, put it on!"

Laura came up as he hugged the boy and squeezed his head in a tender hug.

Alex stood immediately, and gave Laura a long deep kiss eventually leaning her back in the classic welcome-home-sailor pose.

When they broke it off, Laura and Alex had big smiles.

Laura said, "You did it, hero,"

"Yes, but you're the wind behind my sails."

They both seemed to notice the commotion around them at the same time. Glancing around they saw a sea of comm cameras recording their every movement."

"I guess we should have expected that," said Laura, nodding her head toward the crowd.

"Daddy, look!" said Tommy while trying to get his dad to look at what he held in his small hands, "look what we got for you!"

"What have you got there? Mister Astronaut."

"Ah, Daddy, I'm not an astronaut yet, but here, you need to put your medal on." He lifted up the plate-shaped object he'd been carrying.

It was a piece of fiberboard covered on both sides with some sort of sparkling material with a big loop of red, white and blue ribbon attached to the back. On the front in blue, by the hand of a 5-year-old was printed, "My Dad Best Hero Ever Love, Tommy"

"That's beautiful, Tommy, did you make it?"

"I worked on it real hard, and Mommy helped too."

Tommy held it up to his Dad's face. "Put it on, put it on, Daddy."

"I can't put it on. Only the most important person on the Moon can award medals."

"Well, who?"asked Tommy, "Let's do it right now."

Alex said, "He is standing right here,"

"Where? Let's get him; Mommy, do you know?"

"It's you, Tommy, you're the most important person."

Tommy grinned "Ah-w,w, Daddy."

Laura positioned Tommy a little closer to his dad and moved his arm a little higher to reach her husband's bowed head.

The boy looked up at his mom and dad and said, "Ok, you are awarded the best-hero-ever medal." He started to loop the ribbon over his dad's head, but turned to Mom, "Can you help me, I think Daddy's head is too big."

Laura laughed and bumped her hip against Alex. "Well, Tommy, that's for sure. Let's see if we can get that medal over that oversized head." Laughing, Alex looked up at her and smiled warmly as they placed the ribbon and medal over his head.

A little later, after Alex had had time to shower and get a change of uniform. He was pushed by Dr. Severin in front of a crowd in the base cafeteria.

Dr. Severin went to the mic, "Welcome everyone, I know we all want to get back to work."

He paused as a low murmur of displeasure ran through the assembled audience. After a moment he continued, "But I thought we could take just a little time to honor our own. Captain Alex Kijek, who has developed and proven the greatest advanced propulsion system since the wheel. His development will open Mars and the outer system to human settlement and exploration on a grand scale. With this development, we now have a very cost-effective and rapid system that frees the human race from Earth to become a space-faring civilization."

Turning to Captain Kijek, he said, "Captain, a few words please."

Alex smiled and stepped forward to a spot beside Dr. Severin. He was dressed in his dress blues, with the big medal that Tommy had given him dangling on his chest.

"Thank you, everyone, but you know you all helped in this venture, from making the components when most countries on the Earth tried to shut us down, even some of the socialist states in our own America joined in the blockade. So, you all did it. It is your accomplishment. I just jotted down a few notes and sat in a seat for two weeks. Thanks to you and, of course, I want to thank my wife Laura and son Tommy, who gave me permission to go on this little vacation."

There was a scattering of laughter from the audience. Alex motioned to his wife who'd been standing in front of the crowd. Tommy leaned in and whispered something in his dad's ear. The captain nodded.

He faced the audience again. "My son, has awarded me this magnificent medal. He says I'm a hero." Looking down at Tommy with his arm still resting on his shoulder. 'Thank you, son. I'll cherish this forever."

Bending over, he picked Tommy up in his arms and held him up while the crowd cheered.

Dr. Severin stepped to the fore, "Ok, everyone we need to get back to work, there are some critical items that must be completed on the ship and the launch area. We'll plan a more formal celebration once everything is settled down and all the safety checks have been locked in."

Dr. Severin turned to Alex. "You're free to go, have fun for a few days, but we'll need you back soon to start going over the data. Congratulations."

Alex shook his hand, "Thank you, Doctor, are you sure it's, Ok? Do you need me to come for the down-cycling just in case?"

"No, we're good, the same crew that set it up is cycling it down, you picked them yourself, so right now you're on leave. I have to run up to the tower right now, apparently, they caught someone in the wrong area and security wants me there. Thanks, and have fun."

Alex set Tommy down. Then holding his hand, he turned to Laura and said, "Well, should we head home? I have some sleep and a few other things to catch up on." He then leaned in and gave Laura a gentle kiss on the lips.

The three headed out of the cafeteria into the hallway to the elevator that would take them down to the resident area of the base. As the doors swung open, Laura got a call. She started talking rapidly. Finally, she turned to Alex, "Sorry, hon, I've got to get over to the ready room, one of your crew got injured with a fitting or something, and they need another hand for a bit. Apparently Dr. Severin had been celebrating a little prematurely. I'll be right back, give me fifteen minutes." She gave Alex a quick kiss, then bend and gave Tommy a hug and a kiss on the head as she stood.

"You take care of Daddy while I am gone. I will be right back."

Tommy responded back, "I love you Mommy, Oh, hurry back for our plan to Welcome Daddy home."

"I will, love you guys." She then turned and hurried towards the terminal doors.

Alex and Tommy waved to her until she crossed over the emergency seal door and turned the corner.

"Come on, Tommy," said Alex, "Mommy will be back in a bit. Let's go down and talk about what you've been doing while I was gone."

Tommy, who was hanging on Alex's leg said, "OK, Daddy, we are going to have so much fun, and when Mommy gets back you will get the big surprise!"

"Big surprise?"

"Oh no, um, wait, you're not supposed to know that."

They reached the elevator and entered when the door opened. Alex pushed the button to take them down to the resident level, "Ok, Tommy, I didn't hear anything."

Riding down to the resident level Tommy gave Alex's leg a good hug, "Thanks Daddy, Mommy will, aah never mind."

The elevator door started to open to their level when a sudden jolt shook the cabin and the door stopped in a half open position. The implants in Alex's ear began receiving a terminal evacuation signal. He heard the alarms on the residential floor sounding off through the half-opened door.

Alarmed, Alex squeezed through the elevator doorway and picking up his son, he jogged down the resident hallway and into the daycare center. The children were being gathered into the sealed safe rooms in the back of the center. One of the teachers saw Alex with Tommy and hurried toward him. "I'll take him, Captain; we all need to be here until the all clear is given." Alex bent to say a few words to Tommy, but the teacher pulled him away saying, "Sorry, no time!"

Alex saw Tommy running over to his friend Arty, General Holmes's young son.

Turning, he headed back to the elevator at a sprint. He was already getting assembly calls for all personnel to report to emergency stations. On reaching the elevator, Alex made a quick turn and bounded up the stairs. Even though he had not been in a centrifuge since he departed for Mars, he still could move faster up the stairwell than taking the elevator and he did not want to chance getting stuck in one. At the top of the stairwell, he turned toward the terminal entrance that Laura had taken just moments before. As he rounded the corner, he could see other personnel in lab coats and overalls come rushing at him out of the terminal section. The broadcast message in his implant now changed to *evacuate the terminal section immediately*. He continued to the next corner and was relieved to see Laura headed toward him. She and one of the ground crew were helping an injured man.

He rushed to her. "Here let me get that, you get out of here, Tommy's safe down in the sealed area."

"Oh, thank God, we need to hurry, the shell is collapsing."

Alex had already pulled one of the injured man's arms over his shoulder, and started running with him and other ground crewmen toward the seal doors. Laura was running ahead of them.

They were now only a few yards from the doors and Alex

spotted sentries dispatched to make sure the seal doors were clear if they needed to close quickly. They were set with magnetic rails so that they would close with force in seconds if the need arose.

The sentry was waving them to hurry shouting, "Come on! Come on! Let's step on it, people!" The main rush of personnel had already cleared the terminal so they were likely the last few.

As they passed through the exit, they heard the sentry, "Command, all clear visual on T8, Clear check to seal."

They slowed to a walk. As they did so, the crewman they were helping stumbled, dragging Alex to the floor with him. The other crewman was pulled to a knee still holding the arm of the injured man across his back.

As they struggled, a sudden shudder erupted through the entry to the hallway and the floor shifted, throwing Alex to the wall and knocking both crewmen on their faces. Alex snapped his head toward the seal doors, and saw Laura sprawled into the near wall with an arm and hand draped over the support rail that ran alongside both walls of the hallway. She was not moving. The sentry had been thrown back into the terminal, but had already gained his feet and was heading toward the emergency seal panel just inside the hallway entrance.

As Alex took in this view, the outer wall of the terminal section behind the rushing sentry was developing large running cracks. Almost as if in slow motion, pieces of terminal began popping out of the wall and disappearing out into the empty void of the Moon. Alex rose and dove toward Laura, grabbing hold of her arms. He then stood and was about to drape the arm over his shoulder when the whole section of wall in the terminal disappeared. He could see the sentry violently jerked away from the control panel and sucked out to the vacuum of the Moon. Laura's body was pulled horizontally as he held her arm and instantly grasped the support rail. He could see other bodies and objects pass by him and Laura in his periphery. Lights around the seal were flashing as something heavy smashed into him, knocking his head against the wall with a heavy impact. The atmosphere rushing out of the terminal was sucking the breath out of his lungs making it difficult to breathe. He still had a hold of Laura as these seconds passed. Laura's face suddenly snapped up as she revived. Looking him in the face, she seemed to instantly recognize the situation they were in.

He saw her eyes widen as something smashed into him and crushed his hand, pain shooting through it as he lost his grip on the rail.

Their bodies both headed toward the vacuum of the Moon, eyes fixed on each other and somehow Alex found his now mangled hand in hers as these fractions of seconds passed. Their faces mirrored a dual reflection of fear and calm, knowing what was about to happen but knowing also the deep love they had for each other.

A spike of fear hit Alex as his eyes picked up a flash of movement. In mere milliseconds a barrier cut across his vision, then blackness.

In the moments that followed, emergency response crews entered the hallway and found Alex unconscious. He had substantial head trauma and was bleeding heavily. The heavy emergency seal doors had closed at high speed, severing his arms above the elbows and leaving him wedged into the center of the closed emergency doors. The emergency medical personal had to work quickly to seal the open veins, stop the bleeding, then hooking up an IV. He was then quickly moved to the base station hospital.

Six people lost their lives in the T8 hallway that day, the sentry who manually triggered the emergency door, Laura, Alex's wife, and four others.

CHAPTER 2

Alex lay in a white hospital bed, his eyes slowly opening to the low lighting in the room. He recognized that he was hooked up to monitoring instruments with an IV tube hanging down toward his arm. As he tried to move, he realized he was strapped down and his shoulders were elevated. Thoughts raced through his mind as he tried to remember how and why he was here. Slowly, a deep hurt welled up in him as his last conscious memories overcame him. Heavy tears and sobbing choked him. Alex let out a loud cry, and tried to pull loose. It was then that he realized his arms were gone. He screamed, thrashing and tearing at the restraints. But he was bound tight and did not move. A small discoloration occurred in the IV tube attached to his body. A blue icon also appeared on the monitor screen next to his bed. As the fluid worked its way down the tube and into the captain's body his movements slowed. He felt a heaviness in his muscles and mind. In seconds he was still, his eyes closed. He heard someone entering the room, then he was out.

Suddenly Alex was awake. As his eyes popped open, he faced a woman in a white smock sitting on the side of his bed.

The woman spoke quickly, "Sorry about this, but they told me to be quick. I am Doctor Milos. I have been treating you for your brain injuring. Doctor Sinto, who isn't here has been working on your arms. I understand he had only been able to get the electrode implants in before they stopped him."

Alex interrupted, "Hold on here; what is going on? Where is Doctor Severin? Where's my kid, my wife, Laura!"

There was a loud impatient voice from a man in the back of the room, "If you're done, doctor, get out of the way; we need to get this criminal processed!"

The doctor turned her head and snapped at the man, "Officer, I am in charge here and nothing happens until I approve the patient is physically fit. Now back off until I am finished with my exam!"

There was quiet in the room as the doctor turned back to Alex, "Please remain calm Mr. Kijek, you need to remain calm, and trust me. I have very little time."

Alex was a bit shocked by the remarks he heard from the officer. He was also realizing, because of the pull of gravity on his body, that he was not at the Moon base, but was on Earth. He assumed he was in America, but wasn't sure. Alex had plenty of questions, but also realized from the words and tone of the officer and the doctor that he needed to control himself. He focused and reached down into himself. He looked down at the sheet on the bed, paused and in a low voice, almost a whisper, addressed the doctor,

"Yes, Doctor, thank you for your help; please tell me as much as you can."

The doctor pulled her analyzer out of her chest pocket and held it up to his face, she held it there a second and then turned again to look behind her, as if she was checking how close the others were to her.

"Mr. Kijek, you are in the military hospital at New Mexico space port and you are about to be placed under arrest.

You have been here in a coma for almost three months. You were brought down because the facilities on the moon were overwhelmed by the accident. As you may or may not know, the current Supreme Court, at the request of the government of the United States, has interpreted the Constitution as not requiring ongoing elections. In addition, the Congress and the president have passed legislation that the use of a spacecraft can only be powered by propulsion systems approved and manufactured on Earth."

The doctor was almost whispering in her reply; she now held up the instrument in her hand and pulled down his cheek below his left eye and shone a light from the instrument into it while she viewed a monitor to the side of the bed, she then did the same to the right.

Alex whispered, "My wife and son?"

The doctor pulled back, "Mr. Kijek, I am so sorry, but our understanding is that your wife has passed in the same accident where you received your injuries."

The doctor continued, "I am sorry to rush so. I am not sure, but I understand that her remains have been turned over to her father."

Alex paused, tears burning the edges of his eyes. It is what he had expected when he asked the question. He had already felt it in his heart. He managed to choke out, "What about my son, where is he?"

The doctor stopped, "I know he is safe from what I have heard, but I don't know any more."

She stood up and bent over him placing her instrument on his head and making a few adjustments.

"Hold still please," she then turned and looked at the monitor again which showed an image of the brain activity with a readout appearing down the side.

"Mr. Kijek, I am finished now. I won't see you again.

Please be aware that I am very sorry for your loss, but you need to take these next few moments before I leave to brace yourself for some very tough times. These people behind me represent the federal government, and you may not know it but things have changed quite a bit recently. I was hoping that you would be able to regain your full strength but the powers to be say No!"

The doctor rested her hand on the captain's shoulder a moment, "Mr. Kijek, for many people you are a hero, a pioneer, but to the people behind me, you are a scapegoat and you are going to be dragged through the mud. May God himself make you strong!"

With that, she gave his shoulder a final pat, then turned to those standing in the darkness behind her. "Based on the parameters you have outlined the patient is recovered." She then stood and walked swiftly toward the door. Before she reached it, however, the lights of the room were switched on. The brightness was too much for the captain and he instinctively closed his eyes and turned away from the light.

A shadow blocked out some of the glare and Alex was aware that someone had moved up beside the bed to his left.

"Open your eyes, Kijek!"

Slowly Alex opened his eyes and saw a man of smaller stature leaning over him. He had a longer than usual neck for his size and thin narrow head. His eyes were inset and small and he had a pale complexion. The man had on a suit and tie and was handing Alex a document and seemed obtuse to the fact that Alex hand no arms.

As the man stood in that position, he turned his head to someone toward the foot of the bed, "OK, Tina now!"

Immediately, bright lights flooded the area, cameras flashed and again his eyes reflexively closed. The man beside him started speaking while looking down at him, "Alexander Kijek, you are under arrest for the capital murders of the thirty seven individuals on Moon Base Command, and the terrorist bombing attack you committed there. In addition, you are subject to prosecution for violation of the Space Control Act, for defying the lawful orders of CASA." He through the envelope onto Alex's chest.

The man then turned toward the group gathered in the hospital room, As District Prosecutor for the New Mexico Region, I will charge you too the full extent of the Law."

The prosecutor then looked over toward the woman who he had signaled earlier, "How was that, Tina?"

Tina immediately responded, "That was excellent, Jon, you're the greatest." She flashed him a smile while turning a little sideways and winking.

The prosecutor immediately picked up on it and continued, "Please, ladies and gentlemen of the Free Press. Remember to please use my title and full name in your articles. And even though we are all friends, we still must let our comrades in the public know the full truth about the prosecution and conviction of this criminal. And also remember to submit your articles to my office before publication on the net. Remember we are all faithful civil servants and must work together for the common purpose."

Alex had remained quiet while the man in the suit was talking, trying to digest the advice that the doctor had given; even hearing the remarks coming from the suit he struggled to keep his outside manner calm.

A police officer in uniform then pushed his way through the crowded hospital room to the strange man. He bent close to his head and spoke in a low voice, but loud enough for Alex to hear, "Sorry, sir, but a lawyer just showed up saying he represents the criminal."

The prosecutor turned to the officer and in a loud voice with barely concealed anger screamed, "That can't be, I had it all arranged; it is to be one of our people and they were told not to be here!"

"Sir, it is not one of the ones we had arranged for, in fact there are a couple of them and they have all the documents. I have to let them speak to him."

"No, get them out of here, get someone from the party on the line, this can't happen now! I am to do some interviews here. I need this to get the party to back me."

"Sir, look, you can make something up," said the officer, "if this man has to be arrested..." The officer paused, "Here they come now."

The prosecutor looked over toward the door, he then turned to the gathered news gaggle, "Hey, everyone, we need to get moving quickly, Officer Lopez informs me that due to the time constraints the criminal must be processed for arrest immediately and searched by the police as there has been discovery of information for a possible escape attempt by the criminal. Please take over here Officer Lopez. Ladies and gentlemen of the press, we must exit the room and hospital. We can re-group in front of the building. Now we must go quickly."

With that, the prosecutor headed toward the door, jostling people as he went. Simultaneously, the group of suited men Lopez had pointed out to him as the criminal's lawyers made their way toward Captain Kijek's bed.

The prosecutor leaned in toward Captain Kijek's lawyers and said, "You'd better have every 'i' dotted and 't' crossed, because it won't only be me after you, but the Party as well. Didn't you get the warning about this case? What is your firm? I am going to shut you down, not only in my district, but in the whole nation."

The new lawyer, a younger man, and a little taller that the prosecutor, was stone-face while the prosecutor spoke.

"Thank you, sir," replied Captain Kijek's lawyer, "we are here to assure the rights of our client are protected. I assume you are finished since you are leaving. You will find our information here," and handed him an 8 x 11 envelope.

The prosecutor grabbed the envelope from his hand and ripped open the top, pulling out the contents.

Kijek's lawyer continued, "And as you have accepted the envelope, Mr. Prosecutor, it also contains a demand for all the information you collected in this case against my client. It also includes a demand for the arresting documents. This has already been filed and recorded with the court."

Prosecutor, "What? It cannot be, no one was allowed." He stopped looking at the papers and leered up at the new lawyer, "Well, we will see about this...," and turned to leave.

Kijek's lawyer interrupted him, "Sir, may I have the arrest documents and charges? I can scan them, and as you can see from the filing, they are past due in violation of the court order."

The prosecutor turned back to him in a rage, "You will get them when I am ready. I dictate to the court the law in this region. Now talk to Officer Lopez who is in charge of the criminal. I have an appointment I have to get to." He then turned and hurried out the door.

The three lawyers who came to represent Captain Kijek stood by while the rest of the people in the room followed the prosecutor out with their recording devices still on. After their exit, the new lawyers turned toward Captain Kijek. Beside Alex was Officer Lopez and another officer who had moved in while the reporters exited. Officer Lopez was looking over the stumps where the captain's arms had once been. He was starting to pick off one of the bandages that was over a circuit extension for an artificial limb that had just recently been implanted into his arm.

Captain Kijek gave out a moan at that moment.

The lawyer spoke up, "Officer, what are you doing to my client, you are being recorded torturing my client, do you have a license to practice medicine in the district?"

Officer Lopez turned to the new lawyer. "Sorry, sir we are trying to process him, but it looks like he is asleep, and I need a DNA sample for the arrest record."

The lawyer replied, "Officer, this is Captain Kijek, his DNA has been recorded and stored since he was born. You know it appears when you fill out the form."

"Sir, the prosecutor said this is a special case," said Lopez, "and that we need to make sure we had the right person, I mean Mr. Kijek. You know, that sims have been showing up lately for arrests and prosecutions instead of the real person."

"OK, since it is my client, you will permit Mr. Terrel here, my second, to get the sample for you as he is a medical doctor licensed in the district."

That's Ok, sir, I can just call a doctor," said Lopez. "After all, we are in a hospital."

"Officer, I have you and your subordinate there recorded in the process of torturing my client. Do you want me to play it for you?"

"No sir, that isn't necessary, but officially we..."

Kijek's Lawyer was losing patience. "Officially you have been ordered to get a DNA read, you are wasting my time, and you are interfering in the defense of my client. All this will need to go into the record and be added to your record and that of your colleague there. It would be too bad to ruin a career of such a fine young man, and what about you, officer?" the lawyer walked closer to Lopez and bent over to read his label.

"Lopez, Officer Lopez, you have been with the force quite a while now, right? I am sure you have a nice pension coming to you in a few years."

Office Lopez eyes widened and he turned to the younger officer and said, "Spenser, go down to the vehicle and get my manual, I am going to need it for the arrest process."

The other officer, who was shorter than Lopez, but obviously in much better physical condition, had been standing to the side taking in the interchange between the two, "No problem, sir, I have mine right here." Spencer pulled his phone out and started to hand it to Lopez.

Lopez just looked at him for a second without taking Spencer's device, "Spenser, go down and get my manual!"

Spenser looked from the Kijek's lawyer to Lopez, pulled his phone back, and slid it into his pocket. He then slipped his way past Lopez and exited.

"Ok, here, get the record." Lopez handed a small round device to Mr. Terril as he passed him on his way to Kijek.

"Hold up a sec--Terril is it? I will need your credentials."

He pulled out his phone and held it up. Terrel held his hand out as he passed Lopez and the officer waved the device over Terril's hand.

Lopez then held the device up to confirm the document, "Ok, fine, now please hurry."

Terril moved to the captain's bed side, "Captain, are you awake?"

"Yes, I am," replied Kijek in a calm voice.

"Do you object to the DNA Recording?"

"No."

"Please, can you stick your tongue out for a second?"

Kijek complied and Terril held the device to his tongue. There was a small beep.

Terril looked at the info on the screen of the device, then turned the device to Lopez.

"Ok, I need to do a cross check to verify." Lopez pulled his phone device out again, and spoke into it, "App DNA cross check, Alexander Kijek, confirm."' He watched the screen a second, then spoke again, "Send the cross-check confirmation to file open criminal arrest Alexander Kijek, date and time."

Lopez turned his head back toward the lawyer as he started for the door, "OK counselor, the criminal has been processed and is under arrest. He cannot be moved either from the bed or room, we have an officer posted outside the door and, once you leave, there will be one inside also, due to the flight risk of the criminal. You have twenty minutes. If you need more, you know where to file the request. I don't want any problems. Understand?"

Lopez then turned and left the room.

Kijek's lawyer simply nodded. He then turned and sat down on the bed beside the captain. As he did this, Kijek began to speak, but the lawyer quickly held up his hand. He then pulled a small area distortion device out of his suit pocket and laid it on the captain's chest to activate it. Kijek watched the man intently, forcing back the flood of questions oppressing him. The lawyer then withdrew a small pill type dispenser and pressed out two square flat tabs. He took one of the tabs and pressed it on to his top lip and spoke, "Captain, we are here to help you. I am going to apply this tab to your lip as I did to mine so don't be alarmed."

He then proceeded to speak quietly in a rapid voice, "We are not here to explain the situation to you, these devices will temporarily block the bugs they have planted in your room and the tabs distort them from being able to read our lips."

"You are in grave danger, Holmes sent us. We will not tell you more in case our plan fails..."

The captain interrupted, "I need to know about my son,"

The lawyer remained still so as to make sure none of his body movements would give clues as to the conversation,

"Your son is with his grandfather here on Earth, there are some legal procedures that have been pulled, it will be explained later. But be aware you are to be put on a show trial and imprisoned or executed. The Party has not decided yet. They are trying to use you as a bargaining chip to halt development of your propulsion system and try to regain control over near Earth Space, Mars and the extended space colonies.

Listen, we have only a few minutes now. Mr. Terril is going to step in and examine you. As he does, he will inject you with a device, do not react, it will feel like an injection. The rest of your day will be normal, by this evening you will fall into a deep sleep. Listen, this is important. If you wake, if the drug doesn't work properly, you must not react, but remain as if you are asleep. No matter the situation, do not make any noise or take any action that may cause..."

Just then Terril came up behind the lawyer and whispered in his ear, "Sir, I need to start now."

The lawyer immediately stood up and Terril took his place, leaving the device on Captain Kijek's chest. Kijek noticed that Terril also had a tab stuck to his upper lip. In his hand, Terril had a device similar to what the doctor had used earlier. Without a word Terril placed the device on his head in the same manner as the doctor had earlier. He then turned to the lawyer, and nodded.

Turning back to the captain he reached out and held him by what remained of his left upper arm. Terril now held the captain with his left hand on his triceps and his right hand on the end at the stub where the electronics had been implanted.

"Good," Terril said, "just let me check one more thing."

He then reached across the captain and held both arms behind the triceps and pulled them forward, looking closely at the implants, "Can you sit up a little, Captain, and face me?" The captain adjusted his position in the bed even though he felt weak.

Terril continued, "Do you have any pain around the implants, Captain? At this point it should feel as though you still have your forearms and hands. Also please look downward with your head. Imagine you are wriggling the fingers on both hands as if they were still there."

The captain tilted his head down and immediately felt a little pinch under his left triceps where Terrill's hand grasped him. However, he did nothing and kept his head down, focused on moving his imaginary fingers until Terril let go of his arms. Kijek realized that Terril had just injected him with the shot the lawyer had spoken of. Terril then quickly picked up the device that he had placed on the captain's chest. It had slid off to the side when the captain sat up, then he quickly pulled the tab off the captain's lip and himself and placed them someplace out of sight.

Seconds later, Office Lopez accompanied by the younger officer came bursting into the room.

"Ok Counselor, your time is up, please leave the premises now."

"OK officer, thanks for your efforts, I will leave my associate, Mr. Washington, here in case we have a further need to meet with our client."

"No, you are ordered off the premises, the prosecutor has attained an order from his own judge expelling you. I imagine you will be disbarred in this district by tomorrow.

You seem to be on the wrong side of the Party in the New Mexico district, so good luck with that."

Officer Lopez turned to Spenser and said, "Check out the criminal."

He then turned back to Kijek's lawyer and his two associates, "Out into the hall, now!"

The lawyer didn't move, so Officer Lopez grabbed him by the upper arm and started shuffling him toward the door.

The lawyer began protesting, "Officer Lopez, this is assault and against the law and my rights; this is also all being recorded."

Lopez replied, "The Party decides who has rights in this district, do you happen to belong to the Party here?"

"No, but that should not…"

At that point Lopez shoved the lawyer through the doorway and into the hall.

Standing in front of the lawyer in the hallway was the prosecutor with a score of additional police officers.

The prosecutor stepped up to the lawyer and said, "You are going to be arrested, it is illegal to use cloaking devises to interfere with a criminal prosecution in this district. "

"Mr. Prosecutor, there is no such law."

"Oh didn't you know? Judge Amaldod just made a ruling on that for the district. You must be a pretty poor lawyer if you are not up on the current law."

The lawyer paused a second as if consulting something, "You have no proof or evidence to arrest me or my associates."

"Search them, I want the cloaking device and those tabs."

The group was roughly pushed up against the wall and the police began an aggressive body search. They dumped the contents of the lawyers' suitcases onto the floor and began kicking the contents around scattering them across the hallway.

"Prosecutor, you are violating client-lawyer privilege."

"What decade are you from, Counselor."

The prosecutor then stood back from the lawyer to watch the search process. After a few moments an officer came over to the prosecutor and he spoke quietly to him.

"What? That can't be, we saw them, search again."

The officer insisted, "Sir, we searched and scanned, the devices are not here."

"Search the room and the hallway."

The officer walked off, collected a few of the other officers, and headed back into Captain Kijek's room while the remaining officers guarded the three lawyers.

Meanwhile as young officer Spenser approached the captain's bed, he pulled his comm device out of his leg pocket and appeared to be taking notes.

"Sorry sir, orders, it will just take a minute. I need to search you for the record...procedure, you know," as he spoke, he looked around the captain's bedding. He then reached down and placed his com device on the bedding near where Terril had been sitting.

"Lift up your left arm," he said as he reached for the stub where the captain's forearm and hand used to be. Kijek feared the officer would find the spot where Terril had injected him. The captain stiffened a bit as his arm was still tender in the area, but to his relief Spenser said nothing. Instead, he felt Spenser's thumb rubbing over the location. As he did so, the tenderness dissipated.

Spencer then spoke in a threatening manner, "Why did that lawyer look at your implants?"

"How should I know?" Kijek said dryly. "I did what he said, I am no doctor."

"Well, we will find out soon enough, the whole lot of them will be in custody, the same as you, once the prosecutor is finished with them. We don't hold well with crimes against the people in this district."

Spenser then forcefully pushed the captain's arms aside. Kijek was not ready for that and winced and groaned at the sudden soreness he felt in his upper shoulders.

A smile spread across Officer Spenser's face as he leaned in with his face close to the captain's and braced himself up on either side with his hands on the bed.

"You think that hurt, wait till we get you up to the penitentiary, if you last that long. You will pay dearly for your selfish greed and crimes."

Spenser was still in that position grinning when Officer Lopez came back into the room. "Spenser, back off, we need to search the room. We need to find out where they stashed those devices they used."

Spenser pushed himself back from Captain Kijek, and as he did so the captain felt something press against his left thigh, but did not look down. Spenser stood with his comm in his hand. "Yes sir, should I take notes and do a recording."

Lopez, "No, just start searching, and stop taking notes, that is going to get you into trouble someday."

"But Sir, we learned that keeping records is a best practice for strengthening the people's justice. "

"Can it, Spenser! And turn that thing off and put it away."

Spenser closed up the unit and slipped it into his thigh pocket.

"Listen, and you better pay attention," said Lopez, "because this is the real world here. All the mumbo jumbo applies to civilians, not to us, not to the police, to our unit here. If there needs to be any recording done it will be by me or one of our union or party representatives. Keep that advice in mind if you want to move up the ladder. Now, find those devices. "

The group of officers searched the room entirely, moving the captain roughly about on and off the bed a number of times and flipping the bedding and medical equipment into a mess on the floor. Captain Kijek groaned repeatedly as his body was moved, lifted, and shoved around the room. The rest of the small hospital room was also torn apart including parts of the ceiling and walls. After coming up with nothing, Lopez called out the door for the device detection technicians to set up their equipment and do a thorough search for electronics.

As they were finishing up and having found nothing, the floor nurse came into the room. Seeing the activities of the police and that Captain Kijek was lying on the floor partially across the bedding, she started screaming at Lopez and the technicians to get out. She then signaled for the floor manager and orderlies to head to the room. She knelt down and began caring for the captain.

As she did this, Officer Lopez dialed up the district attorney, "Sir, they are kicking us out." He listened for a second, then responded, "Yes sir, this is a secure channel. Ok, I will wait for your assistant, what's his name?" Lopez was silent for a while as he listened. "Yes sir, I understand, I will keep everyone out till the specialist arrives. "

Putting his phone in his pocket he turned to the nurse and said, "This room is a crime scene, you must leave immediately or face arrest for obstruction."

The nurse turned toward him with a look of anger on her face, but before she could speak Lopez pulled out his stunner. The nurse recognized the weapon for the government control device it was and with her head down she stood and left the room without a word.

Lopez then shouted out into the hall, "Spencer, block off this hallway and use force as needed; no one gets into this room until the investigation is over."

Another officer responded, "Sir, Spencer had to take a break, he will be back in a minute." Then seeing Spencer coming down the hallway he added "Oh, here he comes now."

Lopez, "Go get him in here! You men..." Lopez stuck his head into the hallway, "Block this area off, no one gets through, this has become a crime scene. Keep me informed on anyone that arrives from the prosecutor's office. I don't want to talk to anyone else."

When Spencer reached the room's doorway, Lopez asked, "Spencer, did you get that?"

"Yes sir, no one gets through except the prosecutor's representative, anyone we know?"

"No questions, just usher them in as soon as they get here, and don't leave again until this is over."

"Yes sir!"

Lopez then backed into the room and shut the door behind him. He reached down and made sure none of his devices were recording, turning them off for good measure, then he slid them into his special shield pocket when he wanted to be undetected and left alone.

Half-talking to himself and to the captain lying on the floor he mumbled, "Why did I get picked for this? This is out of my league, I'm going back to the street division, this political crap is not worth it."

He then took a look at the captain lying on the floor, thought for a second, then headed to the room's restroom to relieve himself while still talking.

"We were only supposed to be here half an hour, I got work piling up at the precinct and I have to get home early for the kid's soccer game. I guess you have a kid so you must know how that goes."

He stopped for a second, and you could hear him washing his hands and running the ancient style air hand dryer.

He then came back out into the room, and bent over the captain, "Ok, Mister, let's get you straightened out here a little, but don't you ever mention this you see, with you being a vicious criminal and all. Are you even awake? Alive?"

Getting no response, Officer Lopez straightened the mattress, making it level on the floor, then he straightened out the captain on it to what looked like a semi-comfortable position. Finally, he looked around for a pillow and tilting his head up a little he placed it under Kijek's head.

Lopez then stood and, picking a chair up off the floor, he placed it up beside the door and sat down to wait for the prosecutor's representative. He then reached in and pulled his com out from the special shield pocket he had learned to always carry with him these days. He did not, however, turn the device back on.

It had only been a few minutes when there was a knock on the door, "Sir, it's Spencer, there is someone here that says he is from the prosecutor's office, but they have no I.D."

Lopez, speaking through the still closed door, asked, "Do you recognize him?"

"No sir, never saw him before. He handed me an envelope to give you."

Please slip it under the door."

"Yes sir."

Lopez grabbed the envelope as soon as the edge appeared under the door, he was getting to the point that he just wanted this day to be over, the sooner the better, and get home. He quickly opened it to find a small note inside,

It said, "Read quickly. Once you read it the paper will evaporate, but that won't get you off the hook. This is a threat so treat it as such. Have all your men turn off their devices and push everyone off the floor hallway. Do it now, then let me into the room and you stay outside at the door. Do it now."

As his eyes read the last words of the message, the paper evaporated out of his hand and he felt a slight burn to his fingertips but saw no residue there.

Lopez spoke through the door, "Spencer, I am coming out, call the men together and have them hand you all of their communicators and personnel phones, then order them to clear everyone from the hallway except the person from the prosecutor's office."

Upon exiting the room, Lopez looked around for the person who had brought the envelope from the prosecutor's office but only found Spencer and his men standing around the door.

"Where is he?"

Spencer said, "I think he's hanging out around the corner. "What was in the envelope?"

"Special orders, now Spencer, do you have all the comms and phones?"

Spencer pointed across the hallway. "They are all over on that cabinet."

"Ok, it will only be for a few minutes."

He peered down the hall for any evidence of the representative.

Lopez pulled a larger screen bag out of his front pocket and handed it to Spencer, "Put everything in here."

In a few minutes, the young officer had made his way over to the cabinet and placed all the devices inside and returned to Lopez. "Here they are, sir"

Lopez looked down at the bag Spencer was holding out, "Hold on to them till I give the word."

"Captain Lopez, a word please," came a low voice from so close that it startled him.

Both Lopez and Spencer moved back a step from a thin man standing to the side of Lopez and close to the hospital room doorway of Captain Kijek.

Before Lopez could respond, Spencer spoke up, "Sir, this is the representative."

At that, the representative turned to Spencer, "Officer, you may leave us now, keep everyone out of here." He then bent closer to him and said "Spencer" in a low tight voice.

Spencer replied, "Sir" then immediately turned and hustled the remaining officers down the hallway and around the corner.

The representative watched quietly as Spencer performed the duty, then turned back to Lopez.

"Be aware Lopez, that you are not to remember any of this, and whatever happens is a result of your actions, not anyone else's. Any investigation will show that you and your squad were the only ones here or involved. We have all of their names and info. You know the harm that can happen to one's career, a colleague's, or that of a family member's opportunity or even health benefits. Think of your three children."

Lopez straightened and backed up a little at this statement, his eyes widening.

"So you will cooperate. "

Lopez, his shoulders drooping, simply responded, "Yes."

The representative moved toward the room door and, extending his arm toward Lopez, said,

"Excuse me," as he entered the room. As Lopez turned to follow, the representative turned around sharply in the doorway and said, "You stay out there, and guard the door. I will be out when I am finished." He then abruptly closed the door in Lopez's face.

Lopez slowly turned with his back to the door and waited with eyes forward, looking toward the hallway ceiling. It was only a matter of seconds before he heard a loud scream of agony coming from behind the door. He turned quickly and grabbed the doorknob and shoved. But he ended up with his shoulder against the door. It had been locked. There was another scream, and Lopez with his head tilted slightly against the door could hear his men stepping out from around the corner of the hallway. Lopez saw Spencer starting to walk toward him and immediately waved him back, turned again to the door and started banging on it as the screams continued, "Sir, sir, open up! what is happening? Sir."

But there was no response from the other side of the door.

Lopez backed out away from the door and started to lift his leg in an attempt to kick in the door.

Just then, the screaming stopped. Lopez lowered his leg and almost instantly the door opened and the representative waved Lopez in with his hand.

Lopez entered and was shocked to see the patient sprawled across the floor with the stump of his right arm bleeding profusely. The artificial arm implant connector had been ripped out and was lying on the floor close to the stump, covered in blood.

Lopez started to speak, "What the fu...", but the representative interrupted with a sharp blow to the officer's stomach that left Lopez gasping for air.

The representative moved close to Lopez, while holding a small item grasped in his fingers up to Lopez's face.

"Here, you fool!" he said. "Here is evidence on the prisoner's planned espionage against the country."

Lopez started to stutter out, "But we didn't find any..."

Again, the representative interrupted, "Shut up. You did find it, you with your superior detective work, and your team, and that is how you will report it. When you check this device out in your lab, you will find out it is a bug that broadcasts to an unidentified receiver, or shall we say co-conspirator?"

"You will say they planned to infiltrate the nation's superior scientific community to steal our more advanced technology on space propulsion and power systems. Do you understand?"

"But aah, how?

"Lopez, I don't have time to waste. Do you know what will happen to you, your family, your men, if you have an issue here? Now, do you understand?"

Lopez straightened up and pulled his uniform shirt down to straighten it out, "Yes sir, I understand."

"Good, here" and signaled Lopez to watch him.

The representative then backed away from Lopez and bent on one knee over the patient.

"This is the evidence, see where I place it." The representative then set down the tiny chip right at the tip of the implant that had been ripped from the patient's arm.

He then stood and returned to Lopez. Taking a pair of nearly invisible surgical gloves off his hands, he handed them to Lopez while speaking.

"Here put these on." Lopez took them, carefully trying to avoid the blood but to no avail.

Lopez could not help but notice that the representative still appeared to have gloves on his hands.

The representative immediately moved toward the door

still speaking to Lopez, "Hurry and finish up; you can either benefit from this or end up in a ditch someplace."

The representative then headed toward the door. Pausing he turned and looked down at the man on the floor whose blood was creating a small puddle, "And leave him be, this will all be a lot easier if he doesn't make it."

As he passed through the doorway the representative said without turning, "We will not meet again."

Lopez gazed after the representative, then stepped to the door to make sure he was leaving. Looking down the hall toward the corner he saw nothing; he then turned in the other direction and saw nothing.

Lopez gave out a holler, "Spencer, You there?"

Spencer's head popped out around the corner with a "Yes Sir."

"Get back here quick, leave the men there to keep the area clear, but hurry."

While Spencer moved toward the room, Lopez stepped back in and slipped the gloves he was still holding on and picked up the tiny chip that had been placed on the tip of the captain's arm. He stood and turned toward the low white medical cabinet that was against the wall and placed the chip on it. He removed the gloves and dropped them beside the chip, then went back toward the door just as Spencer arrived.

Lopez pulled him into the room by his shirt and pushed him down toward the patient. "Quick, get a wrap on that and stop the bleeding, "

Spencer looked at the man on the floor then at Lopez wide-eyed, "What the hell happened? Did that guy do this?"

Lopez started, "I can't believe that scum..." then he stopped in mid-sentence. Spencer had already grabbed a roll of cloth gauze from the cabinet and knelt down beside the patient. He started bandaging the stump of his arm.

Lopez continued, "Spencer, you need to understand this clearly; there was no one else here, I found this strange chip."

"What are you talking about?"

"Listen to me, clearly, look at me!"

Spencer glanced up at him from his work, "What?"

"I found the device when the patient fell while trying to escape and dislodged his implant."

"What? That sounds ridicula...mpff.," but he did not finish as Lopez slapped a hand over his mouth.

Spencer started to struggle, but Lopez glared at him, pulling the young man's face close to his and holding it there.

Lopez started to talk in a whisper, "Listen, Listen," Lopez's voice reflected a desperate tone that Spencer had not heard Lopez use before, and he stopped struggling. However, Lopez continued to hold a hand over his mouth.

"Listen, it has to be this way, think a second, your family, our men out there, their families--don't even speak--you weren't in here when I found the device. No one else was here." And then for emphasis Lopez repeated, "There was no one else here. Do you understand? Do not say anything to anybody, refer everything to me, just follow my lead. We need to save our asses, do you understand?"

Spencer's eyes narrowed for a second, then he nodded his head.

Lopez released his grip on him and spoke, "Ok, go get the tech guys back in here, get our men out of here and you go with them. Are we on the same page?"

Spencer had been looking down as he listened to Lopez. He did not lift his head, but said "Yes" and simply walked out of the room.

Lopez followed him to the door and waited there to

hear Spencer give the orders to the men still waiting around in the hallway. In a few moments, a single tech came down the hall and stopped in front of Lopez.

He said, "Sir, Officer Spencer sent me back, he said you found something."

"Yes, it is on the cabinet by the gloves. Bag it and tag it. Then get it back to the lab."

Lopez moved aside for the tech to enter the room, then followed him.

"It is right there, do you see it?" he said pointing to the red specks of blood and the gloves.

"Yes sir, it will be just a minute."

He watched as the tech held an instrument over the little blood-covered chip and tapped the screen a few times. The tech then pulled out a kit that was for evidence and pulled bags and tweezers out. He carefully picked up the chip and placed it in a bag; he then did the same with the gloves. He turned and started to bend down when Lopez stopped him.

"That will be all," Lopez bent closer to the tech to see his badge, "Nickels."

"Do you want me to sweep again, sir?"

Lopez sounded aggravated. "Your team already swept the room, you are finished here."

"Yes sir." Nickels packed up the items with the kit and went out the door.

Almost instantly the floor nurse was in the room.

She spoke without waiting for any response from Lopez, "What have you done? This is going to be reported! How can you do this? This is a hospital."

She knelt down beside the patient, placing a sheet over the pool of blood on the floor. She quickly checked his eyes and his neck for signs, then stood and called for help to the room.

Lopez said nothing in response; he just turned and walked out the door. As he made his way down the hall, three or four nurses came rushing past him toward the patient's room.

As he rounded the corner, Spencer was standing there alone with the black bag in one hand and Lopez's phone and communicator in the other.

Without a word, Lopez took them, slid the phone in his pocket, and held the communicator to his mouth while looking at Spencer with the speaker open. "Desk, this is Lopez at the hospital, we are done for the day. Please be advised we need replacements to guard the prisoner."

"Yes, just come on in; the Chief pulled the schedule for that guy. Guess he figured he wasn't going anywhere in his condition. At least that is the report we got."

Lopez, "Copy that." He waved to Spencer, "Let's go."

"I thought the guard was for protection?"

Lopez simply hurried his pace toward the elevator.

Spencer turned to look down the hallway around the corner, shook his head, then turned and followed Lopez to the elevator.

Later that night there was an unexplained explosion that destroyed Captain Kijek's room. An investigation revealed that co-conspirators of the captain had placed a bomb outside the captain's room. Apparently, the police and FBI had discovered an espionage plot by the captain and conspirators against the countries' technological secrets. The co-conspirators supposedly murdered him at the hospital with a high explosive charge delivered by a camo drone to the outside wall of his room. The police tracked them down, but the conspirators died in a fire fight, ending the investigation. It was thoroughly covered on all the news broadcasts and web browsers.

CHAPTER 3

Anther racer flashed by and was gone, only visible on the screen for a second, their acceleration vectors coming out of the Sling. Josh didn't waste time, already on the controls and accelerating toward the well. His tall lanky form was a hard fit for racing space bikes in the first place. It was especially tight now with the extra comptroller installed for the advanced booster tech he and Ron had come up with. Back at the station launch start, Josh thought how his dad had laughed the first time he'd climbed into a racer. Well, he would be bowled over if he could see him now squeezed into the tiny racer bike pod. Everyone called them bikes but that was only because of the prone position the racer pilot was in. They were similar to the old motorcycle track racers that had been outlawed more than a century ago.

His race plan now was to get to the moon's highest gravity well first, using as much fuel as necessary to get the pole position going into the well. Getting to the well at the correct vector on the Moon was critical to gaining the most acceleration with the least variance, thus avoiding the commercial and other traffic in the well. Josh was an experienced racer and he knew that almost all of the ships going into the well were setting up on the same vector.

After entering the well with the commercial transports, he must use his electronics to get even micro-gravitational boosts from the larger commercial ship masses and then continue choosing the right vector and timing to get a small boost from each large ship as he moved through the channel, much as the old auto racers of earth used a leading car's draft. The trick here was timing, the breakaway to the next ship, and avoiding each ship's micro-gravity pull. Otherwise, he would just end up losing any advantage gained from the sling effect.

Passing in the Moon's commercial traffic vectors was the most dangerous part of the race. Next would be angling onto the backside and then leaving the Moon's gravity field. His plan was to avoid any damage to his racer and his untested boost system, then if needed pour it on back to the Earth-Bound Transfer Station at the finish line. The transfer station was at the gravitational center between the Earth and the Moon.

Now in the well, Josh's front monitors displayed the flashing signals of both racers and transports. He picked out his target and worked the controls. Josh headed in his target's direction. As he moved forward applying thrust, a racer tumbled by his left and he dodged to avoid it, but was too late as it bumped him out of his vector toward his target transport. He heard the other pilot give an expletive over the race comm. Josh checked his damage visuals and adjusted to stop the spin from the impact.

Behind him, his friend Slider, in another racer commented over the racer's open comm system, "Who is that yahoo?"

Then to Josh directly, "Hey Josh, how's it going, Mind if I stick with you today?

Slider moved in alongside of Josh. Josh could see Slider's image due to the double screen system on the racers. This system was used to make the space racing more authentic and was a kickback to the past on Earth when all types of racing sports took place.

Josh said, "I don't think so, I plan to win, so that would put you at second, and I'm not sure if you can keep up."

Slider said, "Ha, are you serious? With these basket cases, we would both be lucky just to get to the finish line."

Josh replied amicably while still monitoring and accelerating toward the Moon's gravity well, "I'm serious, Slider. I think I got a chance with the modes I made this time, and besides, this race is also for research testing with data collection for my day job."

Slider, still tagging along, said, "What? I thought you said those guys don't give you a thing for your rig. In fact they were pressuring you to quit racing."

"Yeah, them and my wife, I... Hold on, Slider." A little beeping light started flashing on his upper optical monitoring space, along with a special horn tone that was reminiscent of 21st century police car sirens."

"Slider, are you getting that?"

"What?"

"Looks like the cops are out," Josh said, "I thought everything was signed off with the Space Agency?"

Ball spoke up, "I got nothing, my system is not as hi tech as yours. Why? What have you got?"

"Check your screen, looks like there is pursuit after some of the other racers."

Josh's monitors now showed multiple agency ship signals huddled around a score of racers. They were just out and back a few clicks on the race course from Josh's position.

Slider said, "Hey, yeah, they are taking them out. Shit!"

Both racers could see on their screens now that the racer's blips were being forcibly diverted out of the course.

"Man, I got to stick with you now, I don't have any way of knowing where the agency cops are until they get close!"

"Slider, I can't help that, if we stick here together you know we will both get tagged; we got to split up and now."

Slider paused before answering, "Yeah, Ok, you're right, good luck, this sucks. I got to be back at work Monday too."

With that, Slider's racer dipped down below Josh. Josh saw Slider working the racer controls through the double screens on the racers. He abruptly turned on a different vector, heading toward the traffic on the way to the Moon.

Josh said, "Good luck, it looks like they're headed this way, best to get into the traffic fast!"

There was no response from Slider and Josh figured he had gone silent in case the Space agency was tracking the comm signals. It might work, but Josh knew the Agency had way more sophisticated tracking equipment and probably had him on visuals even from their current distance.

Josh scanned all his monitors, along with the paths of the agency ships, flipped off the siren, then quickly selected another vector and took off with a burst from his thrusters. He added a richer mixture to burn thick fuel exhaust and give a temporary screen to his movement. Then he quickly changed to a more powerful mix with a turbo steam boost. This propelled him away from the vector path he and Slider had been on and put him right into the back of a large commercial transport in a matter of seconds. He tilted to the side and skimmed just along the surface, then out to his next target as the current transport closed with another tug transport and closed the gap between them, just slipping out in time and closing the same vector to those behind him. As he maneuvered the racer in tight, he picked up Slider closing in on his left side. He was not too concerned actually a little relieved that Slider had gotten into some traffic before the Space agency cruisers had had a chance to catch up to him. He made a quick juke to the right as the transport fired a small thruster, probably lining up on the Moon to drop its cargo. He almost skimmed it and based on where Slider had been, he knew that Slider probably had bumped into the transport and had to apply reverse thrust to avoid serious damage.

The fuel usage and velocity loss would cost him on the final leg of the race, but getting away from the Agency cops was the highest priority now. He smiled slightly as he cleared the vessel on vector to the next and picked up the last part of Slider's verbal rant against him.

As he cleared the vessel, his heart lightened because this was this favorite part of the race. Sweeping in and out of the large transports and private yachts, even military vessels. Yeah, the race was on, he was in the mix and would need to emerge from the well near the lead if his plan was to work. He squeezed out of the current ship convergence as a freighter and a luxury yacht closed. He banked up and had to twist to the right as another smaller spear-shaped Space Agency cruiser seemed to purposely try to block his exit forward. He now set up to vector toward the outer well as the commercial ships would be jockeying for the bottom to set up and drop their cargo to the Moon tugs. He twisted for more acceleration angle outward when his screen lit up with "RESTRICT AND BOARD DEMAND." It was from the Space Agency; he checked his screens and saw he was being tailed by a Space Agency pod. The pods were similar to his racer, and more advanced as rumors had it. The rumors claimed that they could beat down anything from Earth, but the Agency would not let them go full speed in the Moon-Earth vicinity because they wanted to keep their full capabilities a secret. That was the scuttlebutt in the pits anyway.

Josh had no intention of dropping out of the race and figured the pod was just out to harass him. He certainly did not want the Space Agency looking over his racer and holding him on the Moon for who knows how long. Josh had to get back to his family and his day job on Monday.

He checked his visuals for fuel, checked the traffic ahead and then darted down into the congestion of the freight drop and tug pick up zone. A quick check revealed that the Agency pod came right after him. His visuals flashed with the board demand and started listing penalties. Josh had no time and he was confident in his racer. This space ahead was full of dropping canisters and large cargo containers all zipping down to the Moon's surface through open space. Only when they got within the range of the tugs would they fire retros and slow enough for the tugs to grab them and deliver them to the settlement or agency. It was amazing that with all the fighting and ill will between the countries of Earth and the Space Agency that so much trade took place.

Josh bolted down through the cargo darting in and out of the dropping canisters. He knew the Agency pod would be right on his tail and maybe closing, he figured it may even be a drone. He based this again on the racing rumors about their performance, calculating that a human would suffer some long-term damage from the accelerating, stopping, and turning the pods could reportedly do. If it was an AI pilot then he figured he needed to outsmart it fast. His alarm blared again; it had closed the distance by half. He flipped a switch by his accelerator and immediately a view of his aft view came up. He spoke to his private AI that he had developed for his racer, "track pod trailing, confirm, the word confirmed appeared on his screen." Close up view of trailing pod 1 meter, confirm." The screen view popped to a close up, X looked over the pic while still darting in and out of falling freight containers. He spotted what he wanted. It was a tiny rounded half bulb on the surface of the following pod. The pod had closed the distance again. A matrix of number boxes appeared across the screen of the following pod. Josh picked out the box he wanted, which was right on the oval he had spotted earlier. "Track, oval he confirms," the word confirmed again as shown on the screen.

Josh sent out a super low frequency crypted radar scan. It immediately painted a picture to his left of the area of the well for 2000 km around him. His alarm blared again, "You will be disabled," was the message. Josh reacted immediately. He slammed on retros. The effect on his body was immediate as blood rushed into his head. He pressed his suit compensator that would divert blood out of his body and into and around back in at his legs. He then flipped the pod over backwards; he had calculated that the pod AI would slow almost exactly at the same time so that would put him directly behind.

It was there. His racer's tracking cameras displayed the pod coming almost directly under him by only a few inches. Josh heard some scratching but had already set his plan up. "Paint C48, repeat continuous, Confirm."

As they passed by within inches of the agency pod little paint balls shot out of Josh's racer and splattered their contents across the spot identified. On the screen the word confirmed shown. Josh spoke, "Stop continuous, confirm" the paint ball barrage stopped and the screen confirmed. As he spoke, Josh hit his retros again, this time pushing blood out of his head and with the flip into a forward angle he blasted his thruster, heading at a vector to a column of canisters that had been in a close compact drop. He moved to the back side of this dropping column of freight directly opposite where the agency pod had been and accelerated at full speed up the column. In seconds he was back into the heavy traffic in the well and again darted in close to a freighter that had dropped its cargo.

As he did, another racer appeared in front just ready to start down on the far side to the canyon run. Josh felt relief at that, having feared he'd lost the pack completely and was out of the race. He started to move toward the other racer and its ID popped on the screen. IT was Andy in the Party racer; this seemed too good to be true. Had he run into trouble? He asked the Ai to do an extended scan of the other races. It brought back a spot halfway down to the canyon run for one and the IDs of the rest were huddled in a pack headed backwards down toward the surface. The vector had them lined up and moving toward the nearest Agency Moon Port. Had they all been chased down and caught? What was the problem? The Space Agency had never interfered in this small bean race before.

Josh didn't waste any more time on the thought but launched on a vector to intercept Randy in the Party racer and get close enough to ID the lead Racer already headed down to the trench leg of the race. The leader would be tough to catch.

He had lost the Agency Pod, he now had to set up to get a status on the race and to set up a vector to race through the trench on the far side of the Moon.

He was getting across when he heard a familiar voice. "Josh?" came the question over his com. "Randy, is that you?" Josh replied.

"Yes, keep it tight," Randy said. "Here is an update, be careful. The Space Agency is out in force and dragging every-one they catch down to the surface. I don't know why, but I had received a heads-up text seconds before they started back at the well. I lucked out because I was in a pack, but everyone else got taken and it was not friendly at all. I think a couple guys got hurt pretty bad."

"Say what?" Josh said as he changed his vector and accelerated to Randy,

"I see you coming, Josh. I still plan to win this though, just be on your toes. They seem to be out for blood for some reason."

"Thanks for the info," said Josh as he pressed for more acceleration and changed his vector down toward the Darkside Canyon, "Do you know who that is out in front?"

"That's the new guy, he seems to skate right through everything; he just headed straight to the canyon vector at full speed.

"Damn, that's sheer luck," said Josh."

"I doubt it."

"I am out of here, I got a race to win."

"Ha, you haven't got a chance in that yard sale," jeered Randy. "I will be on him in a second, he flies like an Agency pilot, eat my carbon."

With that Randy's racer engine flared hot and he dove it down toward the canyon, pulling away from Josh at a high rate of speed.

Their racers swept in a steep angle, and they both hit the Darkside sun glare at the same time and lost a few seconds of visuals as the cameras adjusted to the brightness of the dark side of the Moon.

Josh knew Randy was right, about his racer being slower but he had hoped to be on his tail coming out of the canyon and then pass him on the last leg of the race.

Now it looked like he may have to try out his booster system earlier than expected if he had a chance to win.

The old saying is "Stick to the plan" or is it "a plan lasts till the start of the race or is that the battle?" Josh wasn't quite sure, but he knew he had to come up with something fast."

The entrance to the canyon appeared on Josh's monitor as a tiny dot rapidly expanding every second as he plunged toward its entrance. The canyon's topographical features made it the longest and deepest on the far side of the Moon. That, of course, was dependent on what Moon geologist you were talking to. Josh would definitely have to keep his speed all the way through the canyon till he hit all the track markers. It would then be a drag race straight out on the station's vector to the finish. He needed to have a substantial lead on Randy's Party bike to have any chance of finishing first.

Problem now was where the leader would be by then and how had a newbie attained such a lead over the veterans? Did his ship have some new tech? Was he having an extremely lucky day in avoiding the Space Agency pods? or was this annual high-stake race devolving into the same status as everything on Earth nowadays. You have to have connections and a little qi pro quux if you want to get ahead.

Josh accelerated into Randy's bloom. He would pass him and not decelerate until Randy was behind him. He knew that would be a high risk move because the deceleration would have to be extreme. Picking up that much speed while heading straight at the Moon with its added gravitational pull would be pushing the limits. Sporting a tiny smile, he was sure that his racer and his body could take it.

Josh's fuel level was dropping fast. Randy had to be aware of this when he commented over the comm, "Hey Josh, you're not going to make it back to the station, but don't worry, I'll send out a tow. I hear the Agency has plenty in the area." Josh knew that Randy was pushing on the thrust to the fullest to keep ahead of him.

Josh simply responded, "Thanks, I appreciate your concern."

At that second, Randy's Party racer was just off to Josh's right and the bloom of its engines filled the screens there.

Randy couldn't believe it. "Are you nuts? Screw you!" His alarm sounded and he threw on the retros hard.

Randy yelled into the com, "Josh, pull up, man, pull up, you're too close."

It was a matter of seconds, Josh counted them off to calculate the lead he would need to be ahead of Randy out of this trench leg of the race. He pulled his respirator off the bottom of his helmet and at the same time he blasted his retros. His eyes turned white up into his upper sockets, his stomach emptied out his mouth and nose and he continued to heave while straining to see his forward screen.

He listened to the sound of the computer alarm blaring and counting off the distance to Moon impact. His blood was being equalized in his suit, but he needed it to happen faster. Suddenly he was back and his eyes locked back on the screen. He twisted the retro angle and the vector to the trench entry marker. He had only seconds to react before he'd hit the marker. He popped the retro on and off, still almost plummeting in a death spiral to the surface. Blaring warnings sounded in his helmet and throughout his small racer.

He could hear Randy yelling in his head phone, "Josh! Pull up! Pull up! God! God! Shit! Shit! Shit! Pull up!"

Josh plunged down with the Moon now filling all the visuals and him trying to maintain his high rate of speed. He twisted the retro hard again. His eye did not pop this time but some more gorge came out of his mouth and he turned and spit the drool onto the side screen. He pulled up on the bar and fired the main engine and lowered maneuvering thrusters at the same time. It changed his angle slightly as he passed just over the edge of a mountain peak about 1000 klicks in front of the canyon entrance. He needed to expend more fuel to pull out of the dive and he felt his fear and a slight panic start to grip his throat. His pumping adrenaline drove him to the limit. He shut off the thruster and diverted all the power to the lower maneuvering thrusters. He was still moving at incredible illegal speeds toward the surface but at a better angle than an instant death spiral. He was planning it out at lightning speed. He would make it. He also knew he wasn't finished and the race wasn't close to being over. In his wake, Moon dust marked his path on a direct vector to the trench. He set back into racing mode and checked on his friend, Randy. Even before he could check the visuals, he heard Randy's voice, "You stupid crap head, you're a full on a-hole, you could have killed yourself, what the heck are you doing today, Josh?"

Josh said, "Well, I thank God I'm alive, that's for sure."

As he did, he reached over and hooked in the vac tube to his helmet to suck out the puke and freshen his visor. On the tracking screen he saw that he'd gotten a twenty second lead over Randy.

Randy, almost reading his thoughts, said, "Twenty seconds is not enough Slick, I'll pass you in the trench."

"You're on, and thanks for your concern."

Randy said, "Yeah, well, you're nuts."

Josh was into the trench and his momentum was still with him; he would need to lower his speed substantially and use a lot of thrusting retros to get through the trench. The rules in the trench were no flying above the rim and no dying or crashing because the race sponsors can't afford to look for someone that is already dead. So, recovery only occurs when some explorer or scientific expert or maybe a mapping crew comes nearby and is kind enough to bring back a body.

The trench was normally flown as close to the rim as possible at the highest speed, and it also allowed for an easier escape from smashing into the trench walls even if it meant disqualification. Josh would follow the same plane and burn fuel to keep ahead of Randy. As he started swinging back and forth following the curves of the trench. He had the AI post the other racers' location to the 3-D visual of his visor. On it he could see that Randy had already picked up a second on him. The newbie, however, was dead in the center of the trench. Josh thought that odd based on his location when he'd met up with Randy before diving toward the trench. He should have been close to the end of the trench by now, but he was taking his time, being careful. Was he that confident, was he tracking the two remaining racers or did he believe that everyone had been detained? Josh thought the pilot of the leading pod could not really consider himself a racer if he was the only one in the race. He tried setting a scan for his communication signal to see if there was any chatter between the new guy and his ground support. The scanner was dead except for Randy's constant chatter and threats. This was fine with Josh because it let his system pinpoint his nemesis' exact location. Josh knew he was right on his tail and fought the urge to switch a screen to that view as he knew that would only add one more distraction to the already tight race and the tricky maneuvering going through the craters and the radials with so many different lobatescapes included in the far side course.

Thing is, Josh still had his magic booster in the bag and that would take the smile off Mr. Newbie's face.

The elevations were tricky as the crater course cut right across the main section of the far side bulge, so staying low enough to trigger the course relay checkpoints and then avoid slamming into the rising terrain of the bulge made for an extreme challenge in the course.

He dipped over the edge of the next lobate and down into it for a straight shot to hit the relay signal. He would then race around the outer wall of a towering crater wall to his left. His proximity alarm blasted louder as he barely missed a large outcropping of vertical moon crust. Then the second screeching proximity for contact with another racer blared even louder as he felt Randy tapping the side of his racer with his own. Randy let out a wicked-sounding high pitched scream as he caught Josh on the next transition over the wall of the next crater and down onto the floor.

"See you later; better take that piece of crap back to the toy store before you wipe out!"

Then off he went so fast that Josh lost sight on his visual scanners.

Josh saw his speed dropping, and the readouts on the monitors. The three engines were down to twenty percent efficiency and he was starting to feel the vibration in the controls. He realized that Randy's bump was more than that and that Randy must have tagged the engine with some damage, probably with that little extension arm or with some other sabotage device the Party had installed for their racer's use.

To keep control and stay in the course he would have to cut back on the engines to balance out the thrust. He quickly made the adjustment and then just as quickly made the decision to use his booster way ahead of plan. Still unsure of the effect, he checked his battery power levels since the booster required voltage. The booster didn't work by the current engine design with fuel supplied through the engine. Josh had discovered something through an accident of his research at the institute. The FTL tachyon chips he had been working on seemed to create a small distortion in space. Josh calculated by designing them into the front of his racer he could get a boost to pull his racer ahead at as yet undetermined speed. Josh was hoping he could collect some technical data by doing a test during the race that would lead to more grant money from the Institute. That was his plan anyhow, but that changed. Now he just wanted to win the race and bury Randy in his dust.

He tapped to initiate the finger lever he and Ron had set up and did not see an increase in speed. Still traveling at his max speed, he started checking his instruments.

He then heard Randy over the com. "What the hell! what's going on?"

Josh looked up at his visuals and he could now clearly see the thrust blooms from Randy's engines.

He had closed more than half the distance, but was starting to fade once more. He turned to check out the Moonscape and it had dramatically changed. The crater floor was now flat with the distance he had made up across the crater floor.

"Josh, how did you do that?"

"Do what?"

"The distance, man, how did you make up that distance?"

Josh sounded surprised. "Don't know what you're talking about. Hey, did you mess with my number three!"

"Can't talk right now, be waiting for you at the finish."

Josh quickly checked the course topo map ahead, looking for somewhere that he could use the booster again and pass Randy before he could react or see what happened. Josh still wasn't quite sure how the booster had worked.

He turned off his race comm and switched to talk to Ron, Josh's one and only pit crew. Ron was a fellow engineer specializing in the microelectronic and A.I. of the racer. While Josh could handle the same subjects he was more into astrophysics and sub-atomic particles. They had met briefly at the institute before Ron was fired. Ron said it was because of his advanced ideas. Whatever the reason, Josh and Ron had struck up a fast friendship, mainly due to Josh's interest and participation in the bike space racing and Ron's extreme interest in space exploration and travel. Josh would kid Ron about it since he had never been to space and when asked why, Ron would simply dodge the question.

Now Josh needed to run the booster performance by him to see if he had any ideas on what the effect was, or why he didn't notice anything when it happened.

Josh said, "Ron, you got me?"

"Thank God! Josh, it's Ron, did you use the booster?" Ron was quite a bit older than Josh. In fact Josh thought he should be retired, but he wasn't. Even after the institute let him go, he started up a small business in town. That was where Josh and Ron built the race bike.

"Ron, yes it was great, closed the distance I think in seconds, but didn't pick up any speed."

Ron's voice thick with worry, "Josh, I thought you crashed, I was watching the screen and you disappeared, then you were right behind that guy, Randy. That is not what the simulation predicted."

Josh interrupted, excited, "No, but it worked great. Can you run any data you got from the boost and see if you can work it into the simulation? I didn't feel any physical sensation from it but it did work."

"Ok, I'll see if I got anything, but in the meantime don't..."

Ron did not get a chance to finish his warning to Josh. While listening to Ron, Josh noticed that Randy was extending his lead quite a bit. This would be his last opportunity to use the booster again on this leg of the race if he did not act immediately.

Josh interrupted Ron, "Got to go, thanks," and switched his comm back to the race channel and Randy was already on it.

"Josh, do you copy? Are you still there? You, OK?"

"Fine Randy, just checking with base."

"Oh yeah, going over your strategy, come on,... You're barely going to make it to the finish. You'll be working the rest of the year to pay for the tow. Your wife will be pissed. No shoes for the kids this year. Ha!"

The talking gave Josh one more chance to check his screens and course, as he did his comm light from Ron started flashing, but Josh ignored it. He knew Randy's talking was just meant to annoy and delay him.

Josh responded, "Ok Randy, we'll see who is waiting for who."

"You'd better not try another crazy stunt like back at the trench, you're going to get killed!"

Now Josh realized that Randy was coasting in the race. Randy knew that he had second place locked up and realized that the newbie was so far ahead that only a breakdown would get him to the finish first, so he had plenty of time to converse with Josh.

Coming up was the largest crater on the far side and Randy had already entered it. The course ragged up and over the outer wall of the crater then steeply down into the crater itself, past the relay point then straight across the floor of the crater to the relay on the other side. Josh calculated he could tap the booster twice after he hit the crater floor and would pass Randy and head up the wall on the other side, hoping Randy would not notice the action on his monitoring screens. If Josh could do it and get over the crater wall into the next crevasse before the other racer could detect his signal, the crevasse was a short one and he just had to go down close enough to trigger the relay. Then it was a straight out fight with the gravity well out away from the moon. He got ready and checked to see where the newbie was.

As Josh expected, the newcomer had just exited the well and was heading for the finish line at the E.M. Relay Transit Station #1 which was now traveling toward Earth, opposite the #2 Station from which they'd started.

Simultaneously, the crater wall came up, and Josh was up and over, when the relay signal chimed, he tapped the booster and his screens blurred. He took a second to check distance covered visually and radar, then almost instantly tapped it again. For some reason, his instruments did not give him a read on the speed he had reached. He would have to guesstimate, flying or racing by the seat of his pants.

The swift distortion of the blurred screens was disquieting and Josh's vitals spiked. Sweat dripped off his brow. He knew that hitting anything at the boost speed, whatever it was would totally obliterate his ship and him.

His readings showed he had almost hit Randy's tail by less than a click, and he was less than halfway across the crater floor with everything all clear. After his next tap of the booster, he was less than two clicks from the crater wall and in seconds he was up, over and down the other side. He was sure Ballbuster had detected his racer there but was probably completely confused as to what it was. Josh would be lucky if he just thought there was a glitch with his instruments. He had not picked up any speed from his booster and this was starting to confuse him as the physics did not make sense to him. He should be maintaining at least a little speed from the boost in the moon's frictionless environment. This would all have to be worked out later when he got back to the institute.

He came up fast on the last relay and went vertical with his vector lined up on the station and pushed his thruster to full, pushing him back against the bike straps holding him in position. Seconds later after the acceleration pressure had just eased off, he noted the newbie's position. He would pass him close to the station, but with enough space that there would be no worries of a collision. Just as he started to tap on the booster, he heard Randy begin to rant, "What the F…" and he was gone. The tap brought him up close on the newbie. Josh was right at the edge of his visual and he could see the bright shine of the reflection from the back of the newbie's racer. With a widening smile on his face Josh tapped the booster again. This time nothing happened. He was still traveling with just his thrusters and his fuel was depleting fast. Randy's voice was now coming over the headset in a blistering verbal attack. Josh quickly checked all the instruments, saw Ron's comm line flashing again and switched to it, "Ron, are you on?"

"Josh, did you flip me off? Did you hear what I said? What are you doing, Josh? Please don't use the booster again, I can't track you and I got no useable data from any of the times you used it."

"But I got you now, Josh. Looks good, you almost got it, time to finish. Just go in with your own thrusters. Be safe—we can figure this out when you get back."

Josh broke in, "Ron, I got a problem, last attempt to boost got nothing, but all readings were solid. Got any ideas?"

"Probably the switch, some kind of short, if you have time check the connectors."

"Ok thanks."

Josh checked the newbie's location and Randy's; he realized the race would be over by the time he did a full system check.

"Ron, looks like there is no time for that, let me try it again."

"Josh, I wouldn't…" But Josh had already tapped the lever.

The visuals blurred and Josh found himself with a visual on the Station. He turned to his side screen and to his surprise he could see the newbie ship coming slowly up alongside him. He saw the face of the racer and he was surprised since it was a much older man. Josh thought the guy was pretty old for a bike racer.

Josh was not sure but figured the newbie could see his face too. He could not believe they had gotten so close.

He could see the other racer was in communication with someone and talking rapidly, he could also see that even though he had momentarily passed the newbie and taken the lead in the race the newbie was regaining the lead and passing him. His screen started to bleep out the proximity warning for the police. Had the other racer called in the Moon base to have him picked up? As he checked, he also noticed that the other racer had reduced speed to match his for some reason and was moving in closer even though they were way too close already. The newbie was maneuvering as though he were doing a docking procedure. Josh became a little alarmed as it appeared the newbie was coming after him and not trying to beat him to the finish line.

Josh spoke on the open channel to the newbie, "Hey, are you a cop?" but the newbie continued to move in closer to Josh.

"What are you doing, old man, back off!"

The newbie was less than ten feet away.

Josh, hesitated just a second, then tapped the booster lever again, expecting the other racer to disappear from his vision. Instead, nothing happened, the other racer was just moving a little closer and the proximity alarm kept beeping, Ron's comm line also started flashing.

Josh shoved the booster lever ahead hard with the heel of his gloved hand.

CHAPTER 4

As Murphy entered the reception area, he noticed Herb, the center's facilitator with Sally the storeroom clerk.

Doc waved to them both and asked, "Are you guys in the same Emergency Meeting as me?" He waved his arms around to lampoon the description of the meeting, but stopped when he saw Herb and Sally weren't smiling at his actions.

He turned to Claire at her desk, the Director's Secretary and his wife, and asked, "What's Up? Do you know what's going on?" She looked at him and said "No, but here are copies of what Herb gave me for the meeting and..." She put her hand down on a folder on her desk and then held up a finger to him,

"Hold on a sec," she continued, "I need to tell Juan you're all here." Claire turned, and made a small finger motion in front of one of the monitors on her desk. Doc saw her lips moving and knew she was talking to the director; the sound being dampened to private as all the new comm systems were. When she was done, she turned back to Murphy, who was giving her a confused look. She shrugged her shoulders and said, "It is something that came up fast, so you know more than I do."

She looked him in the eye and gave him that little smile of hers, then she turned toward Herb and Sally who had seated themselves and continued, "You can go in now Herb, Sally, please."

She continued with Doc, "Wait, remember, Henry's match starts at eight tonight and I expect to ride with you, so you need to be home to pick me up by 7:30 and hopefully earlier so you can get something to eat rather than eating that junk at the school."

"Yes, yes", he said, "I'm all set, wouldn't miss it." He turned toward the director's door where Herb and Sally were still standing. They seemed to be waiting on him. Claire shoved the folder into his back, "You're forgetting this. Juan wants you to review it, it is all of Herb's notes, and I am going to call Isabel later and maybe have her and the kids over. It has to be hard on her right now."

"Ok," he said as he took the folder and she turned back to her monitors. Doc walked over, opened the door, and waved them in ahead of him. He wished them a "good morning" as they passed. This time they responded with a smile and said good morning back.

As they passed through in front of him, he could sense their nervousness.

Director Juan Gutierrez was seated, leaning back in the chair. "Please be seated so we can get started," he said without any niceties.

He looked at Doc who had seated himself in the chair on the right side of the office, since Herb and Sally had taken the seats closest to the door.

"Doc, please listen and give me some feedback after Herb and Sally are finished. Feel free to ask anything as they go along as far as details etcetera, but I would prefer they get through the whole thing first before any extended questioning goes on.

"First, I want to say that this started yesterday when we

got a super offer for those old chip processors you made for that FTL computing chip you designed, your little tachyon processor or whatever."

"So, I called down to Herb to get a count and get the ball rolling yesterday on the sale."

Addressing Herb, he went on, "Why don't you start your story, keep it short, how you found the problem, what you found, where you're at now. I don't want any of the financial stuff. We can address that later but give us parts, descriptions and quantity you know, the timing of when things happened."

Herb gave a muffled "Ok" and then looked down at his lap as he unfolded his e-binder. He started blinking and touching his appropriate fingers to get his notes arranged. He also continued to mumble "Ok and Yes" to himself, unaware of the annoying effect it was having on the others at the meeting. After a few seconds he stopped, then giving a quick glance to the director and Doc Murphy he gave a final "OK" to himself.

Herb began hesitantly, "Sir, Doctor Murphy, I just want to say that the problem with the missing chips was discovered as part of the department's routine audit procedure. We do inventory checks on a periodic basis and keep tabs on materials that can be salvaged or have high value. The material came up first as a random inventory check two weeks ago right before the New Year's break. So, nothing was done for another week, well, because it was Monday and first day back after Dr. Shamir's terrible accident. Everyone was kind of upset so not much work was finished that day. Then there was the next day with the service memorial and all, so accounting for the discrepancy didn't get looked at till the next day when you asked."

Doc Murphy was also still upset over Dr. Shamir's

accident. The doctor was Murphy's right-hand man at the research center and they had some extremely important projects that were now jeopardized. He was also a very good friend and Doc Murphy considered him a protege—someone who could easily replace him as head of research. Doc was very worried about Dr. Shamir's young family. He wondered how Claire would have managed with their kids if something had happened to him when they were younger.

Herb looked up from his paperwork and quickly glanced at Director Juan and Doc Murphy. He then paused, taking in a breath.

"To be honest sir, this item kind of slipped till yesterday, and we really hadn't planned to look at it then with any priority until we got your message to get an exact count by end of day. Normally we would take some time and check with different departments to see if they had them just sitting around."

Doc sat quietly, still wondering why he was in on this meeting. He smiled attentively, trying to show interest in the discussion and thumbing through the folder Claire gave him.

He followed Herb's dialogue and smiled at him when he paused and looked over at him as though he would know what this whole discussion was about.

Juan prompted, "Please continue, Herb, we need to get through this faster."

Herb continued, "Well, I sent Sally down right away to check the inventory and she can talk you through what the status is now. Herb turned and gave a little head nod to Sally.

Sally gave a look to Doc and Juan, and then started in with her story.

"Just to let you know, we run into this type of problem all the time, maybe not this big, but we usually find everything. Now, Dr. Shamir had been borrowing those old chips quite often, here and there for the past six months. I don't want to get the doctor in trouble," as she looked over at Doc Murphy then quickly added, "I mean Dr. Shamir, that is, since he's gone and all. Though, you know how the doctor would go down there, and wanting different things, and these chips, especially, without doing the paperwork until later. Especially the last week, he seemed really in a big hurry."

"Well, to go back, initially he would just borrow one or two, and we do have some records, then maybe three months ago he started checking out ten or twenty for a week or so, but would always bring them back." Well, around Christmas, he would come back and forth a couple times a day, bring some back and not return others, and taking more. He started sticking some of the ones he brought back in a separate rack, and said not to let anyone take those. I think actually those had been in the racks that are now empty."

"So, after Christmas, sorry, the Winter Worker Holiday, he showed up late afternoon, the last day before break for New Years and he left for the race and wanted a bunch of them, mainly the ones he had separated and he loaded up a cart."

"Well, I gave them to him and reminded him about the paperwork, and he said he would bring them back same as always so I didn't give it another thought."

"So that's it, until yesterday, when Herb came to me all excited and worried about the parts. I know it isn't the right way to proceed and all but there has never been a problem.

"Well, then after Herb told me to go do a count, I got the key and went down to the storeroom, I also have the key to the chip locker on the same key chain.

"So, I unlocked the door and walked to the back where the locker was and it was already open. I did not think much of that and just figured whoever was down here last left it open or it came open on its own as it is so hard to lock sometimes with those antique key locks.

"I started pulling out the chip racks, counting them and then sliding them back in. However, when I got to the rack with the missing chips, I expected to see the slots for the missing ones empty."

Doc interrupted, "Oh, they were back?"

Sally looked at him a little flustered, "No, all the chips in that rack were gone, and as I continued all the chips in the racks below that were empty too. Once I got to the bottom of the row, I stopped and called Herb to come down to see what I was finding."

When he got there, we went through the rest of the racks and found that there are now two hundred chips missing."

"Yes sir," Herb turned to the director, "that comes to over fifty million dollars right there."

Doc Murphy looked at Herb then the director in alarm, "Hold on," he said, "are we not talking about those Tachyon chips I developed years ago. Those are junk, they don't work and the project failed. They failed big. You," pointing a finger at Juan, "Mister Director! Almost had me escorted off the property for that failure and you would have too, had not the board stopped you. And what moron came up with a sum of fifty million dollars. The whole lot of them wasn't worth half that when they were brand new."

"Now Doc," Juan said calmly, "let's not bring up that old situation, I have apologized to you a number of times about how I acted. I was really under a lot of pressure to get that project into development. When it failed the whole center kind of went to pieces."

"*You* were under pressure?" Doc exploded, "I had spent years working on the design, developing the chip. It was perfect on paper, all the simulations worked perfectly. I was the one that failed. I was the one that got blamed, laughed at and moved out to the library for a few years, or did you forget that?"

Juan just sat still for a minute looking at Doc, "Yes, it was wrong to dump on you, but you turned your career around, headed in a different direction and you're now head of research for the whole center with many successful projects and contributions to the world."

"And as head of research and a close friend of Dr. Shamir, we need your help in this issue, if we can get these chips all rounded up and sold to the government, we could well eliminate most of the current funding problems–maybe even get that advanced theory section set up."

"Ok, Juan, I just had buried that project in my mind and was not really expecting to have to go back to those pieces of crap again. I really don't want to deal with these Tachyon collider chips again, miniature or not. The sooner we offload them the better."

Herb and Sally were sitting there a little wide-eyed at the exchange between the two executives.

Juan looked over at them and asked, "Is there anything else you have?"

She looked at Herb and finished, "That is about all we got right now."

Doc was about to continue when Juan held up his hand and said, "Hold on a minute, Doc."

He turned to Herb and Sally then continued, "Thanks Herb, Sally, You two can take off. Please file your report into the log, and keep looking for them. Make sure you get around to all the other departments to see if they are lying around somewhere. This is your highest priority right now so put everything else on hold till we find those chips." As they left the office Juan asked, "Herb, please shut the door behind you. Thanks."

After the door closed, Juan stood up. "I need a stretch."

"Sounds good," replied Doc.

Both men stood up and twisted their torsos around, stretching out their lower backs.

After that, Juan looked at Doc, "Well, what do you think? Do you have any idea where they may be? Can you look around in his area where he might have put or used them on something?"

"I'm sure they're around somewhere. Do you know if he kept material in a special place in his lab?"

"He usually just had everything all set out on the benches unless it was already assembled. "Were they in his lab at all?"

"I think they did a walk-through. Herb's people have looked around and they couldn't find anything.

So, they would have to be someplace that isn't obvious and they were afraid to go through the files in his office or anywhere in the lab."

Doc shook his head. "It's just a truly bad time with his service just two days ago, and now all this hoopla on those worthless chips just sitting there gathering dust for a couple of years now. My big contribution to the world failed, and I just feel badly that all this is happening now, can't this wait till things settle down a little?"

"Come on, Doc, those things were way out past the leading edge when you developed them. Some of the tech stuff you came up with has been used in the newer faster

AI systems and that is a big deal. We just did not see it back then. Besides, nothing, even today, comes close to the processor speed.

"And now the government wants them, they will take them off our hands, anyhow that's why we're talking about big bucks."

Juan continued, "That's why I had them go down and check again, to see how much we could sell them for and get them off our hands. The other thing is that they gave an exact number of how many they wanted, and until this morning when the count turned up short that is how many we were supposed to have in the storeroom, so I don't want to disappoint them."

Doc had been twisting his waist around in an attempt to loosen up his back and responded as he was facing away from the director, "Well, I just had a thought that it is strange that the government wants those chips after all these years. I mean they were pretty cruel to us after they failed, what did the Pentagon say? 'They would never fund another developmental chip processor with us again.' What changed their minds?"

"Well," responded Juan, "the Pentagon actually did not change their mind, it is the Moon base, one of Space Command's divisions of the agency. I did not get the name, but it may be the whole Space Agency or just one of the research wings. I can't keep up when they start throwing acronyms around."

Doc quickly turned his head toward Juan, "You're kidding, those narcissists, how could they possibly condescend to want anything developed on Earth? To hear them talk, we use abacuses compared to their AI systems. It just makes me mad because they're right. They always get the best people. Ok, let me stop before I get going on my pet peeves again."

"Well, that may be," replied Juan," but their money is as good as anybody's and you know they have plenty of it with what they charge for their research there and using their systems. We could save some bucks if we switched to using their systems.

They keep everything, from high orbit to out past the belts, running smoothly. You're right. All the best people are headed to the moon, or to the cities they are building on Mars. So, the faster we unload the chips, the better. We may be able to snag a few new grads with the money."

Doc said, "What about the safety factor, they are not stable, and when they disintegrate, it is not quietly. If they blow in a pressurized environment, people could die."

"Well, I did not have time to mention that to them," said Juan, "but I'm sure you will be able to go over that with them. I'll make sure the tech advice is not included in the sales price. Consultants like you can name their price, right?" Juan held up his hands making quote signs and winked.

"Can't make any more than anyone else; you know the law, Juan. "

Juan said, "That's here in the US, off planet is free enterprise, remember? And if you spend some time on the Moon, it may be a good opportunity for the center to make some contacts. After all, we are still the leader in some fields."

Doc said, "Not going to happen, nothing would get me off planet, especially money. Besides, now I hear the Party is going to pass a law that you need special permission to go to space. That will cause a stampede for sure. People will be trying anything to get away from the cesspool of equal this, equal that. I figure when everyone leaves, someone here might remember what freedom used to be like. And most important, I hate standing in lines."

"Come on, you always say that," said Juan. "You've been

up in the terminals. I know I would go, and I am sure you would too. I see the look in your eyes sometimes, it is not that bad out there."

"Bad has nothing to do with it." Hearing a chime, Doc continued, "Juan, I have got to get going; I have things to do and a couple meetings today."

"Ok, but find those chip modules, and they want the accelerator part too; they are going to the moon or wherever they want them. Thanks."

"No problem," said Doc, "let them blow up in their faces, maybe you should make them sign a no return, no refunds policy."

"Good, I am glad you have no objection." Juan clasped his hands together, "so if you will look around, see if you can find the missing ones, and maybe talk to his wife."

Doc shrugged and started toward the door again, "Ok, I will take a look–check with Ron too. They were always hooking things up together, especially on that sled of theirs."

Now Juan got a little excited. "Ron! Doc, you mean Ron Brady! What is he still doing hanging around here? I mean when he said he quit, I thought we were done with him and his crazy stunts."

Doc replied as he headed out of the office and hung by the door, "Oh he's not here but they have that building on the way to the port where they worked on the race sled. I saw him at the funeral and tried to talk to him, but he was really in a bad way so I didn't want to impose on him. I still consider him a good friend even though the center didn't like his eccentric approach on his research."

Juan waved and said, "Thanks Doc, please close the door, will you? Thanks."

Doc waved to Claire as he passed her desk and said, "Anything new?"

She looked up and started to say something and then the phone rang and she immediately turned to answer it

Doc's past experience proved it was a waste of time to stick around so he headed over to his office and his wing of the research center.

CHAPTER 5

D oc had made it halfway back to his office when he got the ping from Claire.

He puckered his lips to take the call, "Yes dear, what have you got?"

"He needs you back here right away, there are some suit types that just barged in, one of them is still standing at the door...as a guard, I guess?"

"Who are they?"

"I don't know, they just showed up and walked right in. Didn't even stop at my desk. A few seconds later, Juan pinged me to call you. He said, "Get here pronto!"

Claire sounded agitated to Doc so he stopped. Doc groaned. "I am closer to the front door, maybe I should just leave?" But he turned and trudged back.

Over the comm Claire scolded, "Doctor J. Murphy!"

Doc recognizing the tone in Claire voice, "Ok, on my way."

When he arrived, he saw the suit standing at the director's door so he stopped at Claire's desk and started to ask for an update, "Hi, any more info on these..."

He was immediately interrupted by the man in the suit, who had somehow moved up beside him in the few seconds Doc had taken to stop and talk to Claire.

"Doctor Murphy, you are wanted inside immediately, please follow me."

Doc surprised himself when he reacted immediately and started to follow the man toward the director's door. Only after a few steps did he hold up and stop, wondering why he would respond to such an order.

Doc was not the type to fall in line and just follow what any authority might say. He knew it was one of the reasons he was not running the center instead of Juan.

At this, the man turned immediately, looking him straight in the eye. "Is there a problem, Doctor Murphy?"

"Yes, there is, who are you and what makes you think you can order me around?"

Doc watched as the man, who had a stern stiff expression on his face, took a moment as if thinking and evaluating. The thought flashed in Doc's brain that this man he was facing was no civilian but was definitely military and maybe even some special forces type, although he knew that the military was barely a force any longer and that all the past special elite military forces had been eliminated as unnecessary.

Doc became a little apprehensive as he saw how easily the man's expression changed. A broad smile blossomed across his face and a hint of a sparkle could be seen in his eyes. He spoke again, in a completely different tone and cadence. It was like Doc was an old friend.

"Sorry, Doctor Murphy, my boss had asked me to wait for you. I am Todd Patton--I did not mean to come off that way, I mean pushy, like that. I hope you will accept my apology for being so rude to you. Shall I go in and let them know if you will join them or not?"

"First, can you please tell me what this is about, and who you and your boss are associated with?"

"Well, of course, I thought your director had already discussed with you the purchase of your chip materials. And of course, we are with the Space Command, more specifically the Advanced Astrophysics test facility on the Moon."

"You showed up pretty darn fast, we hadn't talked about it til about ten minutes ago."

Todd's eyes did a side glance for a second, "Doctor, I'm sorry, I'm getting pinged from my supervisor about your arrival; do you think you will join us, I hope so, I think your director could really use your help."

Todd stepped to the side and turned towards the director's door, holding his arm out to let Doc lead him into the director's office.

As Doc started to walk toward the door, he turned to Todd. "Mmm, you are good."

Todd, "Excuse me, sir?"

Doc replied, "Never mind" and walked forward. When he got to the door, he pulled it open then stepped aside and motioned for Todd to precede him. Todd hesitated and Doc motioned again saying, "I insist."

Giving a sidewards glance at Doc, Todd walked into the room and as soon as he did Doc closed the door behind him.

He turned to Claire and their eyes met as they started laughing, Claire slowly shaking her head. This moment was brief, however, because the director's door opened immediately, and Todd was standing there looking from Doc to Claire at the desk. Todd started to smile, then Juan's voice came out of the room,

"Doc, come on, we need to get this done right now. Claire said you have to be out of here on time, today, right?"

Doc looked back at Claire one last time, raised his palm to his lips threw her a kiss, turned and walked into the room as Todd slid to the side and just as quickly pulled the door closed behind him.

As Doc entered the office, two men in suits who had been

seated in front of the director's desk stood and turned toward him, extending their hands. Juan made introductions and Doc shook their hands a bit suspiciously. "Gentlemen, this is Doctor Murphy, the designer inventor of the Tachyon processor chips you are purchasing." Pointing first to the one then the other he said, "This is Mr. Leat and this is Mr. Holter, please be seated gentlemen and we can get this finalized."

"Doc, these gentlemen are in a bit of a hurry because their departure from the port was somehow changed and unless they want to spend a week on Earth, they need to be out of here in an hour."

Doc was barely listening to Juan as he studied the two men he had just met. He was surprised at their ages, as the first had to be about Doc's age, and the other had to be late seventies maybe even in his eighties.

He also got the same impression Todd exuded, that they were military types. He had a moment of deja vu when he met the older man. Had he met him before?

Doc also could not ignore the similarity between the older gentleman and Todd. He would have sworn they were father and son if not for the age difference. Doc took another look at Leat and the similarities hit him again.

Doc asked quizzically , "Is this a family business?"

Mr. Holter's expression was remained unchanged as he responded, "Excuse me, Doctor Murphy?"

Juan said, "Doc, what did you say?"

Doc, fearing he might be stepping on some toes said, "What? Oh, nothing."

Juan interrupted Doc's thoughts though, "Doc come on, what do you say? Do you think the offer is enough?"

Doc quickly recovered, but not fast enough, for he saw that the older man had caught him staring. "What was that again, Juan? Let me recheck the numbers."

Juan, "Ok, I just sent it to you in a text."

Doc pulled out his phone and flipped out the extension part to see the number. He nodded. "Oh yes, that's a good number." Then he checked out the rest of the document and looked over at Juan. "So, they are not buying all of them?"

Doc could see Juan's face visibly cringe at his comment and the heads of the two men turned toward him with a questioning look.

Juan addressed the older man, "Mr. Holter, I assure you this is a complete count, even though you got here a little earlier than expected, we have done a complete count and checked the whole building for the chips and accelerators. This number is everything."

Holter responded, "Thank you, Mr. Valdez, I must then take you at your word." But turning to Doc, he said, "Doctor Murphy, what makes you think that all of the components aren't listed?"

Doc realized he had just opened a can of worms for Juan, and would have to quickly come up with an answer that could nail the lid back on.

"Oh, well Mr. Holter, I'm sorry—I was just referencing the old numbers from when they were initially manufactured. I am sure Juan has told you about a few being damaged and disposed of. There had been some additional research going on with the chips that resulted in their destruction."

Then looking down at the document on the screen again, he said, "Yes, this is the correct number that we discussed earlier this morning."

Mr. Holter gave a quick glance back to Mr. Leat and turned to the director, "OK, good, we'll be taking them with us then. They should all be packed up by now anyway. Can you check that, Mr. Valdez?"

After giving a relieved look at Doc, he typed a message

on his pad. A second later he looked up and spoke to Mr. Holter, "They are all accounted for and packed up; looks like your people down there have signed off on it."

Mr. Holter nodded. "Good doing business with you, Mr. Valdez, the funds have been transferred. Now can we move on to the discussion involving Doctor Murphy and the technical support you mentioned, which I must say, Mr. Valdez, is an excellent idea."

Doc immediately shot Juan an undeniably dirty look, to which Juan burst into an apologetic defense,

"Mr. Holter, that discussion is entirely between you and Doctor Murphy. He is an esteemed member of the center's staff and his inventive brilliance you see for yourself in the design of the chips and accelerators you are purchasing today." Still looking at Doc and not seeing any change in his expression, he continued, "As I said when you arrived, Doctor Murphy is probably the only person on Earth capable and smart enough to get you up to speed on your project. If you want to have the best mind on your project Doctor Murphy is the expert."

Mr. Holter, seeing that the director's eyes were fixed on Doctor Murphy, spoke up now to the director's relief. "Of course, maybe we could spend a few minutes with Doctor Murphy alone to go over the guaranteed and upfront monetary benefits for his assistance."

Juan smiled. "Yes, of course, that would be good," and turning to Doctor Murphy, "Sorry, Doc, I didn't have time to warn you, but the thing with you came up off the cuff when we had just started the discussion on price. I had no idea they would just pay my first price, easiest negotiation I ever had."

Doc Murphy still said nothing, and Mr. Holter broke the silence again, "Perhaps there is someplace private we could talk with Doctor Murphy. I would like to move this along as you are aware of our timetable." Then after receiving some internal message he said, "The shipment is already on its way. Thank you for that."

"Yes, of course, ah... Thinking a second, Juan said, "You're welcome, and you could use my office also, I need a break anyway after that tough negotiation session we had."

Mr. Holter nodded. "Well, thank you for that, but sometime a walking discussion is better, and we do have to be on our way."

Juan said, "Yes, of course." Then turning to Doc Murphy, he said, "Doc, I know you're a little upset at me right now, but could you cut me a little slack on this one and just listen to Mr. Holter's request, please?"

Doc relaxed a bit in his chair, leaning back and looking down at his clasped hands. His curiosity had been aroused, not on the prospect of making some extra cash but on why he seemed familiar with the older gentleman, Mr. Holter. He was not interested in any project they may be working on with the chips but he did want to question the gentlemen on where they might have met and if his assumption of the younger Todd was correct. He was also curious regarding a number of questions related to the Moon and the space command in general to try and find out how much more advanced technologically they were than Earth was.

"OK, Juan, no problem, I'll walk them out to their ride."

Juan said, "Thanks, Doc," Then turning to Mr. Holter, who had started to rise from his seat, he said, "See, Mr. Holter, I told you Doc would be open-minded."

Mr. Holter turned to Doc as they exited the director's office, "Doctor Murphy, I'm sorry to put this on you without much warning, but we really could use your assistance in getting up to speed on the chips, especially the physics and manufacture."

Doc said, "I will help as much as I can, but you do know the history on the chips and why I had to shelve them. Excuse me a second, Mr. Holter."

He then turned back to Juan, "I'm going to be leaving after I finish talking to Mr. Holter. Remember, I need to stop by and see Josh's family and also Ron at his shop. Plus, I'd planned to leave early today anyways."

Juan said, "Yes, that's fine; your assistant is here today, right?"

Doc nodded as he turned back to Mr. Holter who was standing by Claire's desk waiting for him.

Doc hurried over to the desk. "Excuse me one second." He spoke to Claire, "Hi, I'm going to walk these gentlemen out and then I'll be leaving for the day and stopping by to see Isabel and the kids. But I will be home as planned to pick you up to go to the match."

"Oh dear, do you want me to come with you to see her?" Claire asked. "I need to get over there and see if she needs anything." "No, we can go over again tomorrow."

Doc then turned to Mr. Holter, "Sorry about that, sir, but we have some plans for tonight, and we also have had the sudden loss of a friend and associate in my department just recently which has deeply affected the Institute. So, I will have to ask for a little indulgence."

"Not a problem, doctor. I'm aware of your loss, and am sorry to hear about the young man's accident. Whenever you are ready."

As the two moved down the hall, Mr. Holter said, "Doctor, we have a proposal with substantial remuneration for you to consult on this project at the Moon Research Facility and it is under the auspices of the Space Agency."

"Well, you know the rules. I can only earn a certain amount per the Central Party Committee on wages in

Washington, and since I am already at the limit there isn't much you can do in that area. But I don't mind you calling me up if you have a problem or I could hold a few video training sessions for you."

As they proceeded out the main entrance, Mr. Holter said, "Yes, we understand the restrictions you have to live under here on Earth, but they don't apply in the solar system. Men of your quality can make out quite nicely and are in high demand. Even new graduates from Earth institutions are making excellent incomes. So, if we could entice you to actually take a position with the Space Agency at the Moon facility, it would be very beneficial to you and your family."

"Well, you lost me there. I will never go into space. I don't know if you have researched my past or not, but I figured you're the type that would know. I've lost family members in space and now a brilliant young man not a few days ago is lost to his family."

The man stopped and looked Doc in the eye. "I understand, doctor. By the way, what do you mean by my type?"

"Well, Mr. Holter, don't be offended. You are obviously military types, so I would think you know pretty much everything there is to know about me and my family. Right?"

Deciding not to respond, Mr. Holter, started to move forward with more details of his proposal. "Look, doctor, although we believe it would be more beneficial to your research and the Space Agency if you relocated to the Moon or even Mars, if that suits you better, we have ways of passing benefits to you even if you decide to stay here. We have many older personnel that want to remain on Earth because of their health status. We have set up beneficial estates in space for their families and heirs. This gives the opportunity for them to benefit their children and even their grandchildren if at some point they decide to emigrate off planet.

They then have funds available to draw on for whatever reason. Some families take Mars vacations; some even are enrolled in our advance technical institution. I'm sure you are aware; the Space Agency and other organization are a little more technologically advanced than those on Earth."

Thinking for a moment, Doc said, "Well, Mr. Holter, that beneficial estate thing sounds interesting as long as it is legal. You know how they change laws around so quickly here. Why don't you send me the info on that?"

"Ok, good, but it will be by messenger; we don't like using the net on Earth for any reason, but I will also include a proposal for you to relocate."

Doc nodded as they approached a waiting chauffeured vehicle with two additional guards standing by, one male and one female.

Mr. Holter reached out and shook Doc's hand, "Well, here we are, doctor, it was a pleasure talking to you, and please consider our offer. Keep in mind that development in the solar system is expanding daily with numerous opportunities for everyone, and if you contrast that to what is happening on Earth, it presents a very substantial opportunity."

Todd and Mr. Leak came to over to shake Doc's hand and then entered the limo as Mr. Holter stood by.

Doc chose that time to ask his nagging questions, "Mr. Holter, have we met before, maybe a long time ago. I seem to recognize you somehow."

Mr. Holter paused a second at the limo door, "Could be, we can check that later; right now we have to get moving, Thanks for your time and consideration."

As Mr. Holter entered the vehicle Doc asked his other question, "Is Todd your son? He looks just like you."

Mr. Holter spoke as the limo door slid closed, "Thank you, doctor, hope to be seeing you soon."

Doc stepped back wondering if Mr. Holter was avoiding his questions. As the limo moved away from the curb and down the driveway, Doc started to wonder about the offer and even have a little daydream about traveling through the solar system and exploring the canyons of Mars.

He was brought back from his fantasy by a small sedan that sped by him at a good clip and out of the drive. Doc thought for a second and then waited to see if the sedan would turn the same way as the Space Agency limo did at the main road access. When it did, Doc shrugged and started to head back toward the Institute's lobby, but paused remembering he was going over to see Josh's wife. He pulled out his comm and tapped the app to have a car sent to him. Private car ownership had been outlawed almost a decade ago. So now everyone used public transportation, which Doc thought was a big reason for the private economy being in such a doldrum since the law was enacted. As it stood today, the only people with access to autos were the very rich who were mainly party officials, or people who worked for big institutions. The old-style corporations were also ineligible for private transportation access.

The driverless auto arrived in a few minutes out of the institute's car pool, and the passenger door slid open after stopping in front of Doc. Doc climbed in and was about to give instructions on the address, when someone stepped up to the window and tapped on it.

Doc looked up to see Conor, the Institute's liaison from the FBI's Community Protection Division (CPD). Doc knew him because of his monthly required presentation on assuring community safety by reporting on your fellow workers. It was required to report someone if they had made dangerous remarks or actions that could cause harm to the harmony of the community and state.

Doc pulled out his comm and saw that Conor had already opened a conversation with him. If this had been ten years ago, he would have just put the window down to talk, but the government had decided that working windows on cars was an extravagance and so had to be eliminated. Doc figured the real reason was that once the government had taken over the private auto industry, they all started having quality problems with so many parts that the fastest solution was to turn it into a political issue rather than find out the real problem.

So since only the rich greedy corporate robbers would want working car windows, they were made illegal and no new auto was to have them. Owners even had to bring in older models to have them retro-fitted at an exorbitant price. This helped the government in their goal to eliminate the private auto because many middle class and lower income car owners ended up having their cars confiscated by the government because they could not afford the retro fit.

Doc picked up the comm. "What can I do for you, Conor?"

"The main office at CPD gave me a call and said I had to follow up with you to see what you talked about with those gentlemen who just left. Do you have time when you get back this afternoon?"

"I'm not going to be back this afternoon, Conor. The director is sending me out to close up some things with Josh's family. So, it will have to be tomorrow sometime. Get hold of my secretary and set something up."

"Ok, I will let them know; is there anything you can tell me now? They seemed pretty insistent."

"Well, they wanted me to hold some classes on the equipment they just bought from the Institute."

"Ok, uh." His right hand went up to his ear. The conversation was being monitored by someone at the CPD, so Doc could assume his comm was also being tapped.

Not hiding the fact that the CPD was listening in, Conor added, "Doc, they want to know what equipment did they buy?"

"It was that old junk from the tachyon chip project that failed. You know what? Go talk to the director; he made all the arrangements. I just walked them out after he made the deal. Ok? Now if you don't mind, I have to get going or I won't have time to get finished up today. Thanks, bye now."

Doc gave instructions to be taken to Josh's apartment complex. As the car started off, Doc used his comm to place a call to Josh's wife, Isabel, to let her know he was coming over. Afterwards he sat back for the short ride over to the complex where Josh's family lived.

Josh's wife, Isabel, answered the door, holding their youngest child in her arms. The child appeared to be sleeping. Isabel welcomed him in. Doc could see from the redness in her face that she'd been crying.

As Doc entered the apartment, Aadrik, Josh's oldest at five came running, "Is that Daddy? Is he home?"

Looking up and seeing Doc, Aadrik moved in beside his mom and wrapped his arms around his mom's leg.

Isabel bent down a little and pulling him closer with her free hand she said, "No honey, remember Daddy won't be home for a very long time. C'mon now, let's talk to Doctor Murphy for a little or you can go back to your lesson on the monitor. What do you want to do?"

Aadrik didn't speak for a moment, then looked up at his Mom and said, "I will stay with you, Mom."

Ruffling Aadrik's hair with her hand, she responded, "Good decision, Aadrik." Turning to Doc, and entering the small family room she motioned Doc to have a seat at the couch along the wall. "Have a seat, Doc, and thanks for stopping by. Sorry for the mess, but I am trying to sort through things, you know, kind of get a handle on things."

"Oh, that's OK, Isabel, Claire and I are going to stop by tomorrow evening too. We thought we would pick up some dinner for you if that's OK?"

Isabel said, "Sure, Doc, so what do you need today then. I don't think Josh had much here. I checked through his desk over there," pointing to an old small flat antique type dining table over by the window of the apartment.

"There are a few electronic items and his notebook," she continued, "You can take the electronics but I want the notebook. It is in his handwriting and I would like to show it to the kids when they're older so they have a connection to him."

Doc nodded. "I understand, can I look through it, just to make sure there are no sensitive items related to the institute?"

"Sure, go ahead, "

Doc walked over to the table. There were a few notebooks neatly stacked up against the wall, in the middle of the table was a type of testing component and beside it were four of the tachyon chips. Doc turned to Isabel, "Was he testing these here? Do you know?"

"No, he would just bring them back and forth from the Institute and then take them down to Ron's shop. He told me he was testing them over there because they sometimes would smoke and smell bad and he didn't want the kids to be around the fumes."

"And the tester he has here?"

"Oh, he just brought that back from the shop right before he and Ron left for the race--same with those other things there."

"Ok, well, I'll take these with me." Doc pulled out the seat at the table and sat down. He reached over and picked up the top notebook, and started to flip through it. He was looking for any institute type passwords, or maybe notes from certain private meetings at the institute on some of the advance science projects they were working on.

But even as he started leafing through the pages, he started to pick out details of what the body of the notes were about. There were advanced particle physics calculation formulas that had Doc stopping and staring at the handwritten pages in the notebook. He finished one and picked up another. The second book was a little different; it still had the multiple formulas postulated, but it related to performance of the chips and certain performance parameter modifiers. Doc picked up the third book and saw quite quickly expanding the project from the other notebooks.

Doc turned to speak to Isabel but at his side was Josh's son, Aadrik, who had come over to his side unnoticed as Doc was reviewing the notebooks.

When Doc turned, Aadrik immediately spoke up. "Those are Dad's zoom zooms."

"They are? Is that what your Dad calls them?"

"Dad is going to win the race and have a big trophy, because he goes fast with the Zoom zooms."

Doc looked over at Isabel. "Did Josh mention these to you?"

"Well, he and Aadrik talked about racing and how Josh was sure he would win this last race. Aadrik was always looking over his Dad's shoulder and questioning him, and asking to play with him. So, all I got is when I would overhear them talking. But Josh did tell me he was pretty confident about winning this time. I don't know how."

"Isabel, Josh has some important material outlined in

these notebooks of his. I am going to try and get the institute to purchase them from you."

"Doc, I would like to keep them, as I said, for the kids."

He nodded slowly. "Yeah, let me see, OK, these have data file backups on them." Doc pointed to the back binder of the books. Did he give you a password? I can copy them and just have the copies and you'll have the originals."

"If it is a password, it is always the same. Here, hand me one."

Doc handed her a notebook and Isabel held it up and spoke something softly to it. Immediately there were three beeps from the notebook and Isabel handed it back. Doc took a small disk out of his pocket and held it up to the notebook and spoke. "Copy files, password protect random my voice."

He then followed with the other two notebooks and copied them onto the same disk.

"How much do you think they're worth, Doc?"

Doc shook his head. "I don't want to be too optimistic, but it should be good enough to get the kids through college and more. I will bring it up tomorrow with the director, but for now you should keep them in a very safe place."

"And you should make your own copies." He passed the books back to Isabel, "Lock them back up with your password."

She quickly did so. She then stood up and started to head toward the narrow hallway.

Doc reached into his pocket, "Just a minute, Isabel." He pulled another disk out of his pocket. "Use this to back them up, and above all don't use your phone. That is all public info."

Isabel took the disk and looked at the small label. "Ok thanks." She then turned and left the room with the notebooks and the disk.

Aadrik started to follow his mom into the other room, but by the time he got to the edge of the hallway she was already coming back into the room. When she stopped, Aadrik grabbed onto her leg again and looked across the room at Doc.

Doc had watched Isabel leave the room and when she returned, he turned back to the desk and picked up the chips and tester. Isabel stepped into the kitchen area and picked up a tote bag and handed it to Doc as he reached the door of the apartment.

Doc said, "Thanks." He looked down at Aadrik and then up to Isabel, "I will give you a call tomorrow after I talk to Juan, and we can see where that goes, but I am sure that if the Institute doesn't bite there will be plenty of others that will."

"Thanks, Doc. Oh, when can we expect you tomorrow?"

"Well, probably around five, because I think Claire has it planned that we both are leaving work early, and we're going to try and bring the kids but that may be problematic. I don't know what they have planned for after school, but Claire will let me know."

Doc looked down at Aadrik again and said, "What do you want for dinner tomorrow?"

Aadrik shyly turned his head into his mom's thigh.

Doc smiled and looked up to Isabel. "Bye, we'll see you tomorrow."

Doc took the steps down instead of the elevator, and hurried to get back in the car. He had to hustle out to Ron's shop and back home by 6:00 p.m. to pick up Claire and get to his son's match. However, despite his haste, he did notice the nice high end late model car that was parked down the street from him. In the short time it took him to get from the apartment entrance to his ride he examined the car and the two people sitting in it. He got a little tinge of fear along the back of his neck. Doc, very much aware of how the government agencies work, started to wonder if they were there for him. As he gave the address for Ron's shop, he had his head slightly turned to see if they would come for him. When the car pulled out, he was relieved that it did not pull out to follow him.

He sat back in the seat to relax, and realized that they did not have to follow him if it was in fact him they were after. They would just track his car on the grid. They were probably listening to and watching him right now. He looked around in the car to see where the camera was located just to be sure. He then prompted the car to play some old annoying music from his youth and sat back to watch funny cat videos on the monitor.

The thirty-minute ride brought him into an old industrial park that was mostly vacant now of business as all the small local businesses had to close down, being unable to keep up with the government bureaucracy regulations and taxes brought on by one party rule. However, the buildings were full of squatters roaming the area. The local city mayor had declared the park a government control zone and prevented the owners from ousting the squatters. The owners went to the courts and contested that the mayor did not have the authority to make such declarations and was thus taking private property which was against the constitution without just compensation. However, the local judge who heard the case was the local party's chapter president and he set the hearing date out to the end of the current docket and has been doing so for the last few years. Now, the owners had been unable to pay the taxes, so the property would be confiscated eventually. Based on past experience, it would be some party official who buys it for next to nothing at some unannounced government auction. After that, the judge would dismiss the case, and the mayor would say it is time to clean up the neighborhood and use government funds to get rid of the squatters and refurbish the buildings for the new Party owner.

Doc got out of the car and walked up to the front door of Ron's shop; Doc was a little confused. He had been to Ron's shop a few times over the years mainly to drop Josh off when he needed a ride. Doc would drop him off even though it was out of the way. Now, Doc thought the suite he was standing in front of was not correct. Doc checked his phone and the directions were right and the address on the suite was right. Doc tried the door and it was locked, he knocked on it as loud as he could and got no response. Moving to the front window he peered through the drawn blinds to see if he could detect anything inside and could not. He straightened and looked around, wondering what to do next. One of the squatters was making his way down the drive between the buildings toward him. He turned back to the window and moved to a spot where the blind had been damaged. Now he could see the inside. The interior was littered with trash, folded up chairs and blankets. He could also see a few monitors set up in the rubble. He cracked a smile as the scene reminded him of dorm room he had once occupied in college. Backing away, and looking at the address again, Doc walked to the next suite to check the address and it was also correctly marked. He pulled out his comm and was about to try and call Ron when he saw that the squatter was almost to him. A little apprehensive, Doc moved back toward the car, keeping to the opposite side from the squatter. As he moved the squatter asked, "Have any change, man?"

Doc checked up and down the street to make sure they

were not being watched by other squatters. He did not want to end up with a crowd surge round, possibly robbing him.

As he reached the car, he quickly reached in a pocket and threw a small value chip at the squatter. Doc bent to get in the car as the door opened, and he heard the squatter again, "Thanks, Doc, get in and drive around this block two times—then change to manual and meet me at 23016 Suite F, go around to the back. Go now."

Doc didn't hesitate. He had known Ron for a long time and this type of behavior was par for the course with him. So, he directed the car to drive around the block. He looked out the window on both sides as though he was checking addresses on the building and once he had made it around he did it again. When he got in front of the suite again, he reached over to switch the manual control on and flipped out a small control arm from the side wall of the car. Doc dreaded using the manual controls, as did most people these days, since it was almost like learning to drive some old ancient auto from a hundred years ago. As he manipulated the controls, the car jerked forward with a weaving motion back and forth as Doc tried to familiarize himself with the controls. So, it took Doc awhile to get to the suite to which Ron had directed him. However, he made it in one piece with no real damage to the car—just a few dents to an old dumpster he hit on the way. There was also an annoying noise by an old plastic crate he had driven over a while back. His anxiety level rose a bit at the heckles and laughs from some of the other local squatters pointing at him as he drove by. But he compensated by smiling and waving at the groups as he passed.

Doc could now see Ron standing in front of his shop in the same worn clothes he had on when he asked Doc for some change. Doc parked and got out of the car. Approaching each other, instead of a hug, they shook hands firmly.. "How are you holding up, Ron?"

Ron had a trace of a grin. "Fine Doc, how about you? But let's talk inside."

Inside the shop was a mess. Doc noticed pieces of equipment he had developed for the manufacture of his chips and other components.

"Hey Ron, that equipment looks familiar."

"Well, it should," Ron said somewhat absently. "Juan had it all pushed out to the loading dock about a year before I left. I asked Liza what was going to happen to it and she said it was supposed to go to the dump. So I asked her to sell it to me. She got a little mad at me because it took me a couple trips and a few weeks to get it all off her dock but I got it done. Yeah, I had to rent out a fork lift to get it off the truck here. She wouldn't let me bring the institutes with me. "

"Well, that's fine, Ron, glad you got a deal, but that isn't why I wanted to talk to you."

"Yeah Doc, I'm just surprised I haven't been arrested yet."

Doc raised an eyebrow. "Arrested, what are you talking about?"

"Uh, What?" Ron thought a few seconds "What are *you* talking about?"

Doc knew it was normal for Ron to go off in different directions and knew their conversation would end up being a long one.

Doc said, "Well, let me explain. The Space Agency just bought all those old chips and accelerators this equipment was used to make."

Ron stepped back and looked at Doc. "Shit!" He then turned to the wall next to them and opened a large electrical panel box installed there. Looking over Ron's shoulder, Doc could see that it had a number of monitors mounted inside. Doc couldn't see what was on the monitors clearly, but Ron turned quickly and motioned Doc to follow him. Ron quickly darted through a second doorway into another work area where Doc saw another race sled partially assembled. What he saw on the surface of the racer brought him up short.

"Ron, why are you putting those chips on that racer?"

"Doc, you need to follow me. I will explain, but it's not safe here. C'mon, hurry before it's too late!"

Doc was getting that feeling again, as he thought back to his visit with Isabel and then Conor back at the Institute. He started to become a little more distressed thinking he was getting involved in something that was none of his business. Just then Ron turned a corner and disappeared; a second later Doc rounded the corner and a door slid shut behind him knocking him slightly off balance as it swept by his butt.

Startled, Doc turned quickly to see what had happened. There was actually no door there—just a solid wall. He then turned to look for Ron who was standing at the head of a staircase leading down and was waving to Doc to hurry.

When it appeared to Ron that Doc was going to ask him a question, Ron quickly put his finger to his lips.

The stairs led down one level to where there was a heavy steel door propped open. Ron bent over to pull out the door stop and motioned Doc through the door. Ron closed the door behind them and told the older man to grab a seat over by the large monitors. There were two large reclining chairs set out in front of the monitor, along with the latest gaming controllers and visors with other clutter lying atop a small cheap coffee table. Doc looked about the room as he walked toward the monitor, noticing different types of test equipment. Some sat in pieces on tables while others were in different stages of completion or repair. Doc could not tell which, but he did recognize multiple chips and accelerators mixed in among the equipment. This type of mess was typical for Ron and it reminded Doc of Ron's lab when he was with the Institute.

Trying to relieve some of the stress he was feeling Doc made what he thought would be a humorous comment, "Ron, I don't think I have time to stomp you in 'Alien Rage' right now." He thought it was the latest popular video game.

Ron did not seem to hear him—just started fiddling with the controller, the screen flashed on, playing a video of the inside of Josh's Racer.

When Doc saw it, he spoke immediately and emphatically, "Ron, I don't want to see this."

Ron looked over at Doc, "Yeah, well, you need to see it, because I don't understand it, and I'm worried others might have picked this feed up. I need your help. You need to figure this out. Josh was the physics whiz. I was just helping put the thing together and helping with the controls, you know."

Doc said, "Ron, if you think I am going to sit down and watch a friend of mine get blown to pieces, you are nuts. Stop this right now. I need to talk to you about the chips up in your shop. We're trying to track them down."

"Oh shit, God damn it! It's too late." Ron turned and ran over to a cabinet along the wall beside the monitor. He reached in and pulled out two handguns and some full magazines. He then hurried back over to Doc, trying to hand him one.

"Ron, are you crazy? Guns are illegal, you could go to prison for life. I need to get out of here!"

Doc turned abruptly away from Ron and headed toward

the door as Ron begged him to wait and give him a chance to explain.

Doc reached out to turn the handle and it was locked.

"Ron, c'mon I'm starting to get more than a little irritated with you. Will you please get over here and unlock the door?"

"Are you sure? I didn't lock it..." Ron paused in thought, "Damn, this can't be."

Ron had been headed towards Doc, but turned, dropped the guns and ammo on the closest sofa, then picked up the controller again. The monitor screen popped up with six views of the shop and building exterior.

Doc recognized the views of the shop and exterior immediately and could see his car parked outside the front door. What he didn't recognize was all the activity going on in the camera shots. He instinctively moved back into the room to get a closer view of the monitor. He ended up standing beside Ron and watching the large screen.

When Doc got a clear view of the activity he gasped, "What the hell is going on? Looks like you got a break-in. Why are they fighting?"

"That's why the door is locked. I put in a fail safe because I didn't want to walk out of my hideout into a bunch of nasty uninvited guests in the shop. So, my system locks the door instead of sounding an alarm, it also locks up the access panel in the shop so no one can get in down here."

"Are they robbing you and fighting in your shop? I thought you were friendly with the squatters."

Ron studied the views for a second before responding. "Those guys aren't squatters, those guys-and look there's a girl! "Ron pointed at one of the views, "They're some kind of Kung Fu master's squad or something. They are not from around here. Look how well they're dressed. They even have their faces blurred so both sides have money. I bet it's the government; maybe a couple governments."

Doc studied the scenes on the monitor and had to agree. "You're right. Why would they want to rob you? And why are they fighting?"

"Because that's what I was trying to show you. They want what Josh used on his racer."

Doc was watching the action on the screens and it appeared now that there were three fighters in one group and six in the other and despite all their skill the group of three would soon lose the fight. Doc felt himself starting to root for them as he had a tendency to go for the underdog. However, suddenly there was a loud crack and one of the three went down, and then the female's identity was no longer blurred. Doc could see her face clearly. Doc recognized her as the female guard that was with Mr. Holter's car that morning when the Space Agency purchased the chips from the Institute. Doc felt a sudden urge to get up there and help her.

Just then automatic weapon fire erupted throughout the shop. Doc and Ron reflexively ducked down. Watching a view of inside the shop, Doc saw a second wave of figures move in behind the first group of six. The largest fighter in the group of three ducked down and pulled the one that had gone down behind some cover. This left the three whom Doc assumed were all Space Agency people hunkered down toward the far back end of the shop.

All went quiet for a few seconds, then someone from the larger group spoke what sounded like an order in Chinese. Doc was surprised to hear that, as he thought it was the federal government probably trying to arrest the three Space Agency personnel. He'd surmised that the Space Agency was trying to get more chips or something and the feds were out to stop them. However, before he could consider another explanation, a translation of the Chinese was provided by Ron's system, "Surrender now, you are our prisoners, but you will keep your lives."

Doc was even more surprised when there was a response in Chinese from the outnumbered group of three. Doc asked, "What's the translation?" Ron looked at him and smiled. "I know it is old tech but I thought it would come in handy one day. Listen."

The translation came out, "Leave now, and you keep you lives, stay and they are forfeit."

Doc looked at Ron who was just staring at the screens. Ron had been quietly cursing to himself during the fighting. The response from the larger group was to loft what appeared to be grenades at the group of three. From the direction of the three, Doc saw some sort of pulse wave hit the grenades in midair dropping them to the street harmlessly sparking with an electrical charge.

Just then the whole building shook with a loud rumble, the lights flickered, pieces of concrete and dust dropped down from the ceiling and the monitor went blank with static. Doc turned to Ron, "Is there another way out of here?"

"Yes, but don't you want to see what happens first? I mean, these people are nuts."

"Ron, the monitor is dead. We need to get out of here, do you realize I have been here less than twenty minutes? If we stick around here, we may not make it out at all."

"OK, do you want a gun now?"

Doc said, "No, it would only be worse for both of us, and you can bet the police are going to be here any second. It would guarantee prison if we walk out to a squad of cops carrying these things."

"Ok." He picked up the guns with the ammo and put

them back in the cabinet. He then reached and pulled out two shock pistols. He handed one to Doc and said, "These are the latest models, they have twenty slugs in the clips. They'll knock someone out, but you have to hit skin."

Doc was familiar with the protective weapon; they also were illegal but the punishment was just a fine and Doc felt comfortable with that risk. Ron started to show Doc how to use it.

"Ron, I am quite familiar with these things, let's get out of here."

In fact, Doc was quite familiar with firearms in general. When he was a kid his grandfather and him did quite a bit of hunting on his ranch. Doc had won a few three gun contests when in high school and still had his BSA shooting merit badges tucked away somewhere. Doc still lamented not making Eagle Scout even though he could do nothing about it. He still had hard feelings toward the Party for disbanding them and labeling such groups illegal and a threat to the environment and community.

Ron pulled out his comm device while heading toward the door with Doc right behind him. Doc saw Ron had not put one of the guns back; it was sticking out of a concealed carry holster in the middle of his back.

Apparently, Ron had released the lock on their way to the door because it swung open with Ron's push. However, instead of heading up the stairs, Ron went behind the bottom set and pulled aside a piece of plywood that was leaning against the wall. He went down on all fours with gun in hand and went through the hole in the wall that the plywood had been covering. Doc did not hesitate and started to follow him, but bumped into Ron's legs which were blocking his route.

Ron whispered, "Hold on, Doc, I will be up in a second, then follow me up."

In a second Ron's legs disappeared up into the darkness, and Doc went through the hole, bumping his head on the other side. In the dim light he saw the outline of the bottom of a ladder. As he felt with his hands, he stood up in the confined area, bumping into the sides of the chamber. He could smell fresh dirt and could feel that the walls of the escape route were lined with wood. Doc slowly started up the ladder in the dark. As he did, he could feel the ladder shaking. This could only mean that Ron was still on the ladder going up. Doc ventured to look up and see how far Ron was ahead of him, but was greeted with lumps of dirt and other debris falling in his face. Clinging to the ladder, spitting out dirt, and taking measured steps he quickly set a pattern that got him to the top of the ladder. He knew he was there because he felt the top of the ladder and the open fresh air around him. He stopped and was about to try stepping out with his foot to test for a solid surface when he felt someone grab his arm.

"Don't move." It was Ron whispering. "I am going to put this night vision set on you."

Doc felt Ron slip a helmet or something over his head and then flip something down in front of his face. Almost instantly, he could see everything around him as though it was daylight inside the building.

He started to look down for a way to step off the ladder when Ron whispered, "Hold on."

Ron then reached under his chin and attached the straps to secure the night vision on his head.

Still whispering, he said, "Ok, let's go." Doc gave a thumbs up and stepped off the ladder to what appeared to be the first floor of the suite next to Ron's shop, he looked down the ladder and was surprised at how short the distance was, then he turned to follow Ron.

Ron was headed toward the other side of the suite, to a set of stairs that led up to a storage area.

Doc caught up with Ron at the top of the stair and they both went down a row of empty shelves till they stopped at the wall. As they walked down the row of shelves, Ron started pushing a ladder set in runners in the floor and ceiling and rolled along the shelves. It was apparently used when the place was a going business to pick parts from the different shelves. When they got to end of the bank of shelves, Ron turned to Doc and pointed up with his thumb. Doc nodded. It was a short climb of about twelve feet, and now Doc could see Ron climb off the ladder onto the top shelf. When Doc got to the top, he just saw Ron's back slip through another hole in the wall of this suite and Doc imagined into the next.

When Doc poked his head through the hole, Ron was there standing on a truss walkway that went across the top of the next suite. Below him Doc saw that the suite had a ceiling hung below him. He quickly followed Ron onto the walkway and they stepped through another hole that had been made through the wall into the next suite. The suite was the same as the last as they followed the truss walkway on into the last suite. Here Ron bent over and picked out one of the ceiling panels. He then stepped down through the opening onto an old steel storage cabinet that had been placed directly below the panel. Next, he got down on his knees, dropping out of the attic space and onto the cabinet. Lying flat on the cabinet, he slid over the side onto a conveniently placed bookcase, then hopped down onto the floor.

This suite had apparently once been used for office space and had two floors. They were on the second. After Doc followed him down, Ron led him down a carpet covered floor to a staircase that took them back down to the first floor. Here Ron stopped at another bookcase that had been shoved up against the wall and he pushed it aside to reveal a hole in the wall. The hole was blocked by what looked like an old piece of cloth. Ron got down and motioned Doc to get down and help him. Together they shoved against it and moved it out away from the wall. A ray of sunlight slightly illuminated the small space. Ron motioned Doc to stay still and he stuck his head out the opening. He pulled back in quickly and removed his night vision helmet. He then stuck his head out again and crawled out. After about half a minute he returned and putting his hand through the opening he signaled Doc to follow him. Doc removed his helmet and crawled out the hole.

Ron was standing beside a couch as Doc crawled out. The couch was what had been blocking the hole they had just crawled out of. When Doc was standing, Ron pointed to the damaged fence that ran along the backside of the industrial park and Ron's building. They started walking along the side of the building with Doc turning back to see if they were being followed.

Doc reached out and grabbed Ron's arm. At this, Ron swung around, eyes ablaze, pulling out the gun from his back holster, pointing it at Doc. Doc jumped back quickly and raised his hands, saying hoarsely, "No, No!"

Realizing he scared the crap out of Doc and there was no danger, Ron said, "Sorry Doc, I kind of freaked out there, what's up?"

Doc straightened up and said, "There hasn't been a sound since the building shook. I think we should check out what's going on."

Ron said, "Are you nuts? We can be through that fence and be gone, c'mon."

"No, I have to take a look. You can go, but there is a car

parked out front that leads directly to me. I need to see if there's a chance to get out of this fix, or at least figure out what it's all about."

Ron emphatically said, "Doc, I told you what this is about, but you just don't believe me."

"Ok, Ron, why don't you go through it again, but it just seems to me that a lot of detail is missing on how this fighting is related to you and Josh entering a racer in the Annual Moon Grand Prix." Doc continued, "Now I am going to walk back to the corner and take a look."

"Shit, Doc, don't do it."

Doc was fearful of the situation he was in with the local authorities and even the feds for that matter. He felt that maybe if the Chinese were somehow operating illegally on US soil, he could testify or be a witness against them to get himself off the hook for anything the authorities may want to charge him with. He figured Ron could just take off as he had no family that Doc knew of, but Doc had a wife and kids. He couldn't put them in jeopardy.

As he neared the edge of the building, he slowed to a stop to check on Ron. Ron was still standing where he had left him beside the couch. As Doc watched Ron, Ron started backing down along the building toward the fence, still facing Doc and still with the gun in his hand pointed in Doc's direction.

Doc turned back and edged forward, planning to look around the building and down toward where he had left his car in front of Ron's shop. He held the stun gun ready. He planned to keep it hidden around the side of the building. If he had to step out into view for some reason, he could then drop it out of sight. Doc pressed his head against the cool concrete at the edge of the building for a second. He could feel the sweat dripping off his face. He stopped and then dropped down on his knees. Again, he pressed his head against the concrete and slowly moved so that his left eye would have a view down along the building to where his car should be. However, as he peeked around the corner his heart sank. Doc was looking at somebody's legs in a tight black fabric and a type of thin boot, also black. Doc let out a low moan, dropped the gun beside him and placed his head in his hands on the asphalt pavement, unable to move. A feeling of dread started building in him. Next, he heard a shot fired and Doc knew it must have come from Ron's gun. Doc could not move, he remained motionless, bent over on his knees with his head in his hands dreading what was going to happen next. Doc remained so for only a second, and getting his wits back knew he had to stand up and face the situation whatever it was.

As he turned upward and looked into the face of the person in the black clothing, he realized he knew the man. It was Todd from the Space Agency who he had met in the morning in Juan's office. Doc smiled.

Todd spoke first. "Hello, Doctor Murphy, might I suggest you get to your car and head home?"

"Todd? What are you doing here?" he mumbled as he stood. "Get to my car?"

As he spoke, he heard movement behind him and turned. It was Ron being held in an armlock by the female guard from this morning and the more recent fight in Ron's shop. Doc stared at her for a moment realizing that she looked familiar to him.

Doc said, "Ron, are you OK, what was the shooting about?"

However, Ron was silent, his eyes flashing fear.

"Ron, don't worry, I know these people." Turning to Todd, he said, "What are your people doing here and who was that who attacked you? Are you Ok?" then thinking about the fight he asked, "Is the guy that got hurt OK?"

Todd reached out and clenched Doc's arm, "Sorry, Doctor, but you really should leave now, so let us escort you to your car." Doc was a little confused, but let Todd and the female quick step them to his car.

When they arrived at the car, Todd released Doc's arm.

Todd said, "Doctor Murphy, may I suggest you take Mr. Brady with you. This area is about to be swarming with your government's federal police and you both would probably be detained for quite a while if you are caught here."

Doc said, "Sure Todd, I will take Ron with me, that's a good idea."

Turning to Ron, who was still being held by the woman, Doc said, "They suggest you come with me, is that Ok with you, Ron?"

As the woman released him, Ron murmured. "You bet Doc, let's get the hell out of here!"

The car doors were open on both sides and Doc started to climb in, then stopped and took a look at the building. He could see cracks in the concrete and broken glass in the door and storefront windows.

Todd was being insistent, "Doctor, please. "

Doc turned to face him. "Well, Todd, thank you guys for your help. I don't know what is going on but I hope you're successful."

Doc turned toward the woman who had stepped back in a relaxed position after releasing Ron. He said, "Thank you too, young woman. By the way, I know Todd's name, what is yours?"

The woman answered, "Hope" with a smile, then looking at Todd followed immediately with, "Sir."

"Hope, that's a pretty name," Doc said pleasantly. "You

know you look very familiar to me, I'm just trying to place who you remind me of."

At that, Hope seemed embarrassed and started to step forward toward Doc, but Todd interrupted, "Captain, they need you inside."

Hope stopped, looked at Todd with what appeared to be anger in her eyes, then back at Doc, turned and headed toward Ron's shop.

Todd said, "Doctor, please! You have to get out of here now!"

Doc and Ron hurried into the car and the doors closed.

Doc turned to face Ron who was already seated.

Ron said, "That bitch took my gun!"

"Can it, Ron! Let's get out of here." Doc gave instruction to the car. He was heading home. It was still daylight and he was feeling strangely optimistic. He was just wondering if he could make it through the evening with his wife without telling her about his day.

As the car pulled out of the industrial park and headed toward the freeway, Doc closed his eyes and tried to collect his thoughts and sort out the day. The moment of peace did not last long. Ron elbowed Doc abruptly and when Doc looked over at him, he had his finger to his lips again. Doc responded angrily, "Ahh c'mon, stop the bullshit. I don't care. Tell me what you want or leave me alone."

Ron looked behind him out the back window then out the side one before responding in a low voice, "OK, you see my point, this is all related to Josh and his racer. Now please Doc, watch the video. I need someone with more smarts than me to study it. At this point it may be that our lives depend on it." Ron paused a second, looking down at his comm to bring up the video of the race, then said, "Or at least mine might."

Doc could see in Ron's eyes that he was tense as a guitar string so Doc relented, "OK, let's see it, can you project it, it would easier to see." Ron in a more relaxed voice, but still whispering, "I don't know, what about the cameras."

Doc wasn't worried about the cameras set in cars to monitor the citizenry and he turned slightly to look at the one he'd located earlier in the day. There was no attempt to hide the devices and there were multiple cameras in a single car. Some in plain view and some hidden just like the mics.

He was surprised when he saw the device. It had melted somehow. He then turned quickly to look to the other side of the car, checking behind Ron. Ron, a bit confused by Doc said, "What's wrong?"

Doc paid no attention to him but continued to look around the car in the usual locations where he knew cameras were placed. As he did, he could see that the two more he was able to locate were also melted.

Doc turned back to Ron and pointed at the different locations. "I don't think the cameras or mics are working in this car anymore. Those people back at your shop seem to have disabled them."

Ron said, "Yeah, I see, who were those guys? They never introduced themselves to me you know."

"It doesn't matter right now, but they want to talk to you. Also they are probably taking any of my old chips you had at the shop with them."

Ron said, "Yeah, I thought that's what this was all about; do you know if they are good guys or bad?"

"What do you mean? If you mean are we going to get in trouble or arrested probably not. At least not tonight. Ok, no more questions. Let's just look at your vid before I get home. "

"Ok, look up here." Ron leaned back and projected the vid onto the ceiling of the car from his comm. "This is at regular speed." The video showed the inside of the racer and must have been set up right in Josh's helmet. Doc heard Josh's voice yell out, "Back off, old man!" and he saw out the racer's side view of Josh's racer another racer with a much older man angling in toward Josh's. The view then swung toward the front screens and the orbiter station came into view. Doc saw that the race was almost over when the accident happened. Ron alerted Doc, "Here it comes!"

Doc braced himself to see an explosion on the screen and the last moments of his protégé's life. Instead, he saw nothing, the scene on the video showed no explosion, did not turn to static or a black screen. Instead, the screen seemed to freeze the motion and scrabble the screen, like an old digital monitor did when streaming and the internet slowed and started losing the signal.

Ron pointed at the screen as the scrabble on the screen continued getting worse, "Do you see what I mean? It just keeps getting like that. Now, look what I discovered." Doc watched the video as Ron continued, "I ran it at super slow motion and condensed the incoming signal, watch again, I will start it from right when it happened."

Doc watched as the screen at a snails' pace started with the pixelated view out toward the orbiter. However the view showed pixels flashing all over the ceiling to the point that it was hurting Doc's eyes.

"Turn it off, Ron," then turning toward him, he said, "What was I supposed to see? I don't understand!"

Ron flipped the comm close and shoved it into his pocket, "Doc, what you need to do now is see Isabel, and ask to see Josh's notebooks and now let me tell you about Josh's racer."

Outside the car the sun was starting to cast longer shadows now as the day was edging toward late afternoon. Doc looked out of the car window as they were about to pull into his driveway.

"Ron, can you tell me later? You can stay here tonight if you like, but I just don't understand what you are trying to tell me."

Ron said, "Josh was using those old chips of yours to help him win the race. He had set up a controller ..." Ron stopped as he saw Doc drop his face into his hands and he heard Doc sob.

Doc said, "Geez, Ron, how can this day get much worse, I knew I should have destroyed those things a long time ago. My ego wouldn't let me and now Josh is dead because of me."

"Doc no, no, no, that isn't what happened. You are wrong, didn't you see it in the video?"

The car stopped in front of Doc's home garage door, now used as a home office for Doc when he had time to relax and read.

Doc got out and walked toward the front door, leaving Ron in the car.

Claire came out of the front door as Doc approached.

Walking toward him she said, "I was wondering when you were going to get here. Here is a sandwich." She handed him a small brown bag as she passed him and headed toward the car. She stopped short when she saw Ron sitting inside and turned back to Doc. Holding the bag in his hand, he had turned back toward her and the car. She was going to ask why Ron was with him but sensing something in Doc's manner she said, "What's wrong?"

When Doc said nothing, she continued, "Is Ron coming with us?"

Doc still did not say anything. Just then the car door opened and Ron got out and stood beside the car. Claire turned her head to look at him then turned it back toward Doc. She said, "Well, Ron, are you going to tell me what's going on?"

Ron didn't hesitate and started to answer, "Claire, I got the video,"

Doc interrupted him in a loud voice, practically shouting, "Ron, how about a drink?'

Ron stuttered on his words and said, "Sure, I can really use one" and headed toward the door. Doc went into the house, and followed the hallway into the kitchen to the frig with Ron close behind him.

Doc opened the frig, pulled out two green bottles of beer, and handed one to Ron.

Ron mumbled, "Thanks."

Doc reached into a counter drawer and pulled out an opener. He opened his beer then tossed the opener to Ron who caught and opened his.

Claire came into the small kitchen and said, "That's OK, guys, I am not really thirsty right now." Then turning directly to Doc, she said, "So either tell me what you two are up to or let's get going so we're not late."

Doc looked up at Claire, then turned to Ron, "You're welcome to stay here, come with us to the school or we can drop you someplace." He paused, "If it is on the way, that is."

Ron lifted up his beer and finished it off in a few big gulps, "I would like to go with you guys." Then on second thought, to Claire and said, "Hi Claire, how are you, how have you been?"

Doc gave a quick glance at Claire then back to Ron, who shrugged. Doc smiled and took another swig of his beer and said, "Well, that is what I needed, let's get going. I don't want to be late for Matt's match."

On the way to Matt's school, Claire asked Doc in a few different ways what had gone on with him and Ron during the day. Doc dodged her with the "later" excuse the first time and "too tired now" the second time. She was about to try her luck with Ron, when they heard a muffled snore come from him. Somehow, he had managed to fall asleep while they were talking. Claire looked back at Doc and said, "Well, apparently he doesn't want to answer any questions either," and then leaned back in her seat.

The lower weights had already competed when Doc and Claire found some bleacher seats on the home team side of the gym. As they sat down, Claire conversed with some of the other parents in the bleachers. Doc did his traditional stare at his comm to avoid talking to any of them. He noticed there had been a few call messages left. He didn't really care, as none of the calls were identified. He was a little annoyed that there were messages; his phone was set not to let any calls through unless the number was in his list.

He was just starting to relax when he heard Claire say, "Jonathan, what? You're not going to give your Mom a hug?"

Doc started to smile as he looked up from his comm. His younger son had come over to greet them. Doc called him Jack, which Claire didn't like because his full name was a family name from her side. But Doc thought it was too long and it would be too embarrassing to go around calling him Jonathan when he got older and had friends around. So, he always called him Jack. Jack was a freshman and decided to go out for wrestling like his older brother, Matt, who was a senior. Matt wrestled at the 154 lb level and was thin as a rail. Jack was just learning the sport, mostly on the practice squad. He did get to wrestle on the J.V. sometimes, depending on how eliminations went.

Giving the expected, "Ah Mom," Jack bent over a little and let his Mom hug him.

Doc said, "Jack, are you going to sit with us to watch Matt's match?" Doc knew he wouldn't; he much preferred to hang out with his buddies at the end of the bleachers or in the school hallway.

Jack said, "No Dad, I just came up to get you. Matt wants to see you right away, c'mon."

Claire started to rise, "What's wrong? Is he sick? Did he not make his weight?"

Doc had started to rise too. "Well, it's almost time for his match." Then he noticed that Matt's seat on the team chairs was empty. "Ok, let's go."

As they started, Jack turned to his Mom and said, "Mom, Matt just wants Dad, OK?"

Claire looked at Doc and back at Jack. "Well, OK, tell him good luck for me." As she finished, Jack had already made it down the bleachers to the gym floor and was headed to the door of the locker room. Doc had to hustle to keep up with him. Jack turned as they went through the door and Doc immediately saw Matt leaning up against the wall and looking down with Assistant Coach Mr. Simmons talking to him.

Jack walked up to Matt and said, "Dad's here" and moved off to the other side of the hall. Matt glanced up with a worried look on his face as Doc stood before him. The Assistant Coach then spoke extending his hand. Doc took it in a quick hand shake, "Doctor Murphy, good to see you again, since it is almost time for Matt's match, I must explain quickly what happened. It is not Matts' fault, but there is really nothing we can do about it. We only were told this afternoon that the district athletic directorate has been directed by the Party that they must work to eliminate the inequality in scholastic sports. It was explained to the team that this meant winning and losing is discriminatory. Basically, they told us that since our wrestling team is undefeated, they would need to lose tonight because it was unhealthy for them and the community to display such inequality and discrimination. So, you understand... "

Doc held up his hand to Mr. Simmons, "Sorry, Mr. Simmons, but I have had a hard day. Let me talk to Matt."

Mr. Simmons stopped. "Sure, Doctor Murphy," and backed up a step.

Doc said, "Alone please, Mr. Simmons."

"Ok, but he is almost up" and walked over to the door looking out into the gym. Matt's brother moved back in a little closer to his brother.

Doc said, "What's up, Matt?"

"Dad, they told me I had to lose the match because of the new party directive and that it would be good for my future for getting into college."

"What, you're kidding right? That is what all this garbage is about?"

Matt nodded. "I told them I didn't even want to wrestle then, and Coach said I had too, because the other guy is some big shot's kid. Coach says he has to win to demonstrate the benefits of the new policy."

Matt hesitated and continued, "Dad that kid hasn't won all year, I could take him easy. I wanted to go undefeated my senior year, this is crap."

You could hear some booing coming from the gym and then Mr. Simmons yelled over from the door, "Matt, it's time."

Doc said, "Matt, you have to do what you think is right most of all, you have to say 'is this something I can be proud of, or is it something you may regret?'" Doc continued, "You're a tough kid, Matt. Whatever you decide to do is OK with me. You have always done your best, and you should stick to that."

Doc put his arm around the back of Matt's head and pulled him in close in a loose headlock so that they were face to face." So, what do you think, Son?"

"Dad, I'm scared."

Doc still held Matt, "Son, you know what, I'm not, because I know you're going to pin that guy in thirty seconds. Now give him hell." Doc released Matt's head with a little jerk and Matt looked up at him smiling. Jack who had been standing close was also smiling.

Doc released Matt and pushed him toward Coach Simmons, "Now Go!"

Matt hustled to the gym, going right past Coach Simmons without a word. Simmons turned toward Doc and Doc gave him a big thumbs up as he walked toward the gym with Jack at his side.

When he got back to his seat, Matt and his opponent were already in the middle of the mat shaking hands. A second later the referee blew the whistle to start the match. Like lightning, Matt shot down for a single leg of his opponent, yanked it up and swept the remaining leg out from under him with his foot. As his opponent fell to the mat, Mat plowed his hips over his head and wrapped his legs over his opponent's head in a head lock. His opponent fought back desperately but Matt ended up on top with his opponent flat on his back, arching his neck to keep from being pinned. The referee was already down on his stomach with his hand out ready to slap the mat for the pin. Matt looking comfortable on top of his opponent reached out and pulled the opponent's leg in to collapse his back arch. He pulled the foot in with one hand and reached back and pulled the opponent's elbow out from the mat by yanking on his arm. The back arch of his opponent collapsed and the referee slapped the mat, signaling a pin and the end of the match.

Matt jumped up with his hands in the air as the crowd in the stands roared. He ran around the outside circle then headed back toward the center. The referee called both wrestlers into the middle of the mat, grabbed each participant's hand and quickly raised Matt's hand to signal the winner of the match. As he let go, the buzzer rang from the bench and the referee was waved over. A crowd had formed there, mostly of people from the visiting team. You could hear voices at the scorer's table getting louder.

At this point the referee turned and left the gym. Matt had watched this as did the crowd in the gym. At that point he headed off the mat and started slapping hands with his teammates. His opponent had already left the mat and left the gym. Matt's school principal, Mr. Fisher, now appeared at the table, and after a few seconds some of the crowd went out toward where Matt's opponent had gone. Doc watched as the principal came over to the Coach, spoke for a minute and then, with him, came over to where Matt was with his teammates. Doc could see Matt shaking his head back and forth, so Doc headed over. What he heard as he approached was the principal trying to go back out to the middle of the mat again. Doc heard that somehow Matt had been disqualified and his opponent had won the match. Doc could see Matt's face was red and he was furious. Matt was staring straight into the face of the principal with his arms crossed in front of him. When Doc reached Matt, the principal turned to him, "Please Doctor Murphy, I am terribly sorry, and I know it is not correct, but I have been told in no uncertain terms that the new athletic policy must be enforced and that official over there says if we don't do as he says he will get the funding here cut. Can you explain to Matt ?"

Doc looked across the gym and could see the man in the suit that had been pointed out. He also saw that they had rounded up Matt's opponent and had escorted him back into the gym to where the man in the suit was standing.

Turning back to the principal, "What do they expect Matt to do; the match is over."

"Well, we have to go back out and I've been asked to raise the other boy's arm as the winner."

"Are you fucking kidding me?"

"Doctor Murphy, I have to, that guy can destroy us; you know how the party works. The government will take it out on the whole school to get what they want, Please, help us."

Doc looked over and could see that the official had walked the other wrestler into the center of the mat and was holding him there by his arm, looking over toward him and the others in the group. Doc saw the principal look at him and then over at the official. In the background boos were starting to come out of the crowd, as this began the official signaled to someone in the door of the gym and a young woman came out to the scorer's table turned and started videoing the crowd. This brought a quick silence in the gym.

Doc turned to his son and spoke quietly while pushing the others in the group away, "Son, you won the match and you are undefeated, but you know what's going on here is a sham, we can walk out of here now, but a lot of people will suffer, you're old enough to know how this country works. So, I am asking you to put on a show for these government clowns and let's get out of here. Celebrate your victory, Matt, celebrate the truth. Celebrate yourself!"

Matt looked at his Dad, gave a nod, and started out to the middle of the mat saying "Let's go, Fisher!"

As they got there the official stepped to the side and Principal Fisher reached down to hold up his hand. As he did, he also reached for Matt's. As he raised his opponent's arm the boos and jeers broke out again. Matt had a slight grin on his face because as the cameras flashed on him, he had his middle finger sticking out on both hands. One across his chest. A second later, Matt pulled his hand away from the principal and with arms raised high took another victory lap around the mat. The crowd broke into cheers and applause again as Matt exited the gym toward the locker room. Doc and Jack followed him out, and to his surprise so did a group of parents with their kids from the team bench in tow. They were followed by the principal trying to get them back to the match.

Matt was out of the locker room by the time Doc and Jack got to the door. He had not bothered to shower.

Doc said, "Well, that was a short night; you boys up for some pizza?"

Jack, said, "Sure am, Dad, but we've got school tomorrow."

"Well, we'll see about that. You hungry, Matt?"

"I could eat three large pepperonis."

CHAPTER 6

I t ended up being quite late for a school night when they finally headed home from the restaurant. Doc was quite exhausted from the crazy day he'd had and was quite satisfied to just be gazing out the car window on the way home. Jack had fallen asleep while Matt was on his comm the whole time with his friends reading and sending messages. Claire also had been engaged on her comm sometimes by voice, other times texting. According to her, the whole school was in an uproar over what had happened at the wrestling match.

Ron had disappeared while they were in the gym. Claire said she received a message from him that he had to leave, nothing else. Doc had tried to contact him while they were eating, but received no reply.

As they neared the house, Doc noticed a car was parked in their driveway. For some reason he was not surprised and looked glumly down at his hands. His car started to pull into the driveway, but stopped. Over a speaker the A.I. let him know there was something blocking the driveway and all passengers would have to depart at the curb. As Doc started to move to get out there was a tap at the window. Looking out, Doc saw a darkly dressed individual indicating he should get out. Doc noticed that the car was surrounded now by four men all dressed in dark clothing.

As Doc stepped out of the car, he was grabbed from

behind and shoved against the car. His hands were pulled behind him and bound.

Doc shouted, "What the hell are you doing?" As he spoke, he saw the individuals on the other side of the car draw their weapons and point them at him. One of the men behind him spoke, "Murphy, you are under arrest for embezzlement and misappropriation of government property. Any more outbursts from you will result in forceful restraint. First lieutenant, please demonstrate." Moments later Doc felt an intense shock that sent him sprawling to the ground, limbs askew. He must have passed out, for when he could focus again, he could hear Claire screaming. She wasn't near him, however, so he rolled slightly to see what was going on while struggling to get to get free of his bonds. He was aghast when he saw her shoved up against the car with her hands bound. One man was holding her down while another was rapping some sort of muffling device over her mouth.

Shouting to his wife, Doc kept struggling to get up and see where his kids were when a heavy boot was shoved down on his head pushing his face down into the driveway. Doc paused in his struggles.

With the boot still on his face, he heard a man's voice in tense tones, "Again, Jonathon Murphy, you are under arrest for embezzlement and misappropriation of government property. Now, do you need a muzzle like your wife?"

The man paused to look down at his comm, reading through the information there.

He said, "Who is this Tomasz fellow?"

"What? This is a mistake, there is no Tomasz here," said Doc. The man shoved his foot harder into Doc's face, grinding it into the driveway. He then stepped off and gave Doc a hard kick in the stomach, causing Doc to groan in pain.

"Shut up!" he said. "Oh, I see now, "Like father, like son. Appears being a traitor runs in your family, scum."

When Doc did not answer, the man stepped back. "Pick him up, but cover his eyes first."

There was a "Yes, sir" response.

Doc had a dark spit hood pushed over his head, and then he was yanked to his feet by both arms from the back. He groaned at the pain.

"Now, Doctor Murphy, I can call you that, right? Of course I can, I can call you whatever I like. The state has filed charges against you and your wife, and your two sons. Your wife and sons are being charged with felony car theft. Your son, Matthew Murphy, is also being charged with the additional crime of inciting a public disturbance and disobedience of the recently enacted State Equality Athletic Fairness Statute."

Doc said, "What are you talking about? You are not making sense."

"We just came back from my son's high school. No one here stole any cars. It is impossible to steal a car anyway. Who is making these charges? What did I embezzle? This is all ridiculous, besides, you are required to give me my rights."

To this the man gave a short, "Ha, your director at the institute turned you in once he discovered your illegal activities."

"I just met with the director this morning. He did not mention anything to me, let alone turning me over to the police."

"Let me explain, doctor. You sold government property to another government without obtaining the export permission of the federal government in Washington. You conned your director into believing that the material was worthless and then you received a substantial payment from the other entity."

He continued, "We have all the evidence we need with your ex-director's sworn statement. On the other crimes, while fleeing the Institute you stole this transport, damaged the tracking and communication devices on board in order to flee with your family here. However, we caught you before you could get away."

"Our evidence will show that everyone in this transport was in on the scheme."

"I want a lawyer!"

"Of course you do, all criminals want lawyers, but that is not my responsibility. You and the other criminals will be transported to the FBI holding for interrogation and then to the appropriate education center."

Doc heard shuffling and the man seemed to be speaking to others, "Ok, muzzle him and load them up. We've been here too long already."

Doc felt something pulled over his mouth and tightened behind his neck making it difficult for him to breathe with the bag still on his head.

He was being pushed forward, held on each side by the back of his arms. Doc lost control at that point and started swinging his body back and forth, trying to use his head to force himself free. It only lasted a few seconds before he received another shock and was then carried to an open van and thrown in the back.

When Doc came to, he realized he was on the floor of a moving vehicle and the ride was not smooth. He could feel the vehicle being driven at high speed and not slowing down much for turns and potholes in the road. He tried to speak, but all he could manage was muffled yells. Still, he hoped that if Claire and the kids were with him, they might give some type of response. After a few moments he paused to listen for any type of response and there was none. He imagined that his family had been separated and would be taken to different locations. He'd heard stories of how the FBI had secret locations now throughout the country to keep people incognito. Some stories claimed that the disappearance of many of the young people who tried to protest for human rights and freedom of speech were imprisoned in these hidden locations. At this thought, he wondered if he would even get a trial. Nowadays it was only the privileged Party members who received trial. All others simply were placed in reeducation camps.

Doc remembered how this lack of due process had gradually spread across the country after the Party had won the elections for one term and packed the Supreme Court. A case was brought before them in which the court had rendered a split decision. In this one particular case it was a criminal that had to prove his innocence. Judges that ruled in favor of the prosecution wrote an opinion that had little substance. The individual charged would be forced to prove his innocence because the public believed he was guilty and it would be wrong not to punish him even if the police had no evidence of his guilt. This type of decision became commonplace on the court system until eventually almost all individuals charged had the burden of proof placed upon them and the defence. So now, in line with other socialist countries, the Party, which now controlled all branches of the government, was able to prosecute any opposition into bankruptcy and prison.

It was no surprise then that the Party was a very close client of China, the most powerful country on Earth or that they had adopted China's model of government many years ago.

Doc lay quiet on the floor as these thoughts pounded through his head and he wondered if he would ever see his family again.

When the transport stopped for a moment, Doc heard someone enter before it moved out again. He was not surprised when his hood and muzzle were pulled off and that he was looking into the face of two Chinese in military uniforms.

One spoke in perfect English, "Doctor Murphy, I am Colonel Yang. You have been turned over to the People's Republic of China, by your government. Your family will remain here in your country and you will provide our scientists with the capabilities and designs of your so-called tachyon chips and any other assistance that may be required. Understand?"

Doc asked, "Where is my family? I'm not going anywhere or doing anything until I see them and talk to my lawyer."

"Your family is safe for now, doctor, and of course their future status depends entirely on you."

Doc said, "You can't be serious; you are going through all this trouble for something that doesn't work? Besides, this has to be illegal even for my government."

Yang continued, "Doctor Murphy you must adjust to your new reality, as will the rest of your country very soon."

"What do you mean by that?"

Yang simply smiled, then turned to the other man in the transport and spoke something in Chinese.

They picked Doc up and set him on one of the seats that lined the inside of the transport. One of them cut his restraint and had him put his hands in front. They then attached another restraint with his hands in front. The other man then fastened Doc into his seat belt. Doc sat there exhausted. He could barely keep his eyes open, but even in this state he kept on questioning them about the whereabouts of his family. At some point, a damp cloth was held over his nose and mouth and Doc inhaled a whiff. In seconds he was out with his body slumping against the seat belt and his head bobbing as the van traveled forward.

Doc could feel a massive headache as he began to regain consciousness. He heard voices around him. One said "Shoot him, we need to get out of here now!" There was sudden gunfire.

Someone responded, "Just a sec, here we go."

Doc struggled to open his eyes and stand but he seemed paralyzed, even though he heard the activity around him. He felt a whoosh of air at his neck. A warm flow started outward from his neck and his eyes popped open, in seconds his flailing his arms and legs were against hard pavement. He could see he was no longer in the van.

A voice spoke, "Settle down, Doc, you are safe now!"

Doc thought he recognized the voice and shouted, "They have my family!" Then realizing the repercussions that the Feds and Chinese would inflict on his family, Doc panicked, "You can't do this! You have to get out of here, leave now! The feds will destroy my kids, imprison my wife!" In desperation Doc pleaded, "I beg you to stop!"

Doc still could not focus on the masked figure in front of him, his vision was still blurred and occasionally bright sunlight shown directly into his eyes, causing him to squint.

"No can do, Doc." Then came a loud military order from the man, "Help him, let's get loaded up, move it!"

Being lifted up, Doc was standing when the figure spoke again, "Are the implants in? Good, dump them over the side."

Doc was being supported and led down a road. He could

see he was near the old airport which was apparently where the van had been taking him. He still could not clearly see the figure in front of him. As they were moving him down the road, Doc could clearly see the hands and arms grasping him, but not the entire body of his rescuer. They were all in some kind of light deflection camouflage coverings. As he was led, he saw bodies of a number of men seemingly being dragged across the road by an invisible force. They were then all stood up unceremoniously at the edge of the road and pushed over the side, disappearing from sight. Doc felt a small sense of pleasure, when he recognized his tormentor from the prior night tossed by hand and foot into the air and over the side.

In front of him Doc now could make out a large shimmering wall, and he realized that it was also in camouflage and probably an aircraft. He started to struggle, "No, listen, you can't do this. I can't leave! The Feds have my family."

Doc started struggling with the man holding him up. A second later, he felt another whoosh of air to his neck and his legs collapsed beneath him. As he lost consciousness again, he picked up the voice of the leader again, "Sorry, Doc."

CHAPTER 7

D oc woke up strapped in a reclined seat, he was in a small space with a flat monitor on a small pedestal in front of him with the surrounding walls and ceiling covered in monitors.

Doc also noticed a lightness through his body and immediately recognized it. He was in space; his abductors had brought him to space. He looked down at the straps holding him down, and saw that they were not restraints but merely the normal safety belts for space travel. He reached down to release them when a panel in the floor opened and Todd in a loose-fitting uniform of the Space Agency floated up into the cabin.

Doc said, "Todd, what have you done? You have to take me back! I have to get back! You people don't realize what they will do to my kids."

Todd did not respond but moved into a seat across from Doc and started snapping himself in. As Doc had been focused on Todd, he barely noticed that a second man had entered the cabin and taken a seat right next to him.

The individual began speaking to Doc before he even turned his head. "Doctor Murphy, I am the commander in charge of this rescue mission. The captain here has completed his task in the operation and is in this meeting so that you have a familiar face that you can recognize. But please direct your questions to me and I will answer them to the best of my ability at this point. However, Doctor Murphy, you must understand that we are under a time constraint and so we will need to answer your questions kind of on the fly."

Doc had remained quiet as the man spoke; he'd been caught off guard for some reason when he turned toward him. Doc did not know why--maybe because the man was older than what Doc would have expected a Space Agency personnel to be. This guy must be almost eighty for sure. The older man was dressed in the same loose fitting jumper uniform that Todd was in. Doc realized that he too was now wearing a jumper suit. Doc reached to his face and could feel that he had been recently shaven and feeling around himself for the first time that he had apparently been given a bath.

Doc stared at the man who introduced himself as commander, "Sir, you have royally fucked up here, you had no right to kidnap me. Do you realize what is going to happen to my family? Not even the best lawyer and highest bribes on Earth can save my family now. You might as well have condemned them to immediate death! You fucking assholes, now return me immediately!"

Doc's intensity and anger only increased when he saw in the commander's eyes that he was not even listening to him, but was focused on some messaging that was being fed to him. Doc surmised the commander had an implant.

The commander started speaking to no one in particular, so Doc assumed it was someone with whom he was in communication. "Thanks, that is excellent. Good work!"

When Doc realized the commander wasn't even listening to him, he was pissed. Doc unsnapped his harness and reached out to grab the man in a rage, "You fucking asshole!"

Doc clenched onto one of the commander's arms as the rest of his body, legs and butt flew past him and into one of the monitors hanging to the side. He started flailing at the man with his fist as he tried kicking off the wall of monitors behind him using his legs. The commander seemed to almost calmly be swatting his fists away, first one way and then the other. Doc felt himself being grabbed from behind, and something went around his legs, snapping them together. Next his arms were pressed in and another restraint snapped them together. Todd had acted to restrain him and now had him by his jumper and was placing him back in his seat. In a moment, he was back in place with his seat harness on and Todd was back in his seat too. Doc continued to try and get out but it was no use. Catching his breath he said hoarsely "You sons of bitches, you fucking a holes; how can you fucking do this?"

In the next second, Todd was out of his seat again and shoved a mouth restraint into Doc's mouth then reseated himself.

Wasting no time, the commander started again, "Doctor Murphy, we are aware of your concerns for your family as are we all, as any decent community would be."

"Please view the monitor to your left."

One of the monitors on the wall flipped on. In the view, Doc could see his two sons wearing spacesuits with the face plates open. Their seats were located right behind the pilot who Doc recognized as Hope from Ron's shop. Both boys had smiles on their faces and appeared to be relaxed.

Doc relaxed and started shaking his head, trying to spit out the gag in his mouth.

The Commander said, "Doctor Murphy, can you remain civil as we discuss the situation? "

Doc nodded.

"Captain, please remove the gag."

After Todd moved across and removed the gag from Doc and pushed it into a disposal, the commander said, "Thank you, Captain."

"Where are they, and what about my wife?"

The commander held up his hand, "Please just hold on a second and I will update you on your family's status as well as other parts of this operation that have taken place to this point. So far successfully."

Doc, "Claire! Where is Claire? I need to talk to my sons."

"Please let me finish, first your sons as you see are safe and no longer in the hands of FBI. They are currently in a small ship en route to the Moon, and no you cannot talk to them as yet since they still are too close to Earth and could possibly be targeted. The video you are seeing is actually from ten minutes ago. They are now in stealth mode and will be for a few hours. In fact, this ship is also in stealth mode and will be for some time even though we are on a different projectory than the Moon."

Doc, more calmly, "So do you have my wife?"

"Yes, your wife is safe, and will also be heading toward the Moon, although, they are still in very close to the Earth, so there is a higher risk that some country may target them. We have no visuals on her but we were waiting for confirmation we had her safe before waking you."

"Waking me? Wait, why are you doing this? Why has my family been abducted first by the Feds, the Chinese and now I guess the Space Agency?" Doc tried looking around for a clock. "How long was I out?"

"It was only yesterday morning that you first met Todd in your director's office, and let's say it is now actually the following evening if you want a time frame."

"Ok, so what's going on?" Doc hesitated, "commander." Doc paused a second, "Commander who?"

"Commander will do, now let's get started. Please try not to interrupt till I am finished. There's a lot going on right now and time is of the essence."

Doc simply nodded and the commander started in, "First, an update on a number of other important questions that may come up later, so I will answer them now."

"One, your friend Mr. Ron Brady is on this ship as is all the equipment that was purchased from your Institute yesterday and all the equipment retrieved from his shop."

"Two, we also have rescued your Dr. Shamir's family--his wife Isabel and the children. They were picked up yesterday and are well on their way to the Moon at this point."

Doc started to say, "Wait, Isabel had...!"

Again, the commander held up his hand, "Doctor please, I assume you're talking about Dr. Shamir's notebooks? Yes, we have them also. Although it was tricky getting your comm away from the Chinese, along with the backup disc you made. It was good that we picked up Mrs. Shamir and the children before you. She told us about the disc copy you made. Now let me continue; it has now been five days since Dr. Shamir disappeared."

Doc's eye widened, "What do you mean disappeared?"

"Doctor Murphy, so let's get to the why we are all here and why you and your family and many others almost ended up in your country's work camps or prisons whichever you prefer. Your colleague's little racer did not blow up as reported; that was the story we fed your government; it did actually disappear. The fact of the matter is that I was there and witnessed the incident. It was quite amazing."

Doc said, "How were you there, it was clear out between the Moon and Earth; we didn't know about it for hours after it happened."

There was a spark in the commander eyes. "Actually, I

was winning that race until he passed me. I was no farther away from him than maybe ten meters and I could see his face and he could see mine; I am sure of it."

"As I closed on him, I could see he made a decision to do something. He was smiling at me and then he was gone. He disappeared right in front of me. Those chips you invented were plastered all over the front exterior of his racer."

Doc's eyes started to lighten up and his mind started racing as he pieced together the calculations and diagrams he had seen in Josh's notebook and he started to smile. Something else started to dawn on Doc as he sat there face to face with the commander. He was hit with the deja vu feeling again. He knew he definitely had met this guy before and he started to focus on the commander and think back on when it was.

"Doctor, I see that you're catching on, but let me continue."

Doc interrupted. "No, I know you. I am sure of it; where have we met before? Tell me, I'm trying to piece this all together and I need the facts."

Doc could see the commander stiffen, staring directly at him. The man seemed frozen in thought for a few moments. Doc then saw him relax and even glimpsed a slight smile appear on his face. The commander turned his gaze down toward his notes, breaking the eye contact with Doc, then continued, "First, we're in a hurry because I believe that your Dr. Shamir may be still alive, and that time is running out to save him. It is now six days since he disappeared. The question is where?"

Doc guessed that the commander was not going to answer his question so he thought it best to save it for later and focus on the possibility of finding Josh.

"What are you proposing?"

"In the moments after he disappeared, the Space Agency locked down that area and started a search. We are still there with support vessels and personnel keeping the exact location clear—and maybe more important—his racer's trajectory vector."

The display right in front of Doc flashed on.

The commander commented, "Your associate, Mr. Brady, had already tried to discuss his video with you, which was quite inventive by the way. I believe you dismissed what he was doing."

"Well, there was quite a bit going on at the time."

"True, but let's continue; as you see on the display, the location where Josh disappeared is our current destination."

Doc viewed the screen which marked a spot almost ten million miles out in space. He saw that the spot was well outside the Moon's orbit of the Earth. It was obvious that the Earth had already traveled a substantial distance in its yearly orbit around the Sun away from where Josh had disappeared. The monitor displayed the current position of the Earth and Moon as well as the space traffic in the local area. It also identified all the traffic out to the spot where Josh had disappeared.

He noted another highlighted vessel with a counter beside it. The counter was rapidly down-counting the distance on a vector straight toward Josh's vanish point.

"Is that us?" Doc said, pointing to the spot with the highlighted numbers.

"Yes, it is."

"That is pretty fast acceleration, but even at that speed it will take us days to get to the location."

"Well, we're counting on you and your associate to solve that problem."

"How can we do that?"

Trappist

"As I see it," said the commander, "everything that Dr. Shamir needed to build his racer is now on board this ship. Mr. Brady is down in a hangar right now working on building a somewhat larger duplicate of Dr. Shamir's race sled. We need you to help him with the chips. He's told us there were things that Shamir did while building the sled that he was not involved in, and it had to do with those chips and accelerators. Mr. Brady said Dr. Shamir told him it was safer if he did the setup before Brady added them to the sled's matrix. You need to check that matrix setup too."

Doc was deep in thought. "Well, I believe that can all be accomplished, but it is all going to take time. It may take months to analyze the formulation and postulations and do the testing and verifications. I will need to set up test trials etc."

"Stop right there. Doctor, that young man would be dead by the time you even finished talking. We don't have time; you have to decide if you want to try and save your friend or not."

"What kind of a crack is that, you have no..."

"Stop Doctor, we have wasted too much time in this meeting already; your friend's life depends on you. "

Doc looked down at his hands that had gripped the edge of the flat monitor in front of him. "Let me get to work then, and don't bother me or Ron again. We'll tell you when we're finished."

The commander exhaled. "Good." He reached down to his side and pulled out a clear pack and tossed it at Doc. "These are Josh's notebooks; we have already copied them and our best people are working on them. You can interface with them if you wish--some are on the Moon, some are elsewhere."

Doc nodded. "Ok, we'll see."

The commander immediately unbuckled himself and started to head down the hatch. He paused right before ducking his head down into the hatch. "Todd will get you to Brady; if you need anything just ask him."

The commander then disappeared down the hatch headfirst with his legs and feet floating after him.

CHAPTER 8

Todd, still seated, said, "You ready, Doctor?"

"Yes, do you have any gravity on this ship?"

"As a matter of fact we do; this ship was designed as a maintenance ship so all the workshops and bays are under centrifugal force."

Doc's eyes widened. "Really! how big is this thing?"

Todd had now unbuckled and was headed down the hatch. "Follow me, Doctor." Doc slowly complied, moving gingerly over to the hatch, making sure he had a good hand-hold before moving forward.

"Todd, slow down a bit, I'm not quite up to flying across the room yet."

"I am right outside, Doctor."

Exiting the cabin, Doc tried to make his way to Todd, who was hanging in the air beside a ladder that ran down a column leading to the outer rim of the ship. Doc managed to reach out and hold on tightly to one of the ladder's rungs. He was holding himself in place and taking in his new surroundings.

"Lets' stop here a second, Doctor Murphy. I want to show how this central channel system works, OK?"

"Sure."

"Doctor, please watch. Here, I'll hook you in this time. Just watch, Ok? It is not that complicated, but it's good to know if you ever have to use the center channel again."

Todd reached to the belt area of Doc's jumpsuit and pulled back a Velcro cover. There was a snap which Todd pulled and a thin line pulled out behind it. Todd handed the snap to Doc.

Todd said, "Hold onto this. Don't release it yet."

Doc pulled his right hand from the rung and took the snap. Doc could feel the slightest tension on it. He knew that if he released it the snap would automatically wind up back in his jumper suit.

"Now watch, Doctor." Todd took a snap from his suit and reached out into the central tunnel. Running along the wall of the column was a rail and Todd quickly pulled out his line and snapped it onto the rail. Todd then moved out into the central column.

Floating in the middle, he said, "Now you hook on, Doctor."

Doc reached out and snapped in on the same rail as Todd.

Todd hand-signaled Doc to move out into the column.

Doc moved out and gave a quick look around the column. He was in a long tunnel that he estimated went through the diameter of the ship. Doc could see right above him that there was a number of these tunnels intersecting.

Todd said, "As you can see, we are at the center of the ship; as we move out toward the exterior shell you will feel the centrifugal effect. This rail actually has a braking system so if you start moving too fast it will sense it and start braking. These are put in for newbies mostly, because once you get comfortable and have had some training, they slow you down. I'm using it just to demo for you. However, I suggest you or Mr. Brady use them any time you may need to use the tunnels."

Doc said, "It seems like they're not necessary; don't you feel the centrifugal force as you move out?"

"Well, yes, you do, but depending on the ship it could come on fast or slow, and you could very easily plant your face in the deck of the ship at the bottom of the column." Todd continued. "Okay, now follow me and do as I do at the same time when we need to use the ladder. However, you actually should not need to use the tunnels again on this trip."

Todd headed down the tube and within twenty feet flipped around and oriented himself on the ladder, then started working his way down it. Doc followed Todd and could feel that the tunnel wall with the ladder on it was actually pressing toward him and as he flipped to orient himself, he could feel a tiny pull of gravity on his body.

Looking below now, Doc slowly moved himself down the ladder feeling his weight increase and his muscles exerting as he moved to the deck below.

When he got to the bottom of the ladder, Todd was waiting for him.

"Ok Doctor, just unsnap--Mr. Brady is just through here." Todd turned and walked through a bulk head doorway.

When Doc entered the room the dimensions surprised him. There was actually a good amount of room. Its size was about thirty feet across and roughly ninety feet long. Doc could make out a slight curve in the deck.

He saw all the equipment from Ron's shop, plus a number of unlabeled crates. Doc surmised from their size that they contained the chips and accelerator. Doc looked around, but Ron was not there.

"You have a lot of work to do, Doctor, so I will leave you now. I'll be back in fifteen minutes. When I get back, we'll go over the safety protocol and services. Mr. Brady can help you out till then. Ok?"

"Thanks Todd, but I don't see Ron around."

"Oh, he is probably through that door in the hanger."

Todd turned and unlatched an airtight door in the back of the wall adjacent to the ladder and stepped through.

Doc looked around the room again, and walked toward the door Todd had just exited. He could feel a pull on his body as he moved forward. It was very subtle and he figured he was walking against the spin of the rotation in this part of the ship.

When he got to the door, he turned the latch and pushed open the door. Doc had half-expected it to be locked. But to his surprise it opened into a room of people—young people as a matter of fact. They were all in uniforms and were monitoring instruments and talking into headsets. There was a low hum of conversation throughout the small cabin. Doc thought he heard talk about space traffic in their area but wasn't sure. No one turned or even noticed him. Doc guessed they were in their late teens. Doc did not see Todd around and pulled his head back in and closed the door. Turning, he headed across the chamber to the hatch Todd had pointed out. He looked through a clear panel on the door and saw Ron attaching the chips that had been set up on panels onto the exterior of an open-ribbed sled. Doc thought it looked almost like an upscaled racer.

He looked down at the latch for the door and read some instructions for opening. Apparently, this was a hangar deck and the wall and door were safety hatches to seal the ship when the hangar door was open to space.

As Doc entered, Ron heard him and turned toward him. Doc tried to add a little humor to the situation, "Hey Ron, long time no see."

Ron grinned. "Good to see you, Doc, do you believe me now?"

Doc walked toward Ron. "Yeah, sorry Ron, it was just so far out there for me; it's been a rough two days."

"Well, if we are going to have any chance of finding Josh or even just bringing him back, we need to get this thing built in a day or two. It's been six days already, and I don't know how much water he had or food for that matter."

Doc said, "Ok, let's get at it. First, why don't you update me on what you and Josh did and add any comments Josh made about the chips. I need to know anything he specifically said about or did to the chips. Did he ever go over his notes with you?"

"Ok, why don't we head over to the table," Ron pointed to a nearby work bench, "I need to finish this up..." he pointed a thumb back to the sled, "or I'll mess it up." Seeing the notebooks in Doc's hand he said, "I see you got Josh's notes. Hope you can figure them out."

They pulled up a couple of nearby stools and sat down. Ron gave Doc the background on how Josh was using the chips and accelerators. He assumed Doc knew what Josh was working on because Josh had told him to study the chips.

Doc agreed he had done so about two years ago. He wanted to see if they could be salvaged for something but he knew nothing about using them on the racer.

Ron said that, based on Josh's descriptors, he had been testing the chips separate from the accelerators without the tachyon pulses and then he embedded a firmware fix that regulated the path and speed of the particles.

Ron continued, "That's when he gave me a call and asked to test it at the shop, because we had been working on the bike and he was concerned a chip might blow up and didn't want any trouble at the Institute."

Doc nodded. "Yes, I remember, Juan came down on him

and me hard when he blew one up in the test chamber, raving about how much the chamber cost to repair, etcetera."

Ron continued about how Josh blew up a couple more chips and kept tweaking his firmware program. Ron said, "He told me something didn't make sense and he brought in those specialty cameras from the institute. He had me help him set up a program that could work at light speed to put it simply. We set that up and recorded a test. Turns out at that point the chips weren't exploding but were smashing themselves to bits off the ceiling of the test chamber. It was just so fast; we didn't know it till we reviewed the test with the new software that slowed light speed down to extreme slow motion.

"Well, after that he just worked on his laptop and notebooks for almost two months. I was getting on him about the race coming up and that we needed to finish up the racer and he was real upbeat, saying that we were going to win this time. You know he really wanted to have a good race since he promised Isabel it was his last. He then built the testing equipment there, said he needed it to get the physics right. Then he built the chip tester—started to bring more chips over from the institute. Apparently, some of the chips had the correct tolerances and others didn't. Those that didn't would still blow up even with the program. He then gave me the specs for these boards I am attaching. "Ron pointed over to the ship. "He told me to only populate them with the chips he had tested."

Doc queried, "Did he say anything about how they are generating the abnormality?" Doc's brain had kicked into high gear since he'd seen Josh's notes and Ron had gone over what they'd been building for the racer. He opened Josh's notebooks and started through them line by line.

"Well, he showed me how he was doing the testing, and

showed me the results. He explained that when the chip processors were operating in a certain pattern, with the embedded firmware he had developed, they produced a temporal distortion field. That's about all I know."

Doc scratched his head. "Ok, this is going to take me a while. Once I get done, I can get with you on the testing. Is there any critical path right now that would slow you down?"

"I am going to need more tested chips soon," said Ron. "I have enough ready to build about ten more boards, but as you can see, I'm going to need a lot more."

Doc glanced over at the ship and estimated the coverage required, "Do we have enough chips to build that many boards."

Ron said, "Well, we will if the failure rates hold."

Doc put his head back to the notebook. "Well, don't let me hold you up now."

With that Ron got up and went back to assembling the sled.

CHAPTER 9

D oc started at the first notebook and went through every design and expression trying to absorb them as he proceeded through the multiple notebooks. Doc had found that in solving a problem, he worked best by first absorbing all the material and then letting his mind work through it if he could not solve it initially. This is what happened when he finished his study of the last notebook. This had been the second time he'd gone through them, but this time much more thoroughly and actually working out the theories and expressions postulated on their pages.

When finished, Doc sat staring at the books and tried to understand how Josh had made such a monumental discovery in such a short time.

He realized on the final pages that Josh had not written down an expression to tie it all together. Doc thought initially that this was clever of Josh not to write down the overall discovery of how he used the chips to achieve a FTL propulsion system. It struck Doc then. He realized Josh had not tried to tie it all together; he just wanted to make enough progress to make the propulsion work. Doc chuckled to himself.

Josh just wanted to get it to work for the race; that was what was driving him. Once Doc realized Josh had not developed some big complicated unifying theory of everything, he directed his energies to understanding how the components worked and why. He couldn't help grinning, knowing that the Space Agency scientists and even the commie thugs back on Earth were all dug in trying to find Josh's unifying theory. Good, he thought. He could cut to the chase; the real problem facing him was to make the systems work within the specifications and not worry about the how, although Doc had some brain flashes in that area. That research would be for another time. Right now the goal was to find Josh, find him fast and find him alive.

At this point a few hours had passed. Doc went over to Ron and asked him where he might review the firmware program Josh had embedded in the chips. Ron simply smiled and told him he didn't know.

"Well, how do you know he loaded it into the chip?"

"He told me, Doc, remember? I told you, it was one of the things he did to make more chips stable and get the frequency he wanted?"

"Frequency, he said he wanted a certain frequency, for the tachyon?"

Ron nodded. "Yes, something like that, he would have all these chips, and run them through his tester, then hand them over to me to make the boards and put them on the racer."

Doc turned and looked around the work area, "And Ron where might that tester be?"

"Geez, Doc. I am kind of in a hurry here. Can't you help yourself?"

"Well, I would, but I have no idea what it looks like."

Ron kept attaching the board he was working on while Doc stood beside him waiting patiently. After a few moments, Ron got up, placed his tools down on floor where he'd been working, then stood up and looked around the entire room doing a 360. He then walked off in the direction of some of the chip containers stacked on pallets. On one of the pallets was an open bin which looked like it had been stuffed with odds and ends from Ron's shop. Ron bent over and dug through some of the top material, taking some pieces out and dropping them nonchalantly on the deck beside him. He reached way down into the bin, half bent over his pants half falling down with the top part of his butt exposed. Doc had to turn around, looking up at the ceiling, bringing his hand to his mouth to cover his laugh.

A second later, Ron struggled, straightened out, and pulled out a flat heavy nevo plastic-covered box.

"Doc," he gasped, "give me a hand with this, it weighs a ton."

Doc quickly grasped one side of the box and felt the weight. It was indeed heavy.

"This is it then, it is really heavy. What's inside?"

"I don't know, never asked, not my specialty, you know, but he ran every chip we used through it before giving it to me to build an assembly."

At that, they heard the bulkhead door open. Looking over, they saw Todd entering with a cooler bag held in his left hand.

Todd said, "You guys hungry yet?"

Doc instantly realized he was starving and Ron was already on his way over to Todd without even responding.

Both Doc and Ron wolfed down their food quickly and headed back to work, leaving Todd sitting at the small table they had set up for the meal.

Doc went back to the notebooks and started matching the configuration of the testing equipment to pages that had roughly outlined its design. He then started disassembling the tester and laying the parts out scattered across a large work bench. Once satisfied with his understanding of the components he reassembled them again.

By doing this he had determined that Josh had built the tester to embed the control firmware. He then tested the tolerances to ensure that the chip being tested, along with the mini accelerator with which it was matched, were correct . There was no danger in testing the chips; the tester ran a complete test of its own and then passed or failed the combination based on the test parameters. Doc simply had to match up the chips and accelerators to run the test. He gathered a few of the chips and accelerators and started the testing process. He checked his time as it was getting late, and laid his head down on the table for a few seconds to rest his eyes. When he awoke, he saw Ron was asleep in a chair inside the sled's cockpit. Doc checked his watch. He had been asleep for almost an hour, and when he checked the tester it was still running. Doc knew then they were in trouble and he called for Todd on his comm--then made up a list.

Todd came through the airlock a few minutes later, and Doc was waiting there for him.

Doc handed Todd a list. "Here, I need these items immediately; it's best if you get multiples of them because I don't know how many I will need. It is also in your system, so you can check the ship immediately."

Todd said, "Yes sir, may I ask why?"

Doc pointed over to where Ron was still asleep in the cockpit seat, a light snoring sound coming from him in the silence. "The why is that unless I can build a couple more of the chip testers, it will be weeks before Ron can finish a ship that size."

Todd nodded. "Ok, will do, anything else?"

"Also, if you look at the material toward the bottom, I

want those items to build a mock up of the ship here and I want to do a remote test before the real ship is used. So, the list has material needed to build two mock ups. Get some of your drone people working on them. It will be crowded in here but right here would be the best place to do it efficiently."

"That is a lot of work," said Todd, "what is your timetable?"

"The timetable is ASAP, so you better free up some people with some talent to get these things built. You can start sending them in now. I will start them on building the mocks and the testers."

Doc began walking away. "Now, excuse me, Todd, but I need to get Ron back to work."

Doc was getting excited about the work and it reminded him of his younger days at the institute when he had numerous research projects going and many times had worked around the clock.

Waking Ron, Doc gave him an update on the what he had discussed with Todd, and asked him to do a quick design on the two mock-ups with the chip placements for the crew to build, leaving the controls and thrusters to the ship personnel to then upload it to the ship's net.

Minutes later, personnel started arriving through the air lock, some carrying only their tablets, others with storage containers.

Doc didn't waste time talking to them, but sent out a system notice on what was required and where to go for directives on what they had to do. What he did do, however, as they arrived was introduce himself and point out Ron, then ask them their names and what they wanted to work on.

Doc was not surprised, however, this time at the age of the crew members arriving. They were all quite young by his judgment with maybe the oldest in their early twenties and the youngest in their mid-teens.

He observed that the crew organized themselves into smaller groups with a team lead and went right into the work of building the testers and the mock-ups in different parts of the hangar.

At this point Doc heard the tester beeping and went over to check it. Checking the tester, Doc saw that the chip set had passed. He quickly removed them and put another set in, checking the time. It took almost two hours to test just one set. Doc then set about tapping into the firmware on the tester to get it into the duplicates being assembled by the crew. Doc was actually enjoying himself with the buzz of activity around him and he quickly lost track of time again until he heard the airlock open and other crew entered with breakfast.

As Doc made his way over to the line that had formed, he saw the commander come through the airlock, look around, and head straight for him.

It was only a few steps for him since they had set the breakfast up right inside the lock.

"Doctor Murphy, what is your plan here?" he said. "Isn't this going to substantially delay the attempt to rescue your associate, Dr. Shamir?"

"Yes, well this is the best option to rescue Josh and not risk other lives. That's why the mock ups. We just need a trajectory on which to send them so that we learn the results quickly.

"The next factor is that using just Josh's single tester we would need another three days just testing enough for the rescue ship. We need to cut that down and building more testers is the only way."

"Ok, the crew will set up the 3D's on board," said the

commander, to start pushing out the components for the mock-ups. However, we will need to tear down some of the systems equipment to get some of the components for the testers. I will give the word. We are going to have to strip some of the shuttles to get thrusters and enough equipment for the mock ups."

The commander continued, "Doctor, have you uncovered what Doctor Shamir discovered. Do you have the formulation worked out?"

"Commander, I have as a matter of fact uncovered what Josh did and I am sure we can duplicate his system with the material we have right here. The what and the how is not important right now and in all probability requires Josh here in person to finish up his work. Now if you will excuse me, I need to eat and get back to work,"

As he said this, Ron came up to him with one of the covered bowls of food in his hand and a coffee in the other.

Ron said, "Doc, I need to see you right now; it is critical, let's go."

As he said this he continued walking toward the partially built sled.

Doc watched Ron for a second then looked back to the commander, "Excuse me, I have to get back to work."

Doc followed Ron around to the backside of the ship. There was a chair and a small table set up.

Ron said, "Doc, have a seat. I saved you the last of the breakfast; you owe me again."

Doc took the bowl and coffee. "Thanks, Ron."

He sat down and started wolfing down the scrambled eggs and bacon in the bowl Ron had made for him. He'd started sipping the coffee when two of the ship's personnel came around the ship carrying what looked like the base and cover of the tester.

The older male teen said, "Doctor Murphy, sir, may we interrupt, sir?"

"Yes, of course, what is it?"

"Sir, we have assembled this first unit per your spec, but we have no test protocols to check its performance. Can you provide that to us now?"

"Yes, what is your name again?"

"Ensign Belewa, sir."

Doc turned to the younger teen with Ensign Belewa, "And your name?"

"Specialist Ramos, sir."

Carrying the remains of his breakfast, Doc headed toward his work table, "Well, gentlemen, if you will follow me, let's go see what we've got."

On the way, he stopped to talk to Ron, who confirmed that he had helped set up the test protocols in the programming he'd completed for Josh on the tester. Ron also gave Doc the key to copying the firmware to embed on the newly constructed testers.

Returning to the table, Doc could feel his lack of sleep catching up to him as he stumbled on a container that was sticking out a little into the walkway. As he sat down, he saw that the second set of chips had passed. He first removed them, and asked Specialist Ramos to take them over to Ron. Then he pulled out his comm and tapped into Josh's system. It took only a second to download onto his comm and then quickly upload it onto the tester built by Ensign Belewa's crew.

Doc said, "Ok Ensign Belewa; you should be ready to go. Let's keep all the testers here on this table as you complete them. Ok, now watch."

Doc picked up another chip set and put it in Josh's tester and started the test, "I want you to go over to Ron and ask him for a chip set that failed, put that into your tester and run it. It should fail again if everything is working properly– may take up to two hours; if it fails then you can start testing the untested chips."

Doc then opened up his comm again and set up a code to protect the firmware program but make it easier for the ensign to download.

Doc said, "Let's see your comm."

Ensign Belewa said, "Sir, that is not permitted; we are not allowed to download any undocumented systems to our comms."

"OK, take mine, here is the code. You will need to input it to set up each new tester you complete. Can you do that?"

"Yes sir."

Doc said, "Great, let me know of any issues. I need to take a break right now. "

Heading back, Doc looked around the room, checking out all the activity from the crew. He then walked over to the sled, climbed into the co-pilot's seat and checked the time. He made eye contact with Ron who was still working on attaching boards, then closed his eyes and was asleep in ten seconds.

When Doc woke up, he was looking directly at Ron, who was curling up beside him in the pilot's seat, looking like a dead man.

Todd walked up. "Doctor Murphy, sorry to wake you, but the crew is finishing up on the mocks and we wanted to know what your test schedule was."

Doc turned in the seat to look at Todd. He checked the time. He'd been asleep almost six hours and was feeling much better and alert. Doc took a moment to stretch and yawn.

Doc crawled out of the ship, "OK, give me a minute to

wake up and get some coffee. I'll be right with you."

Todd said, "Meet me at the test table to give me an update."

As Doc walked through the hangar, he noticed that all the activity was around the mocks. They looked to him like they were ready to go.

Arriving back at the test table, Doc saw two of the younger crew standing with Todd and that Ensign Belewa and Specialist Ramos were not there. He also saw that the table was covered with testers and that everyone was standing at one end where there was a little clear space.

Doc said, "Ok, let's get started--is Ensign Belewa around? I would like a status report on the testing."

"Sir, Ensign Belewa and Specialist Ramos are off duty right now," said Todd. Let me introduce Ensign Tran, who is handling the component testing, Lieutenant Bukoski is in charge of assembling the mocks and will pilot them, and here is Ensign Abebe who is handling the board assembling and testing of the boards for the propulsion system."

Each of the officers nodded their head slightly as they were introduced.

Doc said, "Thank you, Todd, and thanks to your crew, it looks like they have made good progress while I was ah... hm... gone."

Doc continued, "I think we better wake up Ron and get an update from him, since he has the most knowledge and built the original."

"Actually, Doctor Murphy," said Todd, "Mr. Brady has just fallen asleep and we basically had to stop him from working. He was becoming extremely sleep deprived and was becoming an obstacle to completing the mock ups. But let me suggest we go through the status update first, before you decide."

Doc said, "Ok, let's get going then."

Todd turned to Ensign Tran and gave a nod and she nodded back.

Ensign Tran reported, "Sir, the testing is proceeding as planned, we have completed ten testing units and are producing an average of seven functional chip sets every two hours. We have stopped building more testers, as we have no more earth old-style chips available, but are looking into slowing down some of our older processors to work with the tester software program and firmware. We would, however, need a key, but that will still take time to reprogram. Based on the mock and ship requirements, however, we will still need testing time of an additional 72 hours. Assuming the pass rate holds, sir."

Todd said, "Lieutenant Bukoski, your update."

Lieutenant Bukoski spoke loudly, "Sir, Mock One is complete and is in testing right now. Mock Two will be finished when we get enough chip sets to complete the array and then the additional time for it to go through testing --that is, in approximately three hours after we get delivery of the last set of boards for the propulsion system."

Doc said, "What testing are you talking about, lieutenant?"

Lieutenant Buloski said, "Sir, Mr. Brady provided the protocol program to run system test on the propulsion board system symmetry, which he said is what was on the original test vehicle. The drone system, navigation propulsion etc. on Mock #1 have already been tested and are ready to go. The Mock #2 systems testing is also complete, and so it will be ready once we complete the board array and run the testing symmetry protocols on it, sir"

"How long does the symmetry testing take?"

The lieutenant hesitated. "I am not quite sure, sir. Mr. Brady gave an approximate time, but said it is a testing and programing type of test, so that it will keep running the tests and reprograming the individual boards until symmetry is reached in the whole system. Mr. Brady said there is no fixed time on that result."

Doc turned. "Ok next, Ensign Abebe, right?" This was the final young member of their group, "You're putting the assemblies for the propulsion system together?"

Abebe looked over at Todd who gave him a nod. Abebe then stepped forward and revealed a completed board he had apparently been holding at his side the whole time.

Ensign Abebe said, "Yes sir, my team is assembling the boards. We are 3D printing the base components in the architecture from the boards Mr. Brady provided. These are in low supply with the shipment that arrived from Earth. So, the boards are the critical path to completing enough arrays to meet the production requirements."

Doc was curious. "What is the timeline to complete the assemblies?"

Ensign Abele answered, "We have dedicated all of the 3D capable printers on board to the task; we have also had our escort vessels free up production. So, all required assemblies with allowance for failure loss should be built and ready for accepting the chips and accelerators in forty-eight hours."

Doc gave a sharp look over to Todd, who did not display any change in expression.

"Thank you, Ensign, thanks to all of you, and keep up the good work." Then looking over toward Lieutenant Buloski he said, "Let's go look at that Mock number one, everyone else can get back to their work. Again, thanks and keep me informed of any changes to the schedule."

Doc signaled Todd to come with him to see the Mock up.

It was already sitting by to the large hangar doors next to the vacuum of space.

Doc said, "So, lieutenant, this mock will be ready to test as soon as the symmetry program is finished? There will be nothing else required to push it out the hatch and on its way?"

Lieutenant Buloski nodded, "No sir, everything is loaded in and tested."

Testing Lieutenant Buloski further he asked, "I mean, that the second the symmetry program is complete, you can throw the switch and it's on its way? What is the test flight path and what monitors do you have along its path?"

Lt. Buloski didn't hesitate "Sir, the test flight path is out to Mars station, the station is approaching the planet right now in its rotation, so the distance and navigation should provide a good test."

"What monitors do you have along the route?"

"Sir, we have not placed any monitors along the route."

Doc turned to Todd. "Can you set something up in the way of monitoring this test along the test route, just in case something happens?"

"I will see what we can do."

Doc was feeling new energy. "Good, OK, let's do a dry run. Where is your controller, let's get through it."

Todd said, "Lieutenant, put the process document up on the screen so we can follow as you step through it. And proceed through the complete mission."

The lieutenant reached for his tablet and in a few seconds the screen displayed the drone remote controller. He then proceeded through each step of the mission using the controller to pilot the mock. As he did this, the check list on the screen automatically checked off as an item was completed. Doc noted that it would take almost two hours after the symmetry program was complete to actually begin engaging the mock thrusters and then testing the propulsion system. Doc noted it, and he knew that it would have to change.

The lieutenant continued on how the testing would proceed by turning the propulsion system on and off and collecting data and performance information that would be transmitted both to the ship and to the Mars Station. The initial thrust would be matched to the speed of Dr. Shamir's racing bike before it disappeared.

In addition, there was a backup drone controller system being manned on one of the Mars orbiters just in case something interfered with the signal.

Lieutenant Buloski continued relating how the Mock One would be engaged for different periods of time from milliseconds to up to ten seconds at the completion of the test.

Doc raised an eyebrow at a potential problem. He thought he'd better raise some questions in a general manner just to be sure his concerns were addressed in the test vehicle.

"How do you initiate the test program and what are the parameters?"

Buloski turned to him. "As noted in the check off, once the all clear is achieved, I will initiate the program on the controller and it will engage the system for the tenth of a second, then the program will shut the system down, an evaluation will be completed. At that point, I will initiate the next engagement period and so on until the program as described is completed, sir."

"Good, so to be clear, you initiate the propulsion test and then the on-board navigation runs through the test time and shuts down."

Buloski nodded his head in agreement.

"So once you initiate the test, that is it until the next

phase. The whole test program is contained within Mock One and it shuts down the test after a tenth of a second and then sends a signal to you waiting for the next step in the testing, right?"

"Sir, not quite, since the programing requires encrypting, all the commands must be run through the ship's on-board systems from my tablet controller. So, all the programing is in the tablet and with backup on the ship. There is practically no programing on the Mock as a preventative measure in case it would somehow fall into the hands of an unfriendly party."

Doc turned to Todd, "Have you reviewed with the ship's personnel the speed at which the Mock is going to be traveling?"

Todd looked at Doc looking a bit surprised. "Well, Dr. Murphy, we don't really know the speed, right? The original flight data did not indicate a speed. What is your opinion? We really have no experience other than the video data and the long-range tracking coming in. It appears that if the system is workable, we will substantially cut down the transit time between the Moon, Mars, the asteroid belt and be able to provide access to the outer system."

Doc said, "I see, and is that what your commander said about the system?"

Todd answered, "The commander is a very busy man with a lot of responsibility. I don't believe he has ever addressed the issue of speed. After all, Doctor Murphy, it's only been a few days and we have been jumping through hoops just to get to this point."

"Gentlemen, I can address this now." The commander had walked up behind Todd and no one in the group had noticed him until he spoke.

"Excuse me, Todd." He stepped into the circle.

Doc saw that two men had arrived with the commander. The older man, Doc recognized as Mr. Leat whom he had met in the director's office when the agency purchased the chips. Now, however, he was wearing a uniform of the Space Agency. The other was a tall lanky younger man in just space coveralls, in his late twenties maybe, with a shaven head, heavy eyebrows and what looked like a fat split lower lip and a dark swollen eye from a recent fight.

The commander spoke, "Gentlemen, to Doctor Murphy's point, and also, now that we have gotten to this point, you will follow his direction on any modifications to the controlling systems that may be needed on the ship's systems. These vessels may travel at close to or over the speed of light. At this time the actual speed, how the speed is attained and the physics behind it are unknown."

The commander turned a little toward Doc, "Is that a correct statement, Doctor Murphy?"

"Yes, it is, commander." Doc had an idea of the quantum mechanics that may be involved but knew this was not the time to discuss it.

"Thank you, doctor. Well, gentlemen, the speed of light is a factor so please be sure all your systems take it into account."

He then turned aside and, extending his hand toward the two men who had accompanied him, said, "Let me introduce the pilot, co-pilot and science officer for the rescue mission. I believe you all know the Space Agency's Moon Base First Squadron Commander Arthur Holmes."

Doc smiled at that. These guys knew how Earth worked these days. The Earth governments had figured out quickly what was going on based on the government collusion between the FBI and Chinese thugs. Their attempt to enslave him and his family like they had to so many others with scientific background harkened back to the old forgotten World War II when the Nazis forced cooperation by holding family members hostage. This was a method that was adopted post war by the failed Soviet Union and utilized by America and China. Commander Holmes, as Mr. Leat, knocked them off the trail long enough to get the chips out of the Institute. Lucky Juan was so anxious to get rid of them. Doc wondered what camp he would end up living in with his poor family ripped apart. These thoughts all ran quickly through his mind as the commander continued, "Commander Holmes will be the co-pilot and Mister Joel Dubois is the pilot. We are lucky to have Mister Dubois available in our vicinity to volunteer for this mission."

Doc could not help but notice the dirty look Dubois gave to the commander at that comment. Doc was sure there was more to the story than just volunteering.

The commander continued, "These gentlemen will be making changes to the sled to accommodate their mission requirements; please assist them in every way possible."

"Thanks, dismissed." With that he turned and left.

Doc stepped over to shake Commander Holmes's hand, "Well, it's good to see you again and thank you for getting us off of Earth. I can't even imagine where we would be right now if it wasn't for you."

Holmes waved it away. "No problem, Doctor Murphy, it was a pleasure; but it was all run by the commander, so he is the one you should be thanking."

'Well, yes, we did not get off to a good start, you know he doesn't seem like the type of person that accepts a thank you. He seems like a 'It's part of the job,' type."

Holmes looked him in the eye. "Well, maybe when all this is over, you will get a better idea about him. Anyhow, right now we've got work to do."

Just then Ron stepped in beside him looking bleary-eyed and holding a cup of coffee. "What did I miss, anything important?"

Doc said, "Yes, this is Commander Holmes and this is..." Doc was turning around to try and locate the pilot, Joel, when there was a loud crash of something hitting the floor."

They all turned to see Joel throwing material out of the cockpit of the sled.

Commander Holmes appeared grim. "Excuse me, I'll handle this." And he started toward the ship.

The commander then turned and started off toward the ship.

Doc said, "Ron, you better go with him, you're going to have to work with them to set up the controls. That guy in the cockpit is the pilot and Art there is the co-pilot. We are ordered to accommodate them. Sorry."

Ron said, "That's fine with me, I just wish they had gotten here a little earlier; that chair wasn't quite bolted down anyway. I'll see what I can do. The sooner they get after Josh the better chance he has."

Buloski had come up along with Todd to Doc's side. Ron gave them a quick look and headed over toward the sled where the sounds of Joel rambling and cursing could be heard.

Buloski said, "Doctor Murphy, I have reprogramed the drone to run through the timing of engaging the propulsion and shutting it down with the elapsed time all within the ship's A.I., as a result of the information provided by the commander. Also, the testing on the drone Mock One is complete."

Doc looked at the lieutenant and then at Todd, "Well, then get it out there and send it to Mars, time's a-wasting."

Doc addressed Todd, "Can you get me an update on the chip testing and board assemblies? Thanks."

He then turned and headed over to the ship where he still heard the rantings from Joel and an occasional muffled response from Ron.

When he arrived, he realized that there was no need for alarm. Joel was basically talking and yelling to himself in the pilot cockpit, and Ron was nearly beside himself trying to fit a small conforming seat into the space right behind the pilot. Commander Holmes was sitting in the copilot seat and working on installing the thin screen monitors around him. He had a set of ear phones on and was oblivious to Joel beside him. Doc saw that the seats Ron had put in were gone and new smaller seats of a different design had been installed.

Doc addressed Ron through the side of the ship, "Ron, is everything OK?"

"Yeah, but these guys should have been here yesterday."

"Will this cause any delays?"

"No, they pretty much do their own thing. That guy," pointing to Joel, "is a real basket case, but he knows his stuff. He's just really annoying to work around."

Doc said, "Ok, just do your best."

"Yeah, the same hold points as before, we need the chips and the boards and are running to finish the sync program."

The noise in the area was picking up, and Doc and Ron turned to look in that direction. The airlock was open and heavy crates were being pushed into the space. The crew was pushing the tables out of the way to get them in.

Suddenly Joel yelled out at the crew with the crates and it seemed like it was right in Doc's ear on purpose. "Yo! Yo! Yo! You clumsy squids, that's my stuff. Over here."

The crew started toward Joel with the crates. Doc then heard the sound of a pressure release and instinctively grabbed hold of the ship's frame with his heart skipping a beat.

Joel noticed this and started laughing. "Ha, Doctor, scared, are ya? Ooh hold on, I am going to get sucked out— Ooh! Ooh! Save me! Ha! Just what pitiful bilge did they find you in?" He then mumbled something unintelligible in French. Grinning at Doc, Joel grabbed the side of the ship and started faking holding on and acting like he was panicking.

Art said, "Cut it out, Dubois, we are all on the same team here. You're not helping your cause, pal."

Joel turned to Art and then got out of the sled to start directing the unpacking of the crates.

Doc had regained his calm at this point and he turned to see what had made the sound that almost panicked him. He saw that the hangar doors had slid open to another compartment and Todd and Lieutenant Buloski's crew were pushing the Mock One into the compartment.

Doc turned to Ron, "Ok, looks like you got everything under control here."

Ron gave Doc a disgusted look and grunted, "shit," then went back to installing the seat.

Doc made his way over to the door, but by the time he got there the hangar was already being closed and Todd was standing right at the seal point looking at his tablet. Doc could hear Todd checking down the process with someone in the control room. Buloski was beside him, apparently going through the Mock's controls.

Doc said, "Todd, can you put the test sequences up on one of these monitors?"

Todd, still focused on his tablet, said, "Sure" and a second later all the monitors on one side of the room flashed on with different views. One monitor had a chimpanzee in a space suit view.

Doc said, "Is that for real, you put a monkey in the Mock?"

"Yeah, it's kind of a joke with the crew, because that is how the first space flights started from Earth, and we don't even have a dog on board."

Doc said, "Aren't you concerned something could go wrong?"

"Well yes, that's why it's a monkey and not Lieutenant Buloski." Looking up, he addressed him: "You ready, lieutenant?"

Buloski, "Ready, sir."

Todd said, "Ok, Doctor, give the word when ready."

Doc said, "Go."

Doc had seen the layout of the program; the mock would move away from the ship and set up navigation in the direction of the Mars Station, picking a path that would not intersect with other vessels, planets, etc. Ships en route along the test path had been asked to monitor the space where the mock was expected to appear and relay the information back. Some of the monitors had actual views from ships en route. Each time the Mock shut down the system it would send a signal out to the fleet and calibrate any course adjustment requirements. Then Lieutenant Buloski would send the signal for the next phase.

The test would be out and back, hopefully, and the mock would return to the same general area where the test started near their ship.

Doc noticed the activity in the room had stopped and all eyes were on the monitors as the Mock One was maneuvered out away from the ship to the launch point.

Looking back at the sled, he noticed both Ron and Joel had stopped to watch, but Art was still in the copilot's seat working away.

Over the intercom system, Lieutenant Buloski's voice came on, initiating phase one in "five, four, three, two, one" and the Mock disappeared.

There was a hush in the hangar, then the ship appeared on one of the monitor screens and there was a cheer and some clapping. At this, Commander Holmes's voice was heard, "People get back to work, time is vital here."

Lieutenant Buloski got a signal and he spoke into his comm, "Yes sir, will do sir, thank you sir."

Buloski turned to Doc, "Doctor, I am going to tap into your comm; it will take a second. There will be no more broadcasts on the intercom, so you will need to listen through your comm, sir."

"Here are the stats on the flight, sir. Time .01 seconds, Distance Traveled 80 km, Current Speed 50,000 km/hr."

Doc heard the stats as he watched the monkey sucking on a food tube and no apparent notice of the distance the Mock just traveled.

Doc said, "Any data on the monkey's vitals" as he watched vitals appear on the screen and all the indicators were nominal.

Todd said, "Doctor Murphy, Lieutenant Buloski is ready to proceed."

"Proceed, and just keep going when you are ready, gentlemen. Let's get this done fast to locate any problems."

And proceed they did--in less than two hours the Mock had reached the end of the program test out toward Mars. The only problem was that it had actually gone past the expected test point and reached almost to the asteroid belt. Due to the distance, it took more time to locate it and send the commands back and forth than it did to run the whole test. Based on the data received from the pursuit vehicles and the system on board the Mock, the longer the system was engaged, the distance traveled multiplied at an exponential rate.

When the Mock was located and the lieutenant had

performed a system check, Todd turned to Doc, "We are ready to bring it back, Doctor Murphy."

"Can you change the program, and bring it back in fewer intervals?"

Todd started to nod when Doc continued, "No, this is what we'll do," he said, turning to Buloski. "You need to re-write the program to eliminate all but three jumps, starting with the first two. I want you to set the first interval back too," Doc paused to look at the tracking data from the Mock feed, "So let's see, set it to be engaged for the time of the last interval to the end of the test. Next have the ship's systems calculate the exponential set from the data collected and set an interval to bring it right back to where it started. We are out of the area now, right?" he asked Todd.

Buloski spoke. "Sir, the Mock is lined up and ready for the first interval on the return trip, we are ready to load the revised program for the final leg, do we do it now or wait?"

"Let's wait, we may get more info from the next test. Go when you want, lieutenant."

"Buloski?"

"Check." Buloski took a quick look at his screen, "Ready for return at ten seconds, and five, four, three, two, one..."

The monitor with the monkey was still visible. Doc realized as he watched that the monitor displayed something that would take three seconds in signal travel time to reach beyond Mars.

Doc knew that meant it would be about twenty minutes before they received any new signal from the Mock so he took a seat and pulled out Josh's notebook. He had been carrying it around for reference as he moved from one worksite to the next. At certain points, Doc would lean over and write out a partial formula and statements on the side of the crate next to him. He, however, was still not making any progress in tying Josh's notes and observations to what was producing the FTL effect from the propulsion system.

Doc tried verbalizing a few postulations regarding what was happening, but these attempts all ended in Doc mumbling, unable to finish the initial thought.

Hearing him, Todd turned and gave him a questioning look.

Stretching back in the seat after his last attempt at postulating a theory, he saw the monkey reappear on the screen.

Doc turned, noticing Todd staring at him and added, "Must be about half way back--not bad. That is one fast monkey." Checking out the monkey again, Doc saw that all the vitals were nominal and the monkey was eating again.

Todd looked at his tablet. "The Mock is approximately sixty million km out still on the same path, any suggestions, Doctor Murphy?"

Thinking a second, Doc said, "What do you think? You and the lieutenant there. You want a little challenge. I haven't seen any reason not to press the envelope a little."

Todd looked at him blankly, but Lieutenant Buloski had a smile on his face, "What would you suggest, lieutenant?" Doc continued.

Buloski said, "Sir, I would like to have the A.I. run a time interval calculation and adjust for the travel of the ship and bring the mock right to us for easy pickup."

Doc said, "That sounds good to me, how long would it take?"

"Only a few minutes, sir, let me see..."

Buloski's response was interrupted by Todd, "Doctor Murphy, I would advise extreme caution; I recommend the test be completed as planned."

And turning to Lieutenant Buloski, he continued, "I would advise the test be completed as originally planned."

Buloski, "Yes, sir."

Doc said, "Hold on a minute, we will proceed at my direction on this. Our time is slipping away for the launch of the sled, not to mention the time needed to attempt the rescue."

Doc continued, "What is the closest you would suggest to bring back the mock with a good margin of safety?"

Todd without any hesitation said, "Doctor, taking it back to its point of origin would be a good margin of safety."

Doc smiled a little, realizing Todd was not about to budge on finishing the testing.

"Great! OK, lieutenant, have the A.I. calculate and bring it back to the exact point where the test started."

Seconds later the monkey was on the screen still sucking on the feeding tube in its helmet.

The data screen to the right of the monkey showed the detail. The mock had come to within three meters of the departure point of the test. Doc figured, given the flow of space and time, that it was a perfect flight.

Todd said, "Doctor, do you want to proceed with any additional testing on the Mock One?"

"Well, let's see how long that monkey is going to be able to hold all that food it's been heaving down its throat."

Todd said, "Doctor?"

"No, I'm good, how long before we have the Mock back on board?"

Todd said, "It won't be brought back, at the speed we are moving to the rendezvous point, it doesn't have the fuel to catch us. We have a retrieval ship already dispatched to pick it up."

"That won't do. I want that ship back on board as soon

as possible. If we don't get enough chips to complete the main sled there will be more delays. We need them now. In fact, stop working on the second mock and move all the boards and chips over to the sled. I want the ship back here in ten minutes," he said, looking at Todd and Buloski.

"I am sure two intelligent space guys like you two can find an easy way to accomplish that simple task."

Doc then turned and walked away, making his way over to the testing table where he saw Ensign Tran bent over and looking at the dials and indicators on one of the testers.

Doc said, "How is it going, ensign?"

"Sir, we are developing a few problems with some of the testers. It appears that some of the chip processors we repurposed from the ship are not working as efficiently as the one you brought from Earth. It is moving back our time-table substantially, and there is a higher percentage of failure coming off of the original tester as opposed to the ones built on-site."

"How many more do you need...can you put the numbers up on one of the monitors?" Doc was pointing up behind the ensign to one of the monitors that had been used for the Mock One test.

Ensign Tran said, "Yes sir, just a sec," and the monitor closest to the test table changed from the monkey to the chip stats.

"So it looks like tomorrow, roughly, before you have enough chips."

Tran turned from her tablet and looked up at the screen, "Doctor, that is two days and production is slowing. I believe this particular tester," tapping her hand on the one she had been studying, "should be scrapped."

Doc said, "Ensign, this is an update, we are no longer going to continue with the second Mock. Focus on getting enough chips for the rescue sled. Good work, ensign, keep it up."

Tran said, "Sir, what about the tester?"

"I concur, don't waste your time worrying about it; focus on the ones that are doing the job. Thanks, I will check back later." As Doc said that he realized exhaustion was catching up with him again and he knew he'd need to catch a cat nap very soon.

Doc suddenly remembered something and turned back to Ensign Tran. "Ensign, where is Ensign Abele?"

Ensign Tran, who'd been picking the chip out of the tester she'd been working on, said, "Sir, he is on break, they are all caught up and waiting on more chips. This is the choke point."

"Thank you, ensign." He watched her put her head back down to work on the tester and then headed toward the sled.

As Doc approached the sled, he did not see Ron around. He saw Art was still sitting in the co-pilot seat and seemed to be cross-checking things with his tablet. Standing around the sled at different intervals were ship's crew holding different pieces of small compact modules.

Doc felt something lumpy under his foot and heard an instant, "Yeow, you fuckhead!"

Doc side-stepped quickly, looking down where his foot had been. Somehow Joel had squeezed himself in between a rear seat and the bottom frame of the ship and was working there. Doc had stepped on a hand or other appendage that was no longer in sight.

Glancing around, he saw a mid-shipman standing there wide-eyed looking at him and holding a couple of tiny comm connectors in his hand. Apparently, he was not used to a person of Joel's personality on board ship.

Doc said, "Sorry about that, Joel. I didn't see you down there. You Ok?"

"Shit, I volunteer to help you poor scientists in your stupid sled and you just trample all over me. I need to get back out to the belt and away from you murdering sons of bitches!"

Doc was a little taken aback by Joel's speech but thought it best to ignore it and try for a status update of the ship.

"When do you think you'll be finished, Joel? " asked Doc, bending over and trying to look through the gap from the seat to the inner floor panel.

"Never! This is the worst piece of shit sled I have ever seen; I hate her!"

Not getting the answer he wanted, Doc tried a different line, "So that area down there is called a sled? It's part of the frame, I gather?"

"What kind of a scientist are you? You must be an Earther for sure, Boo! Hoo! Hoo! Hoo! The mean spaceman knows more than me. Put him in jail and raise his taxes. Stay away from me; I need my fingers, boss man."

When Doc looked up from Joel, he saw Art was looking at him with a smile on his face and he waved Doc over.

Doc made his way around the front of the ship past a few midshipmen that were attaching some complete boards to the ship. Here he recognized Ensign Abele holding a board in position while other midshipmen glued it in place. Apparently, everything on the ship was being glued. Doc thought that this was a good solution to get the ship together quickly but was wondering if it would hold up to a ship's acceleration.

Passing Abele on his way around he questioned him, "Ensign, how is it going? Will that glue hold this ship together?"

Thinking a few seconds, Abele said, "Sir, this whole maintenance ship is held together with the same stuff. It will hold."

Doc, a little surprised and not wanting to let on how much of an Earther he was replied, "Carry on, ensign. I was just joking, you're doing good work, Thank you."

"Yes sir, Thank you, sir."

Getting to Art, Doc said, "Well, I'm glad you will be on the flight." He lowered his voice, "I don't know about Joel; he seems to have an innate dislike for me."

Art started to hold up his hand but it was too late. Joel lay right beneath them under the sled. "Dislike you, Earther? You don't know the half of it! Why don't I just trample your frickin hand like a piece of dog shit! You a-hole!"

Art said, "Joel, knock it off." A second later the loud music of an old 20th century group blasted up from below.

Doc recognized the song but the sound was deafening. Art immediately shoved a long thin probe he had been holding in his hand down through a small gap between two modules in the middle panel.

Joel said, "Yeow, you bastard."

Art said, "The music..."

Joel shouted, "What?" Art made a second stab down through the gap.

Joel, "You pile!" and the volume went down to a low drawl as a heavy bass section of the song started in.

Art said, "Doc, you'll have to excuse his behavior; he is kind of here against his will. But we're lucky to have him."

Joel, from below. "You bet your ass!"

Art said, "Enough, already. So we had him on the Moon, and he had snuck into a restricted area out in the belt. It's an area with a lot of 'Rare Earths.' He sneaks in all the time and somehow gets the stuff to Earth and sells it. We haven't quite figured it out yet."

Doc said, "Smuggler?"

Joel said, "It is free space; I'm a free man!"

Art cut in "Not when you're risking others' safety."

"There was no risk, you can't touch my sled!"

Art turned back to Doc, "Well, that's true, his sled is pretty unique, but he is what you would call a pirate on Earth. He is also ex-agency, some say the best pilot ever, and he can handle a sled in the asteroid belt like he is just a shadow. He's like a surgeon the way he can move in on one particular rock and pick it out of a swarm without sending the inner system into panic. His sled is a work of genius."

Art said, "So we, the agency, decided to cut him some slack if he agreed to do this mission for us."

"What about you?" said Doc. "Kind of a risky enterprise."

"Not really, I've studied the data on your colleague's flight and it either works or it doesn't. If it doesn't then we bring it back in and try to figure it out. That would be bad news for your colleague if he's still out there and we can find him."

"Yeah, but he had an accident and disappeared. Why do you think the same won't happen again? Why not just wait and go through some additional testing?"

Art thought for a moment. "Well, you know this, and so does Ron--the consensus is that the control switch for the system failed. It failed to engage before the ship vanished as recorded in the communication between Josh and Ron. Remember from the tape, Ron had recommended that he not use it again."

"So he did and zipped off, but where?"

"Well, that's the part that Ron tried to explain to you when you were back on Earth. The Agency had formulated the same conclusion with better equipment and tracking systems."

Doc said, "So you actually know where he is."

"No, we don't because we're still tracking his distress signal, and based on that he is light years away."

Doc looked down at his hands thoughtfully for a moment then back up at Art. "So the switch must have been locked in the on position for a long period of time. Basically, he is no longer in the solar system, if it has been this many days and you still don't have a final location."

"That is correct, doctor, so to finish answering the question you started with, I plan on being one of the first humans to leave our solar system and explore the Milky Way. Aren't you excited?"

Doc nodded. "Yes, it is exciting and once you're back with Josh we can sit down and work out the physics. I for one will be praying for you."

Art gave Doc a kind of quizzical look, but Doc continued, "Anyway, Joel said he's working on the sled section. Do you know where that is on the ship? I'm trying to learn as much as I can about the ship since it appears I'll be on this project for a long time. I think you used the term also."

"Yeah, we call this type of vehicle a sled because it doesn't really have a supported atmosphere in it. Everyone inside is in their own suit, which has all of the environmental support and radiation protection systems built in. We work in the suits for days and even weeks at a time. It reduces the cost and construction time on this type of vehicle. All of the asteroid miners and private ships are of this type. In fact, the racer, your friend, and the others that do this spacing activity use the same structure. Racing is a big activity out on Mars and the Asteroid. You just don't hear about it on Earth because of the news censoring on the planet. Ok?"

Doc nodded. "Thanks." Just then Doc heard the noise

from the hangar doors opening and turned to see Todd and Buloski stepping through into the opening.

"Looks like the Mock is back, the test was a success," Doc said. "I told them to move all the boards from the mocks to this ship, uh, I mean sled. I guess getting enough chips tested is turning into a problem."

"Well, I suppose we should just be grateful for a success." Doc glanced around. "Hey, do you know where Ron is?"

"I think he's up at a meeting with the commander, he should be back shortly."

"Ok thanks," said Doc. "Right now I'm going to take a nap. I am about to tip over unconscious. I'll be over behind those boxes most likely."

"Here, hold on Doc." Art easily slipped out of the sled and reached into a crate sitting beside the sled. He pulled out another seat for the sled and placed it in the space directly behind him. Apparently, it was lined up with attachments on the base of the sled as it clicked into position.

"This is adjustable and you can tilt back in it and sleep." He reached and grabbed a helmet that had been resting on the floor and handed it to Doc.

"These are pretty comfortable and will conform to your neck and head. You just speak to tilt down the visor, and say 'visor darker' or 'visor lighter' to get what you want--the same if you want to lower the sound."

Doc said, "Thanks," and started to put the helmet on, but Art stopped him and took it back.

Art said, "You'd better climb into the seat first; you'll need practice to enter from the side with a helmet on. These sleds are designed for space and entry is through the top. But since this side is still open, go ahead."

Doc grabbed ahold of one of the sled's rails and stepped through into the seat, with his foot stepping onto an adjoining seat. Then resting on the rail he lifted his butt through and slipped into the seat.

Art now handed Doc the helmet through the opening in the sled, "Just like a pro."

Doc said, "Yeah, tell that to my back," pushing the seat back into a reclining position and pulling the helmet on. Doc gave the brief helmet control commands and then dozed off into sleep.

Doc awoke to a pinging sound coming from the earphones built into the helmet. He tried a voice control, guessing it would be a simple, 'Alarm Off' and the alarm stopped. As soon as the alarm stopped, he heard Art's voice, "Doc, we're finishing up and we need to go over the final plan and clear some things up with you before launching the mission. So, if you are ready, we've got a meeting set up in the commander's conference room."

Doc smacked his lips and recognizing how dried out his mouth was, figured he must have been out for several hours. He had the helmet lighten up and turned the exterior sound back on.

Looking around, he saw he was now in a darkened compartment with different screens flashing on and off showing test data and system checks being run.

Doc adjusted the seat up to a seated position and he could see someone in the pilot's seat. Reaching through a gap in the screens, he tapped the person on the shoulder. He saw immediately that it was Lieutenant Buloski. A second later the screen in front of him came on with the lieutenant facing him.

Lieutenant Buloski said, "How can I help you, Doctor Murphy?"

"Well, lieutenant, apparently there is a meeting I need to get to, so how do I get out of here?"

"The hatch is on top, sir. You need to climb out the top--see the latch?"

Looking up, Doc could see the latch and reached for it saying, "Is this thing strong enough for a spaceship?"

"Yes sir, all it has to do is hold the panels in place; there is no pressure in these sleds."

Remembering the discussion he had had with Art, Doc stood up and pushed up on the latch, opening the hatch above him. Standing erect, the top of the ship was just above his waist and there was not much room to move in or out. Doc also noticed that the sled was now sitting in the hangar. Somehow, they had moved it without even waking him, and he immediately realized he had missed a lot.

Doc said, "Lieutenant, are you getting ready to launch the sled; are you part of the crew?"

"Sir, the sled is running the symmetry program right now; and I wish I was part of the crew, but no, I am not. Mr. Dubois and Commander Holmes asked me to make sure that the tested data and controlling program we used on the mock is in the data base and that they can access and use it easily with an icon on the sled's system. So I am just finishing up here, sir."

Doc was interrupted by Ensign Tran, who came up to the side of the sled while Doc was talking to Buloski. "Doctor Murphy, I am to escort you up to the pre-launch meeting in the commander's conference room--my orders are to escort you there immediately, sir."

Doc said, "Sorry, I just need to get out of here' is there a ladder or something, ensign?"

Ensign Tran nodded. "You reach above you to the straps and pull yourself out and over, sir."

Reaching up for the hand hold straps he said, "Ok, hope

to see you later--maybe we can go over some of the test data later."

Doc noticed as they passed through the hangar it was basically clear, and in the workshop the ship's crew was crating up all the different components of the system. Doc and the ensign went through the air lock and then crossed through a few equipment rooms where ship's crew were monitoring screens. Occasionally, he heard one or another of the crew give a readout or issue a request to check something out. It reminded him of old videos he had seen of the inside of submarines.

They soon entered a narrow hallway, with actual doors to the compartments—the first Doc had seen on the ship. The ensign stopped at one that had no markings and knocked.

"Enter."

The ensign slid the door open and stepped back. As the door closed behind him immediately Joel broke out with, "Well, thank you for your presence, your highness."

The commander, who was seated at the head of a small conference table, said, "Can it, Dubois, we don't have time for your crap." He motioned for Doc to sit.

Seated around the table were Ron, Art, Joel, Todd and the commander.

The commander said, "The sled is in its final stage toward completion. Once the symmetry test is complete and passes, it will be ready to go. Does anyone disagree with that statement--Doctor Murphy, Mr. Brady anything to add?"

Ron said, "Based on what we did with Josh's racer and even the mock testing, I say it is ready."

Doc agreed. "Yes, the only concern is that the sled has a larger mass than either the Racer or the Mock and I have not developed any formulations or even theory to explain what we are doing here."

The commander said, "Todd, give us a quick rundown on the Mock."

"Sir, there were no exceptions, there was no effect on test animal, nor on the components on the Mock, time passed as in normal time on the Mock. The test animal experienced no ill effects at all, either physical or cognitive."

The commander said, "Mr. DuBois, are there any issues that concern you? Can you pilot it?"

Joel said, "Can I pilot it? Sure, I have reviewed everything there is to know. There is basically nothing to do when the system is engaged, the sled will travel the vector it is on when engaged. The only piloting is navigating with the A.I. Piece of cake."

Next, the commander addressed Art by his formal rank, "Commander Holmes, your input please."

Holmes said, "Sir, the sled has been checked out, the on-board systems are running at peak, there are no glitches in any of the systems."

"Then to the final issue," the commander said, "and I am sorry to drop this on you now, Doctor Murphy, but the plan had been all along to have Mr. Brady along for the rescue attempt."

Doc stared over at Ron who was looking down at his hands with a subdued look on his face.

The commander continued. "But it has been discovered that Mr. Brady has a brain aneurism that is very delicate and in fact we will need to get him either back to Earth or Mars if he is to survive. Apparently, Mr. Brady felt it was not an important enough item for us to know until he collapsed on the deck in the workshop earlier today."

Doc looked back and forth from the commander to Ron, "Ron, are you OK?"

Still looking down Ron said, "Yeah Doc, they fixed me

up, but they nixed me from rescuing Josh. That is the only reason I came here in the first place, now the whole mission is caput."

Turning to the commander and eyeing the other members of the conference, Doc said, "What do you mean the whole mission is caput? Everything is ready to go."

The commander stated, "Mr. Brady is a key member of the crew, he is the person that actually built the sled, he knows all the components in the propulsion system. He did the programing; he knows how it works. If something went wrong out there, there would be no way to fix it. The other crew may be able to eventually figure it out but how long would it take? The only person that knows all the programing in the system chip and accelerator boards and symmetry programs is Mr. Brady. We are studying it but it will take days to get up to speed, we are at eight days now, I am afraid it would put Josh's chances of survival near impossible without food, water, and oxygen even with reprocessing."

Without thinking, Doc blurted out, "I know those systems," then stopped and felt his stomach tighten up, realizing what he had just done. Looking around the table he saw all eyes on him.

Doc stammered, "I mean..."

Ron said, "Doc!"

Commander said, "What do you mean, Doctor Murphy? Are you volunteering?" He paused for a moment. "We need to know now; time is running out."

Doc knew that the commander was right. If it wasn't him, then Josh would surely have no chance of making it even two or three more days. Doc thought back over the last few days, knowing that he and his family could not go back to Earth. His family was safe with the Agency and away from the autocrats of Earth. He should talk to Claire. No, that wouldn't work, it would just delay any decision. No! he needed to make this decision on his own and he needed to make it for his family and for Josh's too.

Doc could feel himself getting excited and more than a little tense. He wondered if this was what he was hoping for ever since he found out Josh might be alive and there was some little potential for rescuing him. A chance to get out into space, and on a mission to which he was a vital part. It brought back some memories from his youth when he could get away from his grandfather with the Scouts out into the wild for days at a time, testing himself against the wilderness and the unexpected. Doc grinned. Well, this was a little different than rafting the American River. Well, that was outlawed now by the environmentalists anyhow: "Can't disturb the rocks!" Doc thought to himself.

The commander said, "Doctor Murphy, no problem, we understand and we jumped to a conclusion. We understand your situation, so let's brainstorm for some other possible solutions. Anyone got something we can discuss?"

Doc said, "So the crew for the rescue is Joel, Art and someone to take Ron's place?"

All eyes were drawn back to Doc.

The commander said, "Actually, doctor, there will be four in the crew."

"Four, how is that possible? There are only four seats, were you not expecting to rescue Josh?"

"Yes, we have accounted for that, we've loaded up the sled with enough medical equipment to handle a couple emergencies, in fact. But you have to understand that, once in space, a passenger does not actually have to be in a seat. People or patients can be strapped to different areas of the ship if necessary. We are assuming however that Dr. Shamir will be in a bad way and most likely be on medical monitoring and feeding after rescue." The commander paused. "Anything else?"

Doc sat there thinking. These guys really had it all figured out.

He gulped, his throat a little dry. "I want your promise, commander, that my family and Josh's will have a place out here, preferably on Mars, and that under no circumstances will they be returned to Earth." Doc thought for a second, "Even if they want to."

The group around the table all leaned forward, listening intently to Doc.

"That is the case now, doctor," he said. "You and your family would not be safe on Earth with the current governments running things. So, I can commit to that categorically."

"I want that in writing," said Doc, "and I need to talk to my wife as soon as possible. I will be your tech man for the rescue."

There was silence around the table. Doc glanced around and saw Art staring directly at the commander.

The commander was looking down as if contemplating some inner secret. Again, Doc got the feeling he was not being told the whole story about these people and how they operated, but that wasn't most important to him now. What was important was that things needed to move and move now. If Doc was the one that needed to provide the push, then that is what he would do.

Doc stood up. "So if there isn't anything else, I think we need to get back to work...and please get me a comm line to my wife, and if possible, the kids too."

Ron stood up and started to move around toward Doc. There was look of amazement on the faces of Art and Todd. The commander reached out and picked up his tablet from the table. Standing, he said, "We will notify you when we have the line ready and the documents."

The commander, looking toward Art and Todd said, "Can you get Doctor Murphy set up and fitted with everything he will need for the mission. Let's also make sure we did not miss anything regarding any health issue."

Art and Todd responded in unison, "Yes sir."

Commander said, "Yes, doctor, the meeting is over and thank you for volunteering."

Doc nodded. "No problem." Then thinking a second, said, "Oh, wait a second, Commander, who is the fourth member of the rescue crew. Ensign Buloski?"

"No, doctor, that would be me. I will be the fourth member of the crew."

"You, why would you be on this trip? What about your ship?"

"To your first question, I wouldn't miss this for the world, to be one of the first outside our home solar system, it is a dream I thought I would not live to see. And to your second question. Yes, this is my ship, but this is also my project. Todd, or should I say Captain Holmes, will take over command of the ship in my absence."

Now the commander turned toward the participants in the room, "Any further questions--from anyone?"

There was only a chorus of no's. As they exited, Ron said to Doc, "I'm really sorry about this, Doc. I didn't know. I guess I should have suspected something, but there has been so much going on."

"It's Ok, Ron, I'm kind of getting excited about it. Maybe I was hoping for a chance to ride on the sled in testing or something, but this will work out fine and I think it's the only way to get out there and find Josh, or at least give him a better chance than debating for another day or so."

Ron said, "Thanks Doc. I still wish I was going, I've always wanted to get into space and do something, but with the politics on Earth and at my age, the opportunity never came up or it was nixed. I tried a couple times. It's funny, but I had to turn criminal to get out here, what a pile."

"Yeah, Juan used to always kid me about it," said Doc, "and it was always something I thought I had missed and could never do, but hey, I would rather be a criminal and help humankind take the next step out into the universe, than sitting in a cell with my family, being shoveled that political garbage from the Party and the Chinese. "Besides, I think I'm going to enjoy this, and after we get back, maybe settle on Mars. I think the family will all be fine."

They'd reached the shop now and had a good look at the sled sitting there looking like something slapped together by Doc when he was a kid building a space ship out of Legos."

Doc felt a hand on his shoulder and turned. It was Art. "Doc, I need you to come with me to get fitted up and get a little bit of training before we leave."

As he turned, Joel slipped past him and headed toward the sled, "Don't let his highness get his penis caught in his shorts. You should have thought about what they stick up your ass and wiener before signing away your life. Ha! Hey Commander, make a recording of his screams will ya, for the inflight movie, monsieur."

Doc turned and watched as Joel walked away. He then turned to Art with a bit of a grimace on his face. "Is it that bad?"

Art said, "Well, let's just say I am not going to make a recording."

As they started to walk Doc brought up something from the meeting, "So Art, Todd is Captain Holmes, any relation to Commander Holmes?"

Ducking through a hatch Art replied without slowing the

pace, "Yes Doc, Todd is my son, he is the oldest. I also have a younger boy and a daughter."

Trying to keep up with Art, Doc said, "Hmm, well congratulations, you must be very proud."

"Yes, I am, thanks."

Doc continued his line of questions, "You know when I first saw Todd on Earth, I thought he was the son of a Mr. Holter who was with you on Earth. He was almost the spittin' image of him."

Art stopped in the passage now and turned to face Doc smiling. "Gee Doc, for an Earther you sure don't miss much! Well, to keep it simple, Mr. Holter is actually Mr. Holmes Sr. My Dad, and so he's Todd's granddad."

"Now that all makes sense. Do you have any other family members I might run into? I hope your daughter doesn't look like her granddad."

Art broke into a laugh, "No, Lizzy's very beautiful, follows after her mother. And I don't think you'll be meeting anyone else before we get back." Art turned and started hurrying down the passage again, calling, "But in the agency with security as it is, you never know when family may be right beside you."

Doc answered, "Right," as he went down the corridor after him.

The fitting did not take long as the suits were very similar except for male or female. Doc was relieved to find out that there was no pain involved at all. All the hookups went smoothly and Doc would be wearing the shorts from now on. He would just need to hook up the devices in the lavatories to relieve himself rather than using the old space travel waste system.

Art had told Doc during his fitting that he was the only one onboard that used the old waste system recently, as

Ron had been fitted earlier since he was to be on the mission. So, the ship's engineers were very happy when the system worked with such short notice of Doc's arrival because they had not anticipated anyone using one of the lavatories.

After the fitting, Art left him with a Lt Commander Jenson, who had him sit through a few training videos on suit operations and how to move around using different protocols for surviving an open sled environment. Jenson then had Doc suit up and go through different control commands on fixing his suit as well as the built-in safety system such as damage repair and medical treatment by the A.I. system built into each suit. Apparently, the suits were fitted with A.I. micro fibers that detected damage and then repaired itself. It could do this even if there was extensive damage to the suit. Because of the micro A.I. systems in the suits, they also interacted with a medical diagnostic A.I. that monitored the medical condition of the person in the suit, so it was able to block off appendages if the wearer suffered severe injury. For example, if an astronaut lost an arm, the A.I. would send command to shut off that part of the suit and even constrict it so that the appendage is cut off and sealed by the suit if necessary. The medical A.I. was also capable of injecting a whole host of drugs needed to stimulate, sedate, or put a person in short hibernation, etc.— whatever may be needed to keep the person alive until they got back to a medical facility.

Jenson had Doc practice going through the commands of the suit while fully suited, adjusting cooling, heating, vision, and sound. He could control the video screens around him and even use a tablet designed for use in space with gloved hands.

Jenson suited up and led Doc to the core of the ship where a weightless workout chamber existed. Doc practiced moving around and always snapping in. If he forgot, Jenson would somehow send a zapping shock through his suit and calmly say "You're dead," when he made this mistake.

When Doc started to get pissed at him, Jenson would simply say, "I don't see dead people, if someone wants to try again, go back to the start."

As he went through these exercises, his suit monitor would come on and off, flashing him when it was cooling, heating, changing pressure or injecting fluids into his system if he wasn't hydrating enough.

Finally, Jenson floated over to an airlock and signaled Doc to join him. When Doc arrived, Jenson turned and told him to watch as he removed the air from the chamber and opened the door. Doc backed away as the door opened and saw the open expanse of space beyond the door. Stars shining brightly, the whole Milky Way layout in front of him. Jensen gave him a second then pulled the door shut.

He then had Doc watch as he raised the air pressure back up. When he was done, he turned to Doc and said, "You know you're dead, right?"

"What do you mean?" Doc said. "There is no reason to hook in. Are we finished with training? "

"In a second, tell me why you're dead."

Doc looked around and down; he saw that Jenson was hooked into a catch on the other side of the door, and he saw that he was floating there with his hook in his gloved hand.

Doc moved and snapped his latch onto the closest catch, "Well, I thought we were done with the training, Commander."

"You're right, the training was finished. "Jenson then reached out and pushed a button on the control panel. Instantly Doc was pulled away from Jenson back into the chamber and he struggled to hold onto his safety line. A second later as he tumbled, he was jerked in the opposite direction. Doc was still trying to pull in his safety line when he turned and saw he was being pulled toward the now-open hatch through which he and Jenson had just been looking. He was starting to panic as he realized he was going to be sucked out into space. Doc momentarily stopped himself at the hatch by grabbing an edge. He caught a glimpse of Jenson looking at him with his own safety line synched down tight holding him against the outward flow of air. Doc then saw the huge expanse of the ship as his grasp on the edge slipped and he passed out into open space. In a moment, he was doubled over at the waist and the wind was knocked out of him when his safety line snapped tight and jerked him to an abrupt stop.

While trying to catch his breath, his suit was actually updating him on what it was doing to help and that it was giving him a sedative to calm his heart and control his blood pressure.

He began to struggle at the end of the line, and then he realized parts of the line had started to tangle around him. Doc remembered something from the training video on the line and moved to unwrap the excess line from around his waist and arm. He noticed while working on the line that floodlights on the side of the ship had come on and were focused on his position. Doc used the method he'd seen in the training by holding onto the now untangled line and holding it out at arm's length. He gave the line that extended toward him a tug. The suit started taking up the line pulling him back in toward the ship. He used his extended hand to guide the line in so it would not get tangled. As the slack was removed from the line, Doc felt the pull back to the ship and he also remembered that he could give the suit different commands to control what the line did. He was being pulled back in, and gave a command to increase the speed; he knew he had to be careful since he had no way to slow himself down. When he was able to get a look at the airlock from which he exited, he saw that the hatch was trying to close itself, and this sent Doc's heart rate up again. The airlock door would close down on his line but then re-open completely. It would then try and close again. Doc decided to get some help. So, in an agitated voice he said, "Hello, this is Doctor Murphy, I have been jettisoned out of the ship, please don't close the door," then more calmly, "I am on my way back in."

Master Chief Petty Officer Ashworth with a British accent said, "Doctor Murphy, you have to name the channel you want before you use the comm in the suit. It was covered in your training. You should switch to ships channel M-Alpha for now, sir."

Doc said, "Shit! Are you kidding me? Jensen tried to kill me and you're talking about proper channels! Alert the commander that you have a spy on board!"

Ashworth said, "Yes, doctor, can you please switch to channel M-Alpha so we can proceed."

Doc selected the channel.

Ashworth recognized the switch immediately, "Thank you, doctor, I need to get you down to the hangar; they are waiting on you."

"What? So soon? Is the sled ready to test?"

"Not in my pay grade, doctor. I'm just here to retrieve you and escort you down. I will be at the hatch in a minute."

Doc was still moving toward the airlock. "What's your name? Can you hold that door open; I think it's going to cut my safety line!"

"Master Chief Petty Officer Ashworth at your service

doctor, and I wouldn't worry about that line snapping. The door won't close on a line or anything else, it is a safety measure built into all the airlocks when not on a full alert."

"Ok, that's good to know."

"It was in the training, doctor."

Doc then remembered that safety measure was actually in the training, "What about Jensen? Alert the ship, he tried to kill me!"

Ashworth spoke with a snarky tone, "Well sir, Lieutenant Commander Jensen is pretty busy right now. The commander has him assigned to your project down in the hangar."

As Doc was approaching the air lock, he slowed the retrieval speed down and hoped the mini-thrusters in the suit would work to slow his speed, "What! Hurry! Get some of your MPs or whatever down there!"

Ashworth, still with the phony respect, "Well sir, I think we are fine, Lieutenant Commander Jensen always finishes up his class by sending the student out an airlock. It is a long-standing tradition with ships' training officers. I do believe they get a real kick out of it. I must admit having the door close repeatedly on the line is an excellent added touch, probably because you are fresh from Earth. The lieutenant commander has a real sense of humor. But I am sure you can appreciate that, doctor."

Ashcroft was at the hatch as Doc approached. Ashcroft, also in a suit, reached out and grabbed Doc's belt hook with an extended arm and yanked him in. As Doc passed through the air lock he reached over, grabbed a hand hold, pivoted to a standing position, and gave a command to synch his safety line down so that he ended up standing on the wall of the chamber.

Ashworth said, "OK sir, you'll have to finish up here, and I will wait down at the lower air lock."

"I thought we were in a hurry, chief."

"Well, truly sir, but you haven't completed the training yet, and I wouldn't propose to suggest anything to you, but in space being in a hurry will kill you sometimes, doctor."

Ashworth turned and headed toward the air lock, "Now, if you please sir, hurry now and finish up so I can get you on your way."

"You mean hurry up and wait, chief?"

"Exactly."

Doc just smiled as he worked the panel to shut the air lock and pump up the chamber. When he saw that everything was in order, he headed down to join the master chief at the exit air lock. Doc went to the panel and watched as a small section on the screen changed to green; he then gave the thumbs up signal to the MC. Ashworth spun the lock and pushed open the door. It was getting easier to follow someone around the ship this time as Doc was growing more familiar with the ship's layout. It only took a few moments to slide up into the centrifugal gravity section of the ship and be back in the work hangar, easily squeezing through equipment and around ship's personnel even in the suit.

Ashcroft walked him through to the hangar where the sled was sitting and up to Lieutenant Commander Jensen.

Jensen said, "Congratulations, doctor on passing the training, you will receive notification and your certificate of accomplishment by comm as soon as it is recorded at the Space Agency."

"Oh, thank you lieutenant commander, I was so worried it would fall through the cracks."

Jensen grinned. "No problem, it's part of my job."

Doc glanced around. "Where is everybody at? I thought we were in a big hurry."

"We are, please follow, me. Everyone else has been cleared from the hangar."

"What! What for?"

"Because as soon as you get in, the sled is disembarking."

Doc followed Jensen around the sled to the other side where he saw a low step stool set up against the sled, "But where are Art, Joel and the commander? We need them to do the testing and a shake-down flight."

"They are on board waiting for you, doctor, now let's get you in there."

He started up the ladder and reached up for the lift straps above the sled. "I would have liked to have gotten a shower and shave before this test, though."

Looking down through the hatch he saw the seat in which he had fallen asleep just a few hours ago and wished he had a chance to do it again. He could also see the back of Art's head moving and a partial view of someone sitting in the seat next to him through the opening between them. Doc figured that would be the commander.

Jensen in a somewhat impatient tone, "Doctor, are you ready? Please."

Doc turned and looked down at Jensen, "Hey, how come I don't have any comm with the ship? are they not talking?"

"Look at your visual, the channels are there, do you need my help to get in?"

"Oh yeah," remembering now to check them out. He had not been paying attention to any of the visuals since his experience on the lifeline.

"Jensen, you know it has only been a couple minutes since you shot me out the air lock, so just give me a minute."

Doc verbalized to get on the sled's channel and was immediately sorry he did so, as he got an earful of profanities coming out of Joel accusing him of delaying the launch.

Also, on the comm were the Commander and Art occasionally telling Joel to can it.

Doc said, "Geez," and lifted himself up and into the sled's hatch. In a second, he'd slipped down into the seat and was strapping himself in.

Art said, "Doctor, make sure you engage your environmentals connection into the ship and get a green light. I need it to show up on my monitoring system before we can proceed."

Doc remembered what he had to do, so he unstrapped himself, reached under his butt for the connector and plugged it into the receptacle in the seat. Afterwards he seated himself and strapped in again. Doc then took a quick look around to see if anyone was checking on him. No one was, so he felt a little relieved. They were all studying monitors, and all suited up in the same type space suit as his.

Joel said, "Welcome aboard, your highness, are you going to take the trip with your hatch open?"

Doc looked up and started to reach for his belt again, but the hatch swung closed. Doc reached up and gave it a pull to make the latch set.

"Thanks" he said into his comm, but there was no answer.

The commander said, "Mr. Dubois, I expect you to back off on the crew members with your browbeating language. This isn't one of your smuggling heaps where you can threaten to space someone. Understand, now, I expect you to perform your duties as outlined in our agreement, if not I will declare article 783 of your contract and draft you back into the Agency or Space Command as an E-1 recruit."

Joel laughed harshly. "Commander, are you serious, what with all I have done for you?"

"You mean are you serious? Sir!"

"Je vous demande pardon Sir!" said Joel. "But you are not going anywhere with me in the brig or scrubbing decks on this freight hauler."

"Commander Holmes, will you put on display the item we discussed earlier today?"

Holmes said, "Yes sir." In a second all the frontal screens switched to a small group of asteroids pacing through space with identification numbers and locational data displayed on the screen. The view closed in around one particular piece of rock. Doc thought it was quite a beautiful sight.

Joel was deathly quiet at the sight.

The commander continued, "Now Mr. Dubois, it took quite a bit of effort to locate this little asteroid. But now that we have, you can see it is being tracked."

Joel acted nonchalant, "So, what is it to me?"

Commander, "Commander Holmes, please send orders to retrieve the asteroid identified as IC789002348 and distribute anything of value as charity to the citizens of Earth. No, let me change that...have everything that is recovered given to Italy's National Soccer team."

Joel snarled, "Chiant, bastard, you are the worst."

The commander said, "Do we understand each other, Mr. Dubois?"

"Yes sir, we definitely understand each other."

Just then, Lt Commander Jensen broke in on the comm, "Captain Dubois, all systems are go. Please confirm. Launch ready."

Joel looked around at his monitors–then turning to Commander Holmes he gave a thumbs up. Holmes returned the thumbs up.

"Zumwalt Command, this is the Swift, all systems go," said Joel. "Send us out."

Jensen said, "Confirmed,"

Doc felt a little jolt as the crane arm above them hooked onto the top of the sled. Doc could feel his heart beating faster and brought up his body's monitoring stats. He felt the sled lift up and he looked over at a side monitor that was displaying the launch operation. The floor beneath the sled was opening up while the crane held the sled in place. Doc returned to his medical stats and noticed they had spiked. He knew this without having to look at the monitor since he could feel his tension rising. He adjusted his monitor to include the stats of the other members of the crew. When Doc reviewed them, he was a little disappointed–there was hardly a flutter in the other members' stats. Doc turned again to watch the monitor with the launch operation on it. He felt the jostle of the crane extending the sled out into space.

Doc said, "Is that the name of our ship? The Swift? That's a good name, who thought of that?"

When no one responded Doc started verbalizing different channels and repair functions he had learned, thinking his comm wasn't working. Then Jenson broke in, "Keep this channel clear!" Doc immediately shut up, and decided to wait until someone spoke to him before talking again. He relaxed a little and returned to watching the launch on the monitor.

In a moment Jensen was back on, "Recovery vehicle in position, releasing in three, two, one." At that Doc again felt a jostle and gave a quick look around the sled to see if anyone was reacting to it. He then returned his attention to the monitor. He saw that already the ship he had been on was moving swiftly away and that the crane that had released them was almost back in. Doc realized that the sled was moving out at the vector they were released on and before he saw the crane back in the hangar, that part of the ship had already spun out of his sight.

Joel said, "Thank you, Zumwalt. All systems nominal, we are on our way."

At that moment Doc felt the sled surge a bit as he was pressed back into his seat.

"Set navigation coordinates and vector," said Joel.

Holmes said, "Confirmed navigation and vector set."

"Confirm clear space along vector."

Holmes, "Clear space along vector confirmed."

"Initiating PS in three, two, one."

Doc dropped his head a little. His tension had risen substantially as he listened to Joel and Art initiating what he thought was the first test of the system. He had even been gripping the arm rests on his seat and leaning forward in anticipation of some sort of forward shock. But now disappointment swept over him and he uttered a depressing "Shit."

He looked down at the operation monitor to check how far the Zumwalt was away to figure how long it may take them to get back onboard and figure out what had failed.

Doc was even more disappointed when he saw that the Zumwalt was gone from the screen. To him this meant it would take even more time to get back onboard and check out the sled.

Becoming aware of the chatter going on between the other crew members and Jensen on the Zumwalt, Doc looked around the cabin to see what the crew was doing.

Maybe he'd missed something; he started to focus on their conversation.

Holmes said, "Please confirm Zumwalt, location and vector."

Jensen responded, "Location and vector confirmed."

Joel said, "Commander, shall we proceed to Phase two?"

"Proceed, Captain."

Before Doc had a chance to open his mouth, Joel was doing the countdown again, "Initiating PS three, two, one."

Doc hadn't had a chance to hold on to his arm rests this time, but he still felt nothing and was getting a little agitated that he was out of the loop. Looking at the medical readouts of the crew again, he saw something that surprised him. Where his readings were down and he was calm, the other crew members' readings were way above normal.

Joel broke in, "Zumwalt, this is the Swift, please confirm location and vector."

There was quiet on the sled as the comms went silent, and there was no answer from the Zumwalt. Doc decided it was a good time to break his silence and get an update on when they would be back onboard the ship.

Doc said, "Why aren't they answering, Art?"

In an almost jovial tone, Art answered, "Well Doc, you should probably know that at this distance it takes a few minutes for the signal to travel there and back."

Realizing that he had indeed missed something and with excitement building in his voice, Doc asked, "You mean it worked!?"

Art said, "What? Yes, Doc, it worked perfectly! Commander Holmes, can you set up Doctor Murphy's monitors and provide him all the test data access."

"Yes sir"

Just then Jensen broke in, "Swift, this is Zumwalt, location and vector confirmed."

"Thank you, Zumwalt," said Joel.

Doc's monitor screens were jumping around and he tried to absorb the info and move the relevant data around the screens so he could review the results.

"Thanks, Art," he said and quickly reviewed the data on

the screens. "This all tracks to what we got from the mock. The time to distance traveled is exponential. This is great! Let's get back and get ready."

Joel said, "What? You didn't read the program yet?"

Doc was confused. "What program?"

The commander said, "Doctor Murphy..." He paused, "Art, I will update him; you and the captain keep going."

Doc turned toward the commander, looking directly through the opening between their two seats.

"Update me on what?"

In the background on the channel, Doc could hear Joel checking with Zumwalt for location and vector and confirming with Art.

Turning towards Doc, the commander said, "Doctor, in a few minutes this sled will be lining up from the exact location and setting the exact vector to pursue Dr. Shamir and attempt a recovery. In short, this is the mission."

Doc tensed up a little, still looking at the commander. "But nothing has been checked out, the test results of the Mock." And then getting more agitated, "I haven't talked to my wife, my kids," and with emphasis. "Where is my contract to take care of my family?!"

The commander said, "I am aware of my obligation to you, doctor, and we are even now trying to get a connection for you with your family. But there are some complications that have come up so we're having some difficulties."

In the background, Doc heard Joel counting down, "Initiating PS three, two, one."

Doc noticed nothing. However, immediately on a monitor screen behind the commander a large ship appeared out of nowhere. Doc noticed there were smaller craft around the larger ships.

However, at the moment, Doc was more concerned

about the complications the commander just mentioned rather than the performance of the Swift.

Doc asked, "What complication?"

The commander said, "Nothing serious, but due to the need for silent running on your wife's ship and that there is a pursuit from the Chinese tracking both the ships, we are concerned about any possible interception by them of information related to the Agency's activities--especially about this rescue mission."

Doc said, "Are they going to attack her ship!"

"No, No, doctor, they know better than to do that, and besides, they are not even close to her ship."

Doc nodded. "Ok good, but why can't I talk to her now?" Doc could hear Joel's chatter as he was making contact and exchanging comms with the ship ahead: "Dreadnought Command, this is the Swift, request permission to approach, confirm and verify code."

Doc could hear and feel a shuddering through the ship, as multiple thrusters on the sled fired on and off. He felt as though he was riding in a stage coach from the old West as he tightened his grip on the arms of his seat.

"Dreadnought, acknowledge Swift, this is Commander Payton, Congratulations, and greetings to the commander and Commander Holmes. Please follow vector to hold point, location being held by Typhoon with Captain Jones in command. Handing off control now. Good luck, Swift."

This is Jones, "Welcome Swift and greetings to...."

The chatter continued in the background as well as the changing sounds from the thrusters going on and off as Joel maneuvered the ship.

The commander continued unfazed, "As I said, doctor, we are trying to arrange that, but with the security concerns, and the time delays of communicating over thirteen million miles there are issues."

Doc realized that at the distance they'd traveled in the last few minutes, even the transmissions they'd sent when they were at the Zumwalt's location, would not be received yet. Now, depending on the distance as they'd moved out further in search of Josh, the transmissions may not be received for days or more.

Art broke in on their conversation, "Commander, Doc, we have about ten minutes before we are in position to depart."

"Thanks, Art."

Doc was thinking quickly. "Ok, let me send a message over to the ship there and then they can get it to my wife."

The commander responded. "Art, can you aid Doctor Murphy with his request? Thank you."

"Doc, I just sent you an encrypted file. When you are ready, just record your message and close it. I will send it over to the Typhoon."

"Thanks."

When Doc spoke, he started slowly because he had not really prepared himself to make a recording. He'd expected to speak directly to Laura and give an update of the situation and what he was going to do and when they would be back together. Now he was realizing that he had no idea about what was going to happen or when he may be back. He realized he may never be back or could even die in some distant part of the solar system, never to be found.

He started to speak, then fumbled his words. He looked around the cabin to try and get a sense of what he wanted to say. As he did, he saw the commander studying him.

The commander said, "Doctor, I have switched us to a private channel," and then slowly he continued, "I've found that it is a mistake not to tell your loved ones exactly how you feel. And exactly what you are doing and why. Sometimes you never get the chance to let them know how much you love them, to hold them in your arms that one last time to say goodbye. You just have to hope and pray that they will understand if events go wrong and you can't be there for them."

"Thank, you Commander," Doc said, pausing, "It sounds like you've been through some rough spots before?"

The commander quickly turned away from Doc and looked down toward one of his monitors. Doc again heard Joel's chatter as the Swift neared the Typhoon.

Doc turned his head toward his tablet and began to speak, confirming that the file was recording his face and voice. "Claire, Hi, I don't know how this happened, but we have a chance to maybe rescue Josh. Yes, he may be alive. Anyhow, it requires an expedition in space and it may take a while. For some reason I volunteered, it just came over me and I knew I had to do it. I have worked it out that you and the boys will be taken care of and safe from the Chinese and the Party on Earth. I want to be honest about it, so there are risks in what I am doing and where I am going, "Doc laughed a little at that, "Ha, where I am going, nobody knows. But I am with the best crew I could hope for. So, if anybody can rescue Josh and get us all back safe it is these guys. I know you know it, but I want to say it again because it puts me in my happy place and I need that right now. I love you and always will. Tell the boys what I am up to when you get back together on the Moon and let them know how much I love them, and tell them I am very proud of both of them. Love you all, Dad."

Doc closed the file and sent it back to Art. As he lowered his tablet and looked over the sled, he saw Joel and the commander turned toward him. He then realized he had not switched off the channel during his message. Doc gave a little chuckle but did not feel any embarrassment at all about what he'd said.

Doc turned to Joel, who was still looking at him with a little annoyed look on his face. "Well, are we going to do this or not," Doc said, "why are we still sitting here?"

Joel had the slightest grin on his face and turned back toward his monitors. The commander had a small smile on his face as he also turned back to his work. Doc looked to his side and saw that the Typhoon had moved off some distance. The small maneuvering nozzles of the sled were constantly thrusting on and off now, although Doc could not feel any motion in the ship at all.

Joel said, "Gentlemen, please remain perfectly still, we are in position and on track with the beacon signal from the Shamir racer, we will be running the propulsion with the time program, with manual override if necessary. Commander?"

"Gentlemen, may God watch over us and Dr. Shamir, and help to keep us safe. Amen."

Doc was surprised at the prayer since in most of the countries on Earth and in particular America, Old Europe and China, religious activity had been heavily restricted and discouraged over the last century. So, when even Joel said 'Amen' after the commander's prayer he himself quickly followed up with his own 'Amen.'

"Fasten your seat belts, ladies," said Joel, "no moving about the cabin while the seat belt light is on, for those new to our cruise there are no barf bags in space, so just swallow it."

"Typhoon, confirm location and vector."

Jones responded, "Swift, location and Vector Confirmed, God speed Swift"

"Initiate PS three, two, one."

On Doc's monitors the Typhoon was gone as well as the Dreadnought.

Checking his other monitor, he noticed the higher reading of heart rates on the other crew members.

Doc thought to himself that he needed to get up to speed on the flight plan. He worked on the monitor and brought it up on the screen. The plan called for the initial PS to be five minutes and continue doubling until they reached their objective or needed to make an adjustment.

Joel said, "Location and vector check."

Looking over at Art, Doc said, "Is there anyone out here that can check us?"

"The closest Agency ship is the ED-24; it was a drone that was dispatched about five days ago from Ceres base, that is if we are where we are supposed to be. It will be a few minutes, due to distance."

Commander spoke up, "Doctor, can you set up some method to monitor the propulsion system, to maybe get a heads up on any potential problems."

"Ok, shouldn't be a problem, the code is easy. I will set a system check at every stop."

"Doc, what is the possibility that any of these boards will stop working and how would that affect the propulsion?"

Doc said, "Ok, let me finish this up for the commander," in a few seconds, "OK Art, on the boards, well, there should be no problem at all. With the firmware Josh developed, the system is very stable. The only real issue is that we hit something or something hits us and damages the boards. So, we should be careful about avoiding any type of space debris."

Joel said, "I got a ping from the drone. I am holding on the beacon signal from the racer." He paused a second, "OK, good, initiate PS in three, two, one."

Doc broke in, "Hey, can't you wait a second? Where the heck are we?"

"Oh my god, princess," said Joel, "please may I have your permission to pilot this sled, ahh, I think not. So, foutre au cul!"

Art said, "We were out past the asteroid belt and approximately in Jupiter's orbital path."

Doc said, "Ok, let's see if I can calculate where we will be next..." The ship went quiet as each crew member worked on their assigned tasks. Doc realized that a lot of time was going to be spent just verifying the sled's location and adjusting to the right vector to track Josh's beacon. He had not realized it until the last stop that Joel and Art had spent almost an hour verifying location and the vector and this was in the solar system. Doc wondered what would be the time spent if they had to leave the system. He had wondered about this when the commander and Art first mentioned it. One of their reasons for making the trip was with the knowledge that it may be possible to leave the solar system.

Now Doc began to worry about just how far Josh may be out in space. He looked up the ship's data, looking for the data collected by the Space Agency and what the commander had told him about the signal beacon coming from Josh's racer.

Looking over at the commander, Doc saw that he had reclined his seat and was lying back.

Doc said, "Commander, commander?"

Art said, "Doc, the commander is off line right now, I think he is resting up. Just to update you, we may have to hold up for a few hours so that Joel and I can get some sleep, or we may just trade off with the piloting. Either way, at this point the time in PS will not be long enough to take a nap. I think we all would agree it is important for the pilots to be awake when the PS shuts down."

Doc said, "Well, I don't know how anyone can sleep through this, it is historic."

Art said, "Yes, it is, but we want it to be a successful historic achievement, right?"

"Right, so right now I can't sleep, and I plan to work at some changes to the PS program."

"What changes would those be?"

"Nothing drastic, first, I want it to signal with sound when it shuts down, and now that you mention it, I can have it signal a few minutes ahead of time when it is about to shut down, that way if you are sleeping or accidently fall asleep it would be like an alarm clock to wake you."

"Good idea Doc," said Art. "Tell you what, make the alarm clock one sound for Joel and me and make it go off even if we are off line."

"What?" Joel said. "I don't need no alarms ringing in my head. No!"

"Do it, Doc. Thanks."

Doc said, "Art, do you have an idea just how far we have to go to find Josh?"

"Not exactly, the commander has spent more time on that than me, but I am pretty sure we'll be pretty far out of the solar system." Art continued, "Here, the files and data are in the library..." He paused for a moment. "Oh, I see you already have them, so take a look at them and maybe you can figure it out."

"Radar clear, imaging clear. Commander, can you spare me some time, so we can get moving."

"Excuse me, Doc," said Art and went back to chatting with Joel and checking location and vector. Doc knew they would be at it a while. He figured the Swift must be somewhere near Saturn's orbit now based on just a quick calculation in his head. He looked at the monitor with the exterior view but could only see the brilliant colors and stars of the Milky Way. Using the screen, he moved the view to the aft of the sled and could see the tiny Sun still out-shining all the stars in that quadrant of space. When he lifted his gloved finger from the screen it reverted to the side view.

Going over the data in the library from Josh's flight, it was quite amazing that they were able to pull the stretched-out signal back together. Doc was wondering how the signals could be transmitted through space if the propulsion system had a basis in string theory and created some sort of dimensional vortex. If that were the case, wouldn't any signals produced in another dimension be confined there or at least not escape the vortex until it was closed?

Doc brought up a chart of the solar system. He could immediately tell that it was far more detailed than anything available on Earth. He was surprised when the Swift's location and vector also appeared. He had been pretty close in his calculation of location. The planets were identified as well as their location and orbits. A little curious, he expanded the view and backtracked along the path the sled had traveled. He was curious about how they had traversed the Asteroid Belt, and as he tracked back along the vector, he was quite surprised when he reached it. The display had actual asteroids label and locations in real time. Checking the backup data, he saw that what he was watching was a real time navigational display of where each asteroid was in the belt as well as their travel speed and orbit within the field. Apparently, the space agency had been busy over the years attaching micro-transmitters to millions of these rocks to track and cataloguing them. Seeing that it had been almost an hour now since they had passed through the belt,

Doc worked on the screen to set the time to when the sled had traversed the belt. He then started back along the vector and stopped when he got his answer. Somehow the sled had passed through multiple potential impacts from asteroids in the belt. Doc checked and verified. These asteroids, although small, were certainly large enough to do substantial damage to a ship that had the misfortune to hit them. The sled was traveling at a FTL speed so why no impact?

Doc saved his info and recorded back through the belt to quantify and document the event. He then compressed the view and moved forward along the vector out past all the planet orbits, past the Kuiper Belt and out beyond the Oort Cloud. The vector extended out even past the solar system's arm of the Milky Way and out into the inter-galaxy void.

Doc shuddered, hoping Josh was not out that far. Another concern came to him and he needed to interrupt Joel and Art's conversation.

"Excuse me, gentleman," said Doc, "but we have a problem."

Joel said, "It will have to wait, doctor. I'm going to send this puppy out the vector again."

"What is it, Doc?"

"Go ahead and get going, we can talk with the PS on."

With that Joel said, "Initiate one."

"So we have twenty minutes now," said Doc, "until we stop and do another fix."

Art said, "Yes, we are between Saturn and Uranus now, so we should be ending up out past Neptune on this move. Right, Doc?"

"Right very good, also I was wondering, it is damn cold here now and the sled is not really sealed. Can these instruments operate at these temps. My suit seems fine."

"Is this what you wanted to discuss?" said Art.

"No, but I would like an answer."

Art said, "You can check the specs on how these craft are built when you get a chance, but everything in the sled, even the boards that your chips are embedded in, get heat from the reactor. We won't be having any problems even at absolute zero, Relieved?"

Doc said, "Yes, OK."

"So what did you want to discuss?"

"Well, it may be that we are going to have to go a lot further and a lot faster than what we are doing right now."

"Why?"

Joel chimed in, "Yes, why?"

"I have studied the info on the beacon coming from Josh's racer. And we're still receiving it, but it's still stretched out. The tracking system developed here is taking a signal that has been stretched out over a substantial distance and compression to get the signal." He continued. "This was completed by picking up the signal from a fixed point and waiting for hours and even days to produce a single ping. This from a system that broadcast a ping every second."

Art said, "So?"

"So, as the racer got further away, so did the signal. Right? So, it takes about an hour to get signals back to Earth from here. What about the signals from the racer. How long are we waiting to locate the beacon signal and then waiting to process it? As we get further out are we even going to be able to process it at all?" "It is a problem," admitted Joel, "but we have to wait and confirm if we want to track your buddy down."

"Look, we know the vector the racer took off on, we know the distance that the signal will travel in the eight days is 127 billion miles, so that is in any direction. The question is, what if the racer went out past the Oort Cloud? That means the signal is now coming from light years away."

Art said, "I see--what would you suggest, Doc?"

"What do you do in space when you are trying to track someone down?"

"This type of issue doesn't really come up in relatively close space compared to what you are talking about."

Doc said, "Look, we know he's not within the 8-day time frame, and we can double that because that is the distance the signal would travel in any direction. So that's about 254 billion miles--approximately a 23.5-minute trip in this sled. "

"But here is the next thing: What if we're not getting a beacon signal as in relative space, meaning sixty pings a minute. Then we are not anywhere close to Josh."

"Right, your highness wasn't sleeping after all," said Joel, "so we get out there and there is no signal. Like you say, without using the compression program, then we hit it again. Right? and get the ride over with quick, get your pal, and back to the family, Bing! Bing Bang!"

Joel continued, "Initiate one!"

Art shouted, "Joel stop!" but it was too late; the sled was in PS mode.

"What is the problem, commander? It all makes sense. Connect the dots. We were wasting time."

Art said, "You still should have waited until Doctor Murphy had a chance to finish his proposal."

"He did finish commander," said Joel. "He explained it perfectly, why waste anymore time?"

The commander said, "Doctor Murphy, do you have any-thing else to add?" Apparently, the commander had come back on line and had been listening in on the conversation.

Doc paused, then said, "Well sure, since we know what to expect, and what we are looking for, we only have to do a few things at each stop: make sure we are lined up on the vector, check to see if the beacon is local, and then check to see where we're going is not in a star or something."

Twisting to look back at Doc, Joel said, "In a Star, what the fuck are you talking about?"

"Well, at this point I fully expect that we are going to leave the solar system, based on the data I have studied. So, I haven't plotted anything out yet, but there could be some areas where we just don't want to stop, so we would have to extend or shorten the PS time to circumvent that area of space. I for one believe we should not attempt to travel too close to a star. How about you, Joel?"

Art spoke up. "So we will still be stopping and surveying the path before moving forward, then?"

"Well, I plan to write up a program and using the sled's database on a go, no go basis. The program would use the sled's long range cameras to view the path ahead along the vector. It should pick up anything in our path at only 258 billion miles. The view of the next location will pop up on all our monitors for go, no go decision. If everyone is for going, then the sled takes off, if there is a no, we hold until we resolve the issue and reach a decision."

The commander said, "What do you think, Art?"

"Looks good to me, he's right. If the racer is way out there, we could be tracking for weeks, we don't have the supplies for that."

Joel said, "Doctor Highness, I am sending you a navigation for A.I. control. Please work it into your program. It will document the space we are in at the stops, and will make it easy coming back with all the trip data."

Looking over the material Joel had sent, Doc said, "Will do." Then he added, "So are we all in agreement, Commander?"

"Yes, I agree with your proposal, doctor, just with this last move by the captain: will the arrival space be clear?"

"Yes, we will still be in open space," said Doc. "There may be issues in the Oort Cloud and the Kuiper Belt area, and then the plasma bank at the edge of the system if we have to go that far. But we will be in open space after that. It will be about 40 light years till we hit anything. We are still moving pretty slow; the problem is passing up the beacon signal."

The commander said, "Ah Yes, Trappist-one, um, doctor, commander and captain, I propose we change the approval to just two of us. We are going to need some sleep soon and we should be doing shifts now."

Doc said, "Ok, will do."

The commander said, "Doctor, you and Art can take a break now; you can relieve us in two hours."

Doc said, "Let me set up the system first. I will have it self-adjust for the time passed rather than on a fix on the eight-day value."

"Hey Commander, I need a break too," said Joel.

"Excuse me, captain."

Joel gave a shrug. "Sir, I need a break too, I have had very little sleep since you pulled me out of the brig!"

The commander nodded. "You will get one in two hours, now let's get on moving!"

"Yes sir! With your permission I will send back one of Buloski' s drones."

Joel had reached down somewhere under his seat and pulled out a small cube that looked like it was covered in processor chips. Doc saw Joel send it out through the cabin opening. The mention of Buloski and a drone had piqued his interest.

"We are not that far out yet," said the commander. "I don't see the need."

"He wanted to test one early to see if he could send a signal, that way he could get a normal transmission, if the drones don't make it back to us."

"Excuse me for interrupting, but can you update me on what you're discussing, commander?"

The commander shot a quick glance over at Doc, then touched his monitor's screen. Reconfigured into a small box, the layout of a tiny drone with one of the tachyon chips was mounted in what looked like the mounting board. The drone had everything needed for navigation, storage, cameras and comm systems.

Doc said, "This is interesting, can you hold up on your decision a minute?"

The commander said, "What do you think, doctor, is there a problem?"

"What? No. How many of these little gems do you have, Joel?"

"Joel?"

"Jeez, let me see," said Joel. "I think Buloski gave me about twenty. He said these were left over after finishing the sled so he came up with the idea of making comm drones out of them. Smart kid, that one, not like the old men you normally have to deal with in the Agency."

Art cut in, "Doc, he programed them to be released along our path to send updates or alert the Agency if there was an emergency of some kind. Clever, huh?"

While Doc was listening, he had opened up the crypted programing of the drones, and saw he could reprogram each of them for different tasks.

"This may sound risky, commander, but I have another proposal thanks to our industrious Lieutenant Buloski."

Joel balked. "How long are we going to be sitting here now?" The commander turned to Doc, "Go ahead, Doc."

"It is quite simple, since the lieutenant has done most of the work, it gives us a chance to substantially speed up our search."

"I can change the programming on these drones to spread out along the vector we're searching by calibrating different times for travel in the PS mode for each."

"And instead of stopping and starting as we are doing now, we can send them out straight to points on the vector and check for Josh's beacon. It would only take seconds at each stop–the same as what we will be doing. With twenty--no let's say eighteen, we will keep two in case there is some emergency info we need to send back."

"With our current plan we would be about three light years from Earth in twenty four hours, and that would put us in the interstellar space between stars."

"If we send these drones, heading directly to points further out the vector nonstop, and doing the same check we are, then head back directly to us if they find Josh's signal in real time."

The commander said, "Doctor, but that would still be days out for the drones to travel and then back. How far would you send them along the vector?"

Just then Joel spoke up, "We've stopped, should I go? I checked and we are clear." "Yes, captain go."

Joel said, "Initiate one" and they were back on the PS.

Doc did not even have time to check out the view around the sled, but he continued with his plan.

"It would be based on time, commander, and I don't know exactly how far they will go out because as you know, we have evidence that the time spent on the PS system relative to distance seems to be exponential.

"So, determining how far they go out will be a guess, but it will be multiple times shorter than our expected twenty-four hours and the individual drone times will be relative to the other drones. They will also be doing the same as the sled after they arrive. If they get no signal, they will start the next transit in PS mode at a closer point to the end. Hopefully."

"Commander Holmes, Captain Dubois. Any input on Doctor Murphy's new suggestion?"

"No," said Art, "but commander, we need to have a deadline. As you know we need to be back in five days; that's all the supplies the sled will carry, so my input is that at two and half days we start back."

The commander turned to the captain?

Joel said, "Yes, my plan is to put a gag in his highness's mouth!"

The commander ignored him. "Proceed with your plan. Doctor Murphy. Will you have enough time by the next stop to disperse the drones?"

"Yes, the navigation is already there, should be no problem."

Doc spent the rest of the PS time working quietly, setting up all the adjustments to the sled program and then working on the drones. He put in a few additional adjustments to enable the drones' search to be more efficient.

So, when the notice for the end of the PS mode signaled, Doc had completed the adjustments to the drone software.

Joel reached under his seat and pulled out a number of the tiny drones, "Ok, Doctor Highness, which ones are going out the hatch?"

Doc said, "Here are the serial numbers of the drones to be sent out."

"Are you kidding? I am not going to sit here trying to find numbers on these things."

"Oh yeah," said Doc, "sorry about that."

Doc thought a second and then set the navigation lights to blinking on the search drones to be sent off.

He was rather surprised when brilliant lights started flashing in Joel's hands as the high intensity navigation lights lit up the interior of the sled like an old-time fireworks display. Everybody's helmets automatically switched to the protective glare protection mode.

Holding a handful out in front of him, Joel said, "Stupid! Turn them off!"

"Just open the latch and release them," said Art. "Here, give me some."

Art reached over and pulled some out of Joel's hand; he then unlatched his hatch snapped on his lifeline, released his harness and stood up. Through the hatch Art began releasing the blinking drones. At one point, he stopped back in and handed a non-blinking one over his shoulder to Doc. As Doc took the drone he said, "Here, hold onto this until I'm finished. It is a brilliant view out here."

Doc switched his monitor to view Art releasing the small drones out into empty space and thought about how he used to throw his old Frisbee when he was a kid. A tear formed in his eye as he welled up with emotion at the astonishing site.

Art reached down into the sled over to Joel and said, "More."

Joel reached down into the brilliance coming from underneath his seat and grabbed another handful, handing them to Art. Art then stood up through the hatch again. Joel joined him, going up through his own hatch after grabbing a few more drones and in a few moments the cabin was quiet again and both Art and Joel were back in their seats with their harness belts fasten.

Doc did a double check on the drone systems and then

sent them on their way. The crew watched on the monitors as the drones shuffled around each other for space, then lined up on the invisible vector and disappeared on their individual missions.

Doc looked around the cabin with a smile, happy with what he had completed and knowing that now there was a much better chance of finding Josh. He was not disappointed when no one returned his gaze or commented on his work. He knew now how vital it had become for him to have joined this mission and felt much better about himself as an important member of the crew.

Doc, realizing he was still holding the drone Art had given him, said, "Art, do you want this drone back?"

Art said, "Doc, can you reach through and put it back under the captain's seat?"

Doc took the drone, still gazing out in wonderment

The PS travel progressed forward for several hours and Doc and the crew caught up on sleep and meals. At around the seventh hour mark, Joel started having the heaves, and this progressed through the rest of the crew for the next several hours. There was a discussion on stopping to give their bodies time to adapt, but after Doc reviewed the medical data, he could find nothing abnormal other than the fact that they'd all had extreme cases of motion sickness. He advised waiting until their stomachs were empty before the admission of motion sickness drugs. He also thought for the next few hours they should have the systems feed them intravenously until they had adapted better or the drugs took effect.

Even though Doc was moaning and felt like crap, he could not help laughing when he heard Joel giving it up again and again, as it seemed he was the worst affected. Doc wondered about what the inside of Joel's helmet looked like

Trappist

as he knew his smelled terribly and the interior visor was splashed with his puck.

Eventually, the suit was able to catch up and clean the helmet back to normal. But this took time and he realized that most of the continued sickness was probably due to reflex gagging from being locked in their helmets. Something he thought they may want to consider on future trips with the PS.

Joel spent much of his time during this period cursing at his suit, until he finally asked Doc for some help in getting his heaving under control—almost begging Doc to do something. Doc was able to aid him by getting into the medical program and giving him a mixture of different motion sickness drugs and sedatives. Although Doc was not a medical doctor by law, he was up to date on all the chemistry involved and the sled's medical library actually provided an excellent A.I. assistant as well as cross-checking drug combinations for synergy. Besides, Doc knew that most medical doctors practiced in research these days and that patients never really saw an actual human for medical attention. Everything was run by A.I., exams, diagnoses and treatment or non-treatment as all health care was controlled by the state.

After everyone had gradually recovered with the help of the drug cocktail Doc worked up with the medical A.I., the crew was near exhaustion. On his last shift, (these had been extended to five hours now) Art had mentioned that the commander left him a message with a concern about the crew being physically fit enough to do a rescue. Art and Doc confirmed to each other that they were still a little dizzy. Art said the commander wanted Doc to review any other options he may think of to shorten the mission.

Doc spent most of that shift re-thinking the problem,

213

but had to admit to Art as their shift ended that he was just not up to it, even with the cocktail. When he started to focus too hard working with the data, he would become nauseous again.

Doc heard the ten-minute signal for the end of the PS coming up and the end of his shift. Everything seemed to be going fine but they were not making progress. This would comprise the discussion the crew would be having in a few minutes. Feeling as sick as he did, he imagined the crew would want to end the mission, especially Joel who was still in bad shape.

Doc readied a speech to at least convince them to search a little longer, but he didn't get the chance.

No sooner had the PS shut down than alarms sounded on the Swift. Doc felt a wave of heat come through his suit and its alarms start blaring. The readings on his suit indicated the exterior temperature had shot up to ten thousand degrees and was climbing rapidly.

Doc shouted, "Heliosphere, take us back, we'll burn up!"

Joel, in a rasping voice, said, "Something's wrong! I'm locked out!"

Thoughts flashed in Doc's mind that they would die here, burnt to a crisp in the hellish temperature where the Milky Way's gamma radiation hit the solar systems heliosphere shield made by its solar wind. The last thing Doc remembered was the glare coming from the monitors displaying the exterior inferno before passing out.

Doc awoke to the commander's voice, "Doctor, are you OK?" He felt a hand on his shoulder gently nudging him. "Doctor, Doctor Murphy!"

"What, ah, um?" struggling to speak, his mouth felt as dry as burnt ash, "Commander, what happened? How are we…?"

The commander finished, "How are we alive? I don't know...I don't know how we even got that close to the edge? But right now I need to check on Joel and Art. Is there anything you can do for them? They haven't responded yet."

"Sure, where are we, do you know?" Moving to sit up straight, and taking a sip of water–he quickly regretted it, spitting it out with a "Yow!"

"Yeah, it is still pretty hot, the tank is more forward in the sled, we're definitely lucky the tank didn't explode."

Checking the health monitors for the crew, happy they were still working,

Doc said, "They've been sedated commander by the A.I. It appears they got some doses of radiation and the A.I. shot them up with treatment drugs and sedated them to relieve pain and convulsions. They are going to be under for a few hours."

"Well, that is a problem."

Doc said, "Why, where are we?"

The commander said, "As best I can tell, we are in the PS mode. I don't want to try and override anything without talking to Joel or Art. I don't know if they did something to get us out of that spot back there, but whatever happened, it saved our lives."

The commander continued, "Doc, any thoughts on how we got so close to the edge?"

Doc noticed that the Commander had called him "Doc" instead of the formal "doctor" which made him feel a little better, but he decided not to mention it.

Doc said, "No, it could be anything, even a random fluctuation from something in the Kuiper Belt or the Oort Cloud. There haven't been many studies on their interactions this far out into the interstellar medium."

"Oh," said the commander, looking over at him, "you keep up with that do you?"

"One tries," Doc said, "but, going through the data, I might be able to figure out what happened with the ship."

"Good Idea, I can help—feed me the info when you find something. I'm going to start a system check to see how the sled is holding up."

As Doc reviewed the data, he was surprised to find that they had been in the PS mode for more than two hours, and another thought hit him. He was not feeling nauseous at all.

Doc turned to the commander, "Sir, how do you feel?"

"What do you mean, about what?"

"No, I mean physically, any nausea?"

As though noticing it for the first-time, he replied, "No, actually I feel pretty good now as opposed to burnt toast."

"Yeah, strange isn't it, and just to let you know, we have been under PS for more than two hours. Were you up the whole time?"

The commander said, "No, I just came to a little bit ago, and tried Joel and Art first, then you."

Doc said, "Oh, why not me first?"

"Well, nothing personal, but I could see on the monitor with the data feed from your suit that you were OK, and I needed to know what action they may have taken."

"Let me keep going on the review then," said Doc. "Maybe we'll have some answers by the time they wake up."

"Good, keep me informed," and he turned back to his monitors.

It did not take Doc long to discover what had happened and it brought a smile to his face. Even though he was excited, he decided it best to verify the data. When he finished, he again turned to the commander.

"Do you have a minute?"

"Is that a rhetorical question, Doc?"

"Well, no, just being polite, but I have what we need. And I have good news and bad news, what do you want first?"

The commander acted a little irritated. "You know, Doc, we are light years from Earth, and we don't know where we're going with both pilots out of commission." Then becoming stern, he said, "But I see you need to add some humor to the situation. I don't, so just lay it out there as fast and simply as you can, I don't have time for that and haven't for a long time."

"Gotcha," Doc said, "first, we are in PS drive due to a slight error in the program I wrote for the drones we sent out."

"Yes?"

"I had added some extra actions to save time, when notifying us if one of them located the beacon in real time."

"What should have happened, was if the drone located the signal, it would calculate an interception course, proceed to the spot, and start broadcasting the info to get to Josh.

"So, I programmed the drone to be sure that we on the Swift got the info before traveling to the next spot, was that the Swift would disable the PS if it received a signal from the drone with a positive outcome. "

"Yes, go on."

"Well, the drone also transmitted the navigation information to the beacon location.The error was that it was written as a command. So, when we hit the last spot, the drone signal was there waiting for us. So, the PS was disabled, and the information to get to Josh was loaded in, navigation set and then the PS engaged."

"So what was the error, exactly?"

Doc said, "Well, it should not have been automatic and

with the command as it was, it over-rode all of the on-board controls."

"Doc, is that the good news or the bad? And how long did that take?"

"What? Oh, maybe about a thousandth of a second," then continuing, "And well that is the bad news, along with some other less significant details."

The commander's face relaxed. "Then the good news is the location of the signal. Good, so the drone setup worked."

"Yes, we are headed to the signal now."

"Good, and where is that?"

"Commander, that is one of those other less significant details … I don't know. I will have to go back through the data transmitted and try to figure it out."

"Alright, sounds like a plan, keep me informed of anything significant. Thank you, doctor." The commander turned back to his work again.

Doc now began digging into the flight data from the drone and what it passed to the sled. He identified it by its serial number. It was one of the drones that was sent almost to the end of the search vector. It was drone Number 16, and its time had been set at eight hours. This meant that they still had quite a while in the Swift with the PS on.

Doc thought this would put Josh's racer somewhere out maybe close to twenty light years or so. A wrench was thrown into Doc's calculations when he saw that the drone had gone on PS the same as the sled before picking up the beacon signal. 'No, matter' thought Doc as he plotted it out. It would just require another 20-minute period to hit the spot. This checked out when Doc was able to tap into Joel's controls and bring up the PS system data on his screen.

This is when he discovered another problem; the numbers did not quite work out, not even with rounding.

If the drone traveled the vector for eight hours, and then returned on the same vector to intercept the sled, how did it manage to be there at the plasma storm location waiting for them? Either something was wrong with his math or the sled and the drones were traveling at different speeds. Which would mean Doc had no idea where they would be when the PS shut off. Doc spent some time on this without coming up with an answer. After taking a few moments to lean back and rest his eyes, he fell exhausted into a fitful sleep.

Doc heard a voice as if far away. "Doc, it's Art, wake up, we're here." There was the sound of the morning news going off in his helmet, but it was all scratchy with a lot of static. Doc thought it was a recording of some old documentary Art was running through the ship's system.

Doc was waking up, "You guys record all the old stuff for your travels? You must have quite a library."

"Actually, Doc, it is not a recording," said Art, "it is a live broadcast we're picking up."

Doc sat up straight immediately, "We found life out here?"

The rest of the crew broke into laughter, and Art chuckled, "Yeah, we found life, it's on a little blue planet about forty light years that way." Doc could see Art's gloved hand and thumb pointing back toward the way they'd come.

Doc then realized what he was hearing. Apparently, they were picking Earth broadcasts up from more than forty years ago. "Well, at least we have a beacon to follow back if we lose our vector."

"Ok, can we get started?" Joel croaked, "now that sleepy head is awake."

Art said, "Commander, ready?"

"Let's update the doctor first. Captain Dubois, you can lay a course to the source and initiate at will. Go ahead, Art."

"We have arrived close to the Red Dwarf star labeled Trappist-1, and we have pretty much identified that the beacon from Dr. Shamir's racer is coming from the fifth planet of the system. Trappist -6."

In the moments Art was talking to Doc, the view in the monitor shifted and became ablaze with the Red Dwarf, practically filling the screen.

Art was focusing on the view. "As you can see, it is a pretty crowded neighborhood."

"We are just outside the orbit of the outer most planet," said Joel. "When we go in, I will need to be on the thruster to get into the planet. As you can see from the monitor all six of the planets are moving pretty damn fast. I will need to move in fast to the planet so I don't burn up all our fuel."

Doc asked, "Why is the planet all orange like that?"

"Readings show a high surface temp," said Art, "and a heavy iron make-up. It appears to have a molten surface with multiple volcanic activities along certain rift areas."

There was another shift in the monitors, and the planet loomed large in the screen with the dwarf star's reddish glow filling the rest of the screen as background.

Almost instantly Doc's body was jerked back into the seat as Joel threw the thrusters into full acceleration. Doc could feel his skin pressing against his face and pulling back along his cheeks.

There was a moment when the weightlessness of the past few days returned as Joel guided the ship toward the beacon, then he was popped back into the seat again as Joel went to full throttle. Looking over at the commander, Doc saw that he also was enjoying Joel's piloting skills.

Then it was over. The sound of the main thruster stopped, and a blazing vision shone on the monitor screens. In front was the glowing iron orange planet, and behind, off to the side, was another dark planet with a bluish halo around it, and then there was a very small planet even further off to the side, but with a brighter yellowish halo around it.

Doc said, "Jeez, it is beautiful!"

The commander spoke, "Give me a status captain—you have anything?"

Joel said, "We are right at the edge of the gravity well for the planet." The sound of particles started pinging on the exterior of the sled and carried into the system's monitor systems.

Instantly, the Swift's thruster fired up and Doc was thrown back into his seat again as Joel lifted the sled back out to a higher orbit.

"There seems to be debris all over that altitude," said Joel.

Art spoke. "Commander, it appears the particles being thrown up by the planet's eruptions are reaching orbit; it is a very active planet probably due to the tidal effect from the other close in planets."

"It is going to be hard getting down much closer," said Joel, "with that cloud of debris at that altitude."

Art said, "There are very strong magnetic bands shifting all over the planet, but very restricted in locations. There are also a lot of ice particles in orbit, some very large, some tiny. That's what we ran into down below."

"How am I supposed to get through that?" Joel snapped.

"Hold on, I have him, I have the racer,"

The commander and Doc said in unison, "Where!"

Joel said, "I have him too," picking up the location from Art's input.

Joel said, "Orders, commander!"

"Hold on a second," said Art. The racer is at the edge of a magnetic band that is rotating with the planet below. It is moving at two thousand km/hr. The problem is that the debris is moving at a much slower rate that ranges from approximately seventeen hundred down to one thousand and less. Not much moving at slower speeds. That must be the range when it falls out of orbit and back down to the surface. How is it still there? The debris should have pounded the racer to pieces by now."

"Well, that makes it easier," said Joel.

The commander said, "Develop a plan to get in there, captain. Art, can you pick up any life signs from the racer?"

"Yes, I have his broadcast channel." Art paused a second. "He is alive!"

"What the hell? Bullshit!" shouted Joel. The commander said, "Your plan, captain?"

"Yeah," said Joel, "flip this sled over and head home!"

"Captain, there is a man alive down there in that mess, I don't know how, but this is why we are here--get on with it."

Joel flipped the ship over and headed to a higher orbit.

Looking toward Art, he said, "I need a big piece of ice and thick--it needs to last long enough to get into that maelstrom. Otherwise, we will be beat to hell in a matter of moments."

Art said, "Got you," looking over his side monitor and switching the view to his front. "Check to the ID'd location, captain."

Joel echoed, "Got it," and the Swift's thrusters fired again.

A second later the front monitors were filled with a gigantic chunk of ice.

"Ok, sit back and watch a pro," said Joel. Doc then saw the arms that had been attached to the sled back on the Zumwalt appear in the screen moving toward the ice.

Doc watched as Joel guided the arms out to embrace the

ice, then as the arms secured it, small robots came out of compartments in the arms and crawled onto the asteroid. As they did so, Doc could see they were attaching some kind of fiber as they swarmed across the ice. Doc was amazed at their speed. The tiny robots continued to flow out of the compartments by the hundreds it seemed—each trailing a line out. Soon the lines intersected and the whole aster-oid was held in a loosely woven net. Doc kept watching as somehow the lines tightened into a snug then tight clamp on the chunk of ice, securing it to the Swift.

Joel swung the sled around and headed down into the lower orbit.

Doc's frontal view was now the backside of the ice chunk the Swift had latched onto.

Doc said, "Joel, how are you going to get in to Josh? Can you see anything?"

"Check it out, my little pets are well trained."

A small icon appeared on Doc's monitor and he tapped it. It opened up to the view in front of the ice shield. Apparently when the robots had secured the shield they'd also installed instruments for monitoring and navigation to the shield.

Doc shook his head. "Brilliant."

Joel said, "Yes, I am."

Art looked skeptical. "Do you have the racer on track, captain?"

Joel said, "I have him.... commander, are you sure about this?"

The commander said, "Proceed with the operation, captain."

CHAPTER 10

With the large rock of orbital ice held firmly in place, Joel carved a path through the debris. Joel eased the ship down lower into the maelstrom following the signal that would lead them to Josh's bike.

At this level they could see individual swirling spirals created by the magnetic bands generated by the glowing planet below. Joel guided the Swift into a void in-between two of the spirals. The ship started jerking with the movement of their protective ice shield. The commander asked Joel, "What is causing the ship to move like this?"

"I don't know, it's the shield that's jerking us around. It may be hard to hold onto if this keeps up."

Art spoke up. "It appears that that protective shield we picked out is loaded with iron particles. So, our shield is being pulled around by the magnetic fields surrounding us."

"Can you handle it, captain?" said the commander.

"I can for now--our target isn't too far in. If the racer has any iron at all in it, it may be locked into position with the movement of the bands. We will be using a lot of our maneuvering fuel to keep in a clear area and maintain speed."

The commander nodded. "I will monitor the fuel with you. Will we have enough to get out once we do the retrieval?"

"Coming out will be a bats-out-of-hell ride if we make it,

so if our guest doesn't lose his lunch going in, he will lose it coming out."

Commander turned to Doc, "What do you think, can these fields be a problem?"

"They could be, if his ship is locked in a field, it may be moving erratically with the field, so it may be impossible to get in close enough to get him out. He may also have iron formulation in his helmet and suit so we may not be able to pull him out, depending on the strength of the field. With these high magnetic fields, we are in danger too. If we get caught in a strong magnetic field, it could kill us. We may be unable to process oxygen normally enough to keep us alive..."

The commander broke in, "How high is dangerous, Doctor?"

Doc turned and looked at his panel, "We are approaching him now, but we can only be at this high a level for a few minutes. We may not die but we will probably pass out if we are here longer. Josh is probably unconscious and has been for some time, but he is possibly still alive. You know we should probably increase the oxygen mix so we have more in our system before we start reacting to the loss of iron."

Commander was acting like they were close friends. "Good idea—Doc! Joel! Art! You read, take the oxygen up to max till we exit the field."

As he spoke, the ship jerked violently to the side and the few loose items flew across the tiny sled. Doc felt his stomach turning but managed to keep it down.

Joel yelled, 'We are in it now! You haven't ever been on a ride like this! Please fasten your seat belts and sign those liability waivers!"

That was the last anyone spoke for the next few minutes as the ship jerked and jabbed its way forward down the void with the maelstrom of white ice iron swirling around them. Joel, however, was making all kinds of strange yells and screams as he fought to guide the ship and fought the growing grip of the bands tearing at the sled's makeshift protective shield.

Joel burst out, "Commander! We are approaching the target, but we have a problem with our shield, it is fragmenting fast with impact and it appears to be attracted into the fields around us. It is starting to rupture!"

Doc said, "This ice is probably loaded with iron particles; see the rusty tinge when some light hits it."

Commander said, "I see, can we lock onto the target?"

Joel shook his head in denial. "No, I'm going to sideswipe it in a second. I can't use the arms, there is too much going on. If we drop the shield, we'll get pummeled to pieces almost immediately!"

Art said, "I can slip out and attach the tow line." As he spoke, he pushed up on the latch above him and stood, his safety line already hooked in.

Doc checked his screen. "No, we have to pull him out of the racer, look at its movements, it's locked into the field. We could never pull the racer out. It must be loaded with steel."

They were zooming up on the small racing bike fast.

Joel shouted in the comm, "We need to do something now, we're here!"

He continued to maneuver the sled into the side of the bike, then slammed on the forward thrusters to stop dead even with the racer.

The sled's occupants jerked forward with the abrupt stop.

Without a word, Art was out the hatch and from the top of the sled hooked a line onto the rear of the bike. His own safety tether was already hooked to his suit as it had been for the whole trip. As Art tightened up the line to draw the sled in tight to the racer, they moved into the dim red glow of the dwarf star and the molten planet below. They crossed the planet's terminator, casting both ships in a pernicious glow.

Watching the monitors, Doc saw the glow of the red molten planet below, lighting up the swirling arms of the magnetic spirals emanating out, trapping the iron-laden ice in the reddish hellish maelstrom.

Art said, "Ok, I will pull him out," as he moved a little forward to the side of the racer.

Doc could see on the monitor that the racer had some damage from impact but was still intact.

There was no view of Josh or the interior of the racer.

Watching on his monitor, Doc cautioned Art, "Be careful!"

Doc switched the view to Art's helmet view and saw Art's hand reaching down toward the pin that held the hatch on the bike in place. He could see the chip assemblies arranged over the hatch in the same geometric design Ron had set up on their own sled. He also saw the glow of the swirling maelstrom reflecting off the framing to which the chips were attached. He thought the image was similar to something he had seen before. But as the shout to stop came out of his mouth it was already too late. Art's hand had already reached the latch and a large flash erupted.

Art was thrown back with a cry of intense pain coming over the comm. His body was thrown toward the back of the sled. Instantly his safety line ripped taut and he slammed into the sled's side. He stopped right at the edge of the rear maneuvering engines that were at full throttle, keeping the sled pinned against the racer.

Doc turned to the commander to ask what they should do but all he saw was the commander's leg as he had already pushed out of the seat and was exiting the sled. Doc watched on his monitor through the link in the commander's helmet and on the multiple sled screens as the commander attached an additional safety line onto where Art's was attached and anchored himself in the hatch. He reached back toward the thruster, clutched Art's line and started pulling him.

The commander, sounded winded. "Joel, what's the status?"

"He had a few rips, but they have sealed, he may have lost some fingers. Right now, he appears to be unconscious."

By the time Joel stopped, the commander had pulled Art back up to the hatch. Holding him by the safety line hook on his suit he stepped over to his hatch and shoved Art headfirst down into his own seat. Doc reached across the opening and helped pull Art down into the seat.

Commander said, "Ok Doc, strap him in tight; I will be right back."

Joel shouted, "Commander, what are you doing? We need to get out of here! The ship is getting pounded! We are going to be trapped in here. We're using too much fuel, we are on "Eat It!""

Doc said, "Commander, you can't get to Josh, the chips appear to be still active at some level; that energy field will burn you just like it did Art."

Commander's face was grim. "We'll see. Joel, you hold it till I say so; now stop the jabbering." As he spoke, he moved back across the ship to Josh's bike. He pulled on the line Art had used to latch their sled to Josh's racer.

Sensing that the commander may need help, Doc took these moments to pull Art's unconscious body through the opening between their seats and belt him down in his own seat. He then squeezed through to the commander's seat and hooked his safety line onto the sled before standing up through the hatch. He was immediately hit with the immensity of the swirling maelstrom outside the ship. He focused on the commander, who was standing at the edge of the ship and reaching toward the racer.

Doc said, "Commander, you may be able to go in from the back, away from the chips field."

Commander turned toward Doc who stood in the open hatch, "No, I already checked, that would take hours," the Commander paused, got down on his knees, then adjusted his safety line. He snapped another line down from his suit to a hook ring below him on the sled. He synced it to hold him down tight onto the sled as it jerked around in the maelstrom.

"Joel, give me a couple seconds here," said the commander. If it doesn't work and things go bad, take Art and Doc and get back," pausing again he turned toward Doc, "You were right, we have met before." He paused again. "Ah, Thomas," the commander's voice was cracking, "I just want you to know that I could not be prouder of you and I know your Mom is too."

With that the Commander cut his comm.

Doc said, "What? What do you mean? Are you talking to me?"

Doc started to move out of the hatch even though he had no idea of what he was going to do or why. He just knew he had to get out over to the commander.

What he saw next happened in seconds. The commander reached toward the bike's hatch. As his hands touched the side of the racer the energy field flashed again. However, the commander took the full brunt of the force. Doc could see the man's arms and hands shred away in an instant. Doc scrambled out of the hatch, knowing he would need to retrieve him. Doc ended up face down on the top of the sled. When he raised his head, he saw the commander was still anchored to the sled and the panel on Josh's racer was in pieces. He saw the Commander reaching in towards Josh's motionless body. Doc gasped as he saw the commander's arms and hands were still intact. The arms of the suit were gone and there was no flesh on the arms—only shards and pieces of burnt space suit singed onto prosthetic metallic arms and a large burn area on the front of the commander's suit.

Doc saw those arms knock out the panel and then reach through the opening to unsnap the latch. A second later he was bent down into the bike, unbuckling Josh from his seat. The commander unhooked one of the lines from himself and hooked it onto Josh's suit as he pulled him out.

Joel came on. "Commander, you need patches! Your suit has lost too much pressure!"

Doc was right behind the commander now and reached out for one of Josh's hands. The commander, seeing Doc, let loose of Josh and then slumped over, still fastened to the top of the sled. Doc turned quickly to pull Josh over to the sled's hatch. As he moved the short distance to the hatch, he hooked a short snap line onto Josh and released the one the commander had attached. When he got to the hatch, he snapped Josh down to a handhold just outside the hatch. He then turned back to help the commander who had not moved.

Doc stepped over to him and peered through his helmet. He could see the inside of the helmet had frozen over. It meant that there was probably severe pressure loss in his suit. Doc hooked another safety line to where the commander had his and pulled himself down tight beside him.

Joel called out, "Commander, Doc, what's going on?"

Doc then reached over and released the line holding the sled to Josh's racer. The sled jerked away violently sending Doc's face into the sled.

Doc barely heard Joel scream into the comm, "It's breaking up--duck!" but it was too late. A large chunk of the ice shield collapsed and struck the commander full on against the helmet, buckling him over backwards against the sled.

As the pieces of the shield disintegrated, they pelted all three of the men. Doc yelled into the comm, "Get us out of here!" He could feel and see his suit getting pelted with thousands of ice particles. His alarm went off instantly with multiple breaches.

Wasting no time, Joel flipped the sled over and accelerated out of the finger band of the maelstrom that had closed in around them. The motion banged Doc and the commander brutally against the sled again. Doc felt lightheaded and he started to see frost on the inside of his visor. Extreme cold gripped his leg.

Doc thought he would pass out, but he fought it and the continued violent movement of the sled helped. Doc felt his suit tighten up, squeezing around his leg as well as a blast of heat hitting his face from the suit's environmental system. Still bouncing on the sled's frame, he reached out and grabbed a handhold. He pulled himself around on the sled to glimpse the commander. He was still sitting in the same position. Doc looked over to see Josh still attached beside the hatch. There was no sign of movement from either.

He was now aware of Joel on the comm, "Commander,

Doc respond! Commander, what is your status? Doc, are you there? I have no visuals on you!"

Doc called hoarsely, "Joel, we're still here, but our suits have suffered heavy damage. Can you assist?"

Joel said, "Negative on that, at least for a couple minutes till we clear the debris and magnetic fields. We are low on fuel and I want to get out of here. Give me a few!"

Doc reached for his repair kit and ripped off the patch material as it pushed out and he slapped it on every hole he could see. His suit monitor was flashing the location of the tears onto his visuals. In seconds his suit's environment had stabilized. However, Doc's left arm was in agony and he believed it was broken.

Doc pulled himself back up to the commander with his right arm. He began slapping patches onto the holes in his suit. He switched his visual to the commander's suit status by command and located a few more holes. At this point the man's visor had completely frozen over, but Doc could see that there was still positive pressure in the suit and figured that would have to do. He switched the status back to his suit and ordered the left arm to stiffen for the broken arm protocol that was programed into the suit. When prompted, he affirmed the injection of a pain killer.

The sled had stopped jerking around as it moved out through the thinning cloud of ice particles surrounding the planet. Smaller particles were still hitting Doc's suit but the fabric was holding up.

Still in pain, Doc used his right hand to snap a safety line onto the commander and released the ones that had held him down to the sled. As he released them, they would retract back into the suit. At this point the ship burst out of the end of the icy maelstrom encircling the planet. Doc held the commander by the line and made his way back to the hatch where Josh was tied down. As he got there, a head popped out of the hatch. It was Art. He looked up at Doc and pointed to the side of his helmet, indicating he had no comms. He quickly examined Josh's suit and started slapping patches on the holes. In moments he turned to Doc and signaled him to hold up. Art hooked onto Josh's suit and released him from the handhold. In seconds, Art had pulled Josh down into the sled.

"We are out," Joel said. "I will be up in a sec."

Doc said, "Joel, Art is up, we got it. Keep going!"

Inside the sled, Joel turned in his seat to see Art working on strapping Josh into Doc's old seat. When he saw Joel looking at him, he gave him the thumbs up and indicated his comm was dead.

Joel nodded. "Well, that's great. At least he's back from the dead. I may get what he owes me after all."

As he spoke Art stood up in the hatch again and reached up with a safety line for Doc. Doc took the line and hooked it onto the commander's suit and unsnapped his from the commander. He then maneuvered the commander within Art's reach who pulled him down into the compartment. Doc waited a moment, then moved to peer down into the hatch to see when he could enter the ship. He saw Art strapping the commander along the side of the small compartment. Art then removed the suit controls cover and snapped in a cable that directly tied the suit to the sled's medical systems and he spent a few seconds watching the control panel. Doc figured he was monitoring the commander's vitals and suit performance. Doc switched to that view and saw that the commander was still alive but suffering with the bends from the decompression of his suit. Art had entered the status gauges to give the A.I. a heads up on treatment. So, it was now up to his suit holding up to the increased pressure and getting back to the closest solar system hospital for both the commander and Josh.

Doc realized he needed to check on Josh's status also. Art looked up at him just then and signaled him to go into the hatch where the co-pilot seat was. Giving a thumbs up, Doc turned around to find the hatch. It had slammed shut in all the activity on the sled's exterior. Doc moved over and pulled open the hatch and stepped down in with his feet on the seat. He turned back toward the other hatch just in time to see it pulled down by Art. Still in the open hatch, Doc checked Josh's vitals on his helmet visuals. Doc could see that Josh was still alive, but in a severely weakened and dehydrated condition. Doc also saw Josh was hooked into the ship's medical bay and should recover in time. Smiling a little in relief, Doc turned in the open hatch toward the rear of the ship to get a final view of the planet they were leaving. He leaned back on the front of the opening and just stared in wonder at the sights he was witnessing. Doc took in the full scene over the glow of the fully throttled main engine backdropped by three Trappist planets spinning in space in front of the glowing Red Dwarf star.

He became aware of someone tugging on his suit from below, it was Joel. "Come on, Doc! Just take a picture will ya."

Doc said, "Sorry, I just..." as he sat down in the seat and pulled down the hatch. He looked over at Joel.

Joel said, "You just wanted a moment to take it all in, huh? Yeah, you 'll have many moments, Doc. You're still a young man. Look at the old man back there. He's seen plenty. You know he's one of the ancients around here now. Yeah, he's been here from the beginning."

Remembering the two injured men in the back, Doc turned to check out the compartments behind him.

He saw Art working on Josh, wrapping him in some type of material that sealed itself as he moved up his body. Art did not stop at his head but continued up over the head until he was completely enclosed as in a cocoon.

Art then slapped a control box onto the cocoon over one of Josh's arms. The box appeared to penetrate the cocoon Art had formed around Josh, and he then pulled a sort of umbilical cord out of the side of the compartment and plugged it into the box.

He then did the same to the commander, slipping through the small opening between the two compartments. When he was finished, he strapped the commander securely to the side of the cabin. He then moved back over to where Josh was and strapped Josh in also, but more to the upper part of the cabin wall. This provided more room for Art. Art then sat down in the seat, seated a little sideways with Josh's body barely touching his helmet.

Seeing Doc watching him, Art pulled a line out of a front panel and plugged it into his helmet. This restored his comm, so he filled Doc in on what he'd done, "Both suits were too badly damaged and would continue to lose pressure. The wrap will keep their atmospheres up and will help stabilize them. They should both make it, if we get back in time."

Joel said, "Well, we can make it back a lot faster--I mean if that guy made it out here in a couple of hours, we should be able to get back pronto just by running the track backwards. So, give the word."

As he finished, the view on the monitors shifted to the blackness of space. Joel had made the move to take the Swift back to where they entered the system.

Doc grabbed his seat for a second, then turned to Joel, "Can you warn me before you do that next time?" Joel smiled over at Doc.

"Maybe?" Doc just shook his head.

Joel turned to Art, "Ok, Art, what do you say, it's the same as back home; each stop and adjustment we made coming here we will take on the way back. If the program hits a problem the sled will stop."

Art said, "Did you get a chance to check it out with diagnostics before we left?"

"It checked out," said Joel, "the Swift went right through it with a sim run."

Art said, "What do you think, Doc? You know more about what is going on with this propulsion system than we do. We could get these guys into Mars a lot faster than we took to get here."

Doc turned to look at Art, and then turned back to his visuals. He called up his tablet and dropped it down onto the monitor in front of him.

Doc continued, "Joel, are we exactly where we came into the system?"

"Yeah, I think so. I used the A.I. to bring us back, by the way."

Doc said, "OK, listen, we've been here for a few seconds now. Do a status and see if you have an exact match with our arrival spot."

As Doc watched the monitor, the info popped up.

"Yeah, Doc," Joel said, "it looks like a match."

Doc studied the data info on the monitor and agreed. He then reached out and extended the decimal out to thirty points and ran a comparison.

Doc said, "Do you see the problem, Joel, Art?"

Joel said, "No, Doc, we don't have to worry about that, extending it out that far never affects us."

"It may not matter when you are just tooling around in our little solar system," said Doc, "but when you are talking about trillions of miles, we could completely miss our little system and have to try and locate it by backtracking."

"Let me see the miles' A.I. input. I need to adjust its decision methodology a bit." The screen popped up and Joel had already loaded in his security protocols.

Joel said, "Here you go, what are you going to do?"

Doc said, "Nothing complicated." He paused "What language is this?"

Joel said, "Oh, I don't know, it just came out from that lab on Mars about six months ago, but it works great and is easy."

"Oh, yeah! Recognizing some patterns, very intuitive--this shouldn't take long."

Looking over at Joel, Doc said, "In the meantime, make sure we are in the exact entry location, give complete control to the A.I. if you have to."

He added, "I'm just adding a few changes, standard deviations and an extension of the standard decimal places out to 100."

Joel said, "That will slow us down."

"Well, we're still in a race with time; also take a sec and review my changes to the program. Art, do you know this language?"

"Yes," he said, "it has been adopted very quickly throughout the system."

Doc said, "Fine, then you can look it over too."

It only took a few seconds for the review and Joel made a slight change that they all reviewed before closing out the A.I. instruction on the program.

Joel said, "OK, are we all ready now, Art, Doc?"

"Just a quick question," said Doc. "Is Josh's bike still sending a signal?"

Joel did a check, "No, I got nothing. Is that a problem?"

"Ok, if it's alright with you guys, I would suggest we go back to the solar system a quarter of the way and check ourselves with the existing signal, and at a spot where we stopped on the way out—just to check our progress."

Joel said, "OK, pick a spot, Doc." Joel sent the screen over to Doc and Art's monitors with certain stops highlighted.

"Any of those will generally be at an eight-hour mark."

Doc said, "Okay, but no more racing please. The Swift can be a turtle, only at FTL, OK?"

Joel said, "Ok, but it will be a race with the signal."

Doc picked a spot and ID'd it on the monitor.

"Ok, Doc? Art? We are locked into position and go on five, four, three..."

But Joel didn't get to one before he engaged the drive, and Doc looked over at him giving a sarcastic "Ha, Ha."

The trip back was less tense than when they'd been just engaging PS for a second or minutes at a time, and all members of the crew had a chance to relax and take a breath after the prior exhausting days.

When the drive stopped, Joel was on the navigation and spotting the signal immediately. In a matter of seconds, he sent a status to Doc and Art.

"What do you think, guys; it looks good to me. That was eight hours, can we go for another eight? It will get us just outside the orbit cloud. Could it be too close?"

Doc said, "Are we lined up with the signal?"

"Well, the signal is coming from directly behind us, but I think the final move into the system for Mars is going to be the most important."

Doc interjected, "Are we in the exact point we stopped on the way out?"

"No, but the A.I. is moving us in," said Joel. "It was less than a few kilometers, see it?"

"OK, yes, close enough for light years." He turned to Art, "I'm sure we can go to just outside the Oort cloud to the spot that Joel has laid in."

Doc turned toward Joel, "Eight more hours, Right, Joel?"

"Yes, ready, I like this little ship you made, Doc. Next trip, I'm going for my own planet with the wife and kids."

"You're married?"

"Yes of course, a couple times."

Art interrupted, "Joel, I think we're ready, go when ready."

Joel nodded. "Oui, oui, Capitaine." A few seconds later it was a fast "three two one" with no pauses and the Swift was on its way.

After a few minutes in propulsion, Doc turned to ask Art the question that had bothered him since the Commander went to rescue Josh from his bike.

"Hey Art, do you know the commander very well?"

"I guess so, I've known him for as long as I can remember. Why?"

"Well, when he went out to rescue Josh, he said something odd on the comm, and I got the feeling he was talking to me, but I had no idea what he was talking about."

"What did he say?

Joel cut in, "Art, can you check that med on Josh, something seems loose."

Art said, "Yeah, Joel, it's good, do a diagnostic on the med system, but his vitals are good."

Doc said, "Anyway, let me know when you get a chance. I'd like to know more about the Commander. "

Art said, "I'm good, what was it he said?"

"Well, it sounded like he was talking to me and he was proud of me and that my mom would be proud of me, and I think he called me Thomas for some reason. Do you know what he might have been talking about?"

Doc continued, "He didn't act like it out on top, but you think he may have become disoriented somehow with the PS travel?"

"Doc," said Art, "I was kind of unconscious at the time. I didn't catch what he said."

"Yeah, but you know him? Do you know if he knew my mother back when they built the Moon base?"

"Well, it sure is possible, but I don't know for sure. You should ask him after he recovers."

"Ok, but you say..." and then he stopped. He did not want to put Art on the spot. Doc realized that Art was probably just a kid also back when his mom died and maybe even knew her--or himself when he was a kid. Doc thought these were questions that could wait, no reason to bring it up now.

But Doc couldn't drop it, and he began running over memories he had from his youth. He began to realize how much he did not remember about his time on the Moon. He did remember how his granddad had him change his name to Murphy. What was it before that? Did he also change his first name? Why did his granddad get upset when Doc asked questions about the Moon and his mom and dad? He was forbidden to talk about it.

The ship stopped outside the Oort cloud as planned, and the A.I. confirmed that they were in fact looking at the Earth's solar system. So, they progressed quickly on the return using the PS. They planned to enter the inner solar system at the orbit of Neptune. They figured it was a good spot since Neptune had already passed and it would not be back in the area for another 187 years. Lining up again only took minutes and then shortly they were back in the solar system and making short steps to Mars.

CHAPTER 11

D oc was visiting Josh in the hospital. All of Josh's family and his were crammed into the small hospital room below Tharsis base on Mars. Josh was recovering but was asleep most of the time. He was asleep now as the families updated each other on recent events.

Doc said, "I'll be right back, Claire, I want to run down the hall and check on the commander. I understand he is still in rough shape."

Claire nodded. "Ok, I don't know how much longer we'll be here. They want us all at orientation class in about an hour."

"OK, maybe I'll just see you at home then; they're setting me up at the center and I need to be updated on the systems they use here. They want to set up a station just outside the Oort cloud with one of the newer telescopes to locate systems with Earth-like planets. Isn't that great!"

Claire said, "I don't know whether to call you Doc or master. You know, everyone I meet seems to know who I'm married to; everyone is always smiling at us. I now know what it's like to be married to a superstar. By the way, do you get the feeling there's some secret here that no one will tell us?"

Doc nodded. "Yes, I feel that too, I think it has something to do with me when I was at the original Moon base as a kid and with my mom. I believe there is a statue or memorial to her on the Moon, and I've been doing some research on the Space Agency's history. The problem is they still treat everything as 'top secret' and my clearances are just for the Research Center." He gave Claire a hug and kiss, "Anyhow, got to get going, Bye."

Claire said, "Bye, I'm glad we are here, though. It just feels more comfortable and safer compared to Earth."

"Yeah, I know," said Doc. "I don't have to be looking over my shoulder constantly, anyhow. Bye kids, make sure you do well and pay attention at the orientation." They replied "Bye, Dad," without lifting their heads, thoroughly engaged with their comms.

When he got to the commander's hospital room, he stopped at the window where the status was displayed on the glass. The commander's room was different than Josh's because apparently the commander had a big fol-lowing here in space away from Earth. Doc had mentioned that neither he nor anyone on Earth had ever heard of him. When he talked about this, Doc would get responses like, "That's not surprising" or "Oh, really?" but no explanations or detail. When he tried to inquire of the people around him about the man, they would give him a pleasant brush off. He tried looking up the commander on the space agency system but just found the general net but no information would come up.

After seeing there was no change in the commander's status, he noticed there was someone off to the side in the commander's room. He watched as she came over and sat down beside his bed. Doc recognized her. A second later the window went blank. Doc stepped back a little, then turned and walked around the corner to find the room's door. He saw Todd standing there almost like a guard and went over to talk to him. Doc was happy to see a familiar face. He had not seen Todd since he and the others left on the rescue mission.

Doc saw Todd turn toward him and Doc thought he saw a look of concern appear on Todd's face.

Getting closer, Doc said, "Hey Todd, good to see you. What are you doing out here on Mars? I thought your area was closer to the Earth and the Moon."

Todd nodded. "Hello, Doctor Murphy, I'm glad to see you well."

"Have you been assigned to guard the commander?"

"Can't answer that, Doctor, sorry."

"Of course, say, I see Hope is in there with the commander, is she on the mission with you?"

Todd looked at Doc and paused. Doc knew he was checking his comm system and security before he answered.

Todd said, "Doctor, I'm cleared to tell you that the captain is on a personal visit to the commander as am I."

"Personal, that's great--so you are related to the commander. Your dad didn't mention it; perhaps you can fill me in on him a little? Is he married to an aunt or something?"

Doc thought a second when Todd didn't respond and added, "Is it a great aunt, maybe your granddad's sister?"

Doc started to enjoy himself because it was the first time he'd seen any type of expression on Todd's face and Doc knew he was squirming to answer Doc's questions as briefly as possible.

Todd spoke slowly. "Well, I really can't, Doctor." A worried look appeared on his face which Doc picked up on. Even though Doc had only met Todd a few times, he'd never seen any emotional changes in his facial expressions. Doc thought this was new and that maybe Todd was more relaxed here on Mars and off duty. Maybe it would be a good time to get some of Doc's questions answered.

Just then the door opened and Hope stuck her head out and spoke to Doc smiling, "Oh, hello Doc, good to see you. I understand you guys had quite the adventure."

"Well hello, Hope, it's good to see you too. Yes the commander saved the day out there. He saved Josh's life and also saved Todd's dad all at the same time."

Hope said, "Well, I heard that it was you who was quite the hero of the mission."

Doc said, "Whaaat? No, no I was just along for the ride you know." Doc saw a chance to change the subject, "Hey, so you get to see the commander; are you his family, his granddaughter?"

Hope peered over at Todd who was looking like he got caught at something and didn't want to be there.

Hope said, "Todd, you can go into the room if you like while I talk to Doc."

"Sounds good to me" and Todd slipped past Hope into the room.

Hope moved out into the hallway a little and let the door close. She reached into her pocket, pulled out her comm and began inputting some info, then placed her finger on it.

Hope placed the comm back in her pocket and smiled up at Doc, "There, now we can talk in private at least for a little while."

Doc said, "Oh, good, so you're the commander's granddaughter."

"No, actually he is my dad, and I have you to thank for bringing him back to me."

Doc looked a little embarrassed, "Well, not really--anyhow, changing the subject, "I have you to thank for rescuing mine and Josh's families from the FBI and the Chinese."

"You're welcome, it was very important to me and the commander that we get you all out safe."

"I'm glad that you did. Say, it may not be a good time, but can you give me any info on the commander. He said some things to me immediately before he was injured and I'm trying to follow up by doing some research, but everything seems to be locked down to me."

Hope nodded. "Well, you'll be able to ask Dad yourself in a couple weeks so just sit tight. I am sure he had his reasons; he is a very deliberate type of person."

"OK, so does the commander have any other kids running around that I can hit up with questions?"

"You know what, I have an older brother, but I can tell you now that he won't have a clue what you're talking about."

Doc said, "Oh, is he on Mars?"

With the biggest smile on her face, Hope said, "As a matter of fact he is."

At that moment her comm started buzzing loudly, and she quickly reached down and looked at it.

"Got to go, Doc. We're just out here for a quick visit and need to head right back to the Moon, so I'll see you around, I'm sure."

Doc said, "You mean you aren't stationed here? How did you get here so fast?"

"No, we're not stationed here; Joel came and got us in the Swift."

"The Swift, I would think that it would be in for repairs."

"Well, Joel is not the type to ask for permission; he spent more time on the Moon getting permission to come back than in transit!"

Doc nodded, "Yeah, I got that impression real fast,"

"So we'll see you soon, stay safe." Then to Doc's surprise, she stepped forward and gave him a hug.

Doc hesitated a second then hugged her back.

Stepping back as her comm continued to buzz, she said, "I am just so happy, you are all safe and here with us."

It looked to Doc like Hope reached up and wiped an eye as she turned and went back into the room.

Doc quickly refocused on his search and blurted out, "Hope, what is your last name?"

But it was too late, the door to the room had closed.

Doc continued to research the agency web over the next few days, searching for any information on the commander. He now included the commander's daughter, Hope, in the search. In fact, Doc included everyone he had met in the search since the meeting in his director's office when the Space Agency purchased the chips. All with no luck.

Doc did not see Hope or Todd the following week at the commander's room and the window remained blacked out.

His family had finished with the orientation classes and had settled into a condo with a great view of the Valles Marineris as their new home. The boys were starting back to school this day and Claire had a few interviews for different positions she was interested in. Doc was spending his days in the lab organizing it for the future.

Josh had agreed to work with Doc in the Space Agency Research lab on Mars. They planned to set up and improve a production facility to manufacture the tachyon chips and accelerators there.

Ron was also on his way out from the Moon to Mars to join his department. Ron was coming by regular transport and would be there in a few weeks along with all the remaining parts and equipment from Doc's old department on Earth. However, Ron was due for some medical treatment upon his arrival and so would be laid up for a few weeks afterwards.

Doc received word from Art that the Swift would also

arrive about the same time as Ron. It had been disassembled and the parts crated up and placed in an Agency ship transport hold. Apparently, after Hope and Todd were dropped off by Joel on Mars, he tried to take the ship back to the Asteroid Belt with him and the agency had to disable the Swift to stop him. The report did not say how the sled was disabled, but there was damage to the Swift's array and Joel is in the medical bay on board the ship. The Agency was still weighing whether to charge him or not. Art told Doc that Joel is quite the celebrity in the system for some of his exploits and run-ins with the Agency. Doc checked him out on the net and was amazed Joel was not in space prison permanently. When Doc asked Art about it, Art responded that Joel was too valuable to waste in a prison and that the Agency didn't really have a prison anyway.

Now, after spending a few hours in the lab that morning, Doc made his way to the cafeteria on his department's lab floor. He was enjoying a cup of coffee when he noticed furniture and stacked moving containers being moved down the hall outside the cafeteria's entrance toward his department.

Thinking it was something being delivered to his lab, Doc took a last sip of coffee and headed down the hall after the movers.

The delivery did not go to his lab, but stopped at an empty suite of rooms next to it. The crew continued on with the material in through the big double doors of the large suite.

Curious, Doc followed the crew in through a large reception area and into a large office space. There they stopped and started unloading the crates and stacking the contents. As he walked into the main office, Doc noticed that another crew was working on installing a heavy set of security doors at the entrance.

A young man in a Space Agency uniform, appeared to be in charge. He seemed to be about the same age as his son, Matt. Doc made his way over to him.

Still not familiar with military rank insignia, Doc questioned the young man, "Hello, is the material for the lab, Mister? Ah," Doc bent down at his name tag, "Mr. Nigle?"

The young man responded, "Sir, it is Lieutenant Nigle, and no sir this is for the commander's office. His Command will move here while he recovers from his injuries."

"Oh, that's good, I'm glad to see he's starting to get around. When will he be starting? Do you know?"

The lieutenant stopped what he was doing and looked at Doc; he then looked down at Doc's ID and security clearance.

Lieutenant Nigle said, "Oh, Doctor Murphy, It's a pleasure to meet you. You were with the commander on the Mission. Thank you for saving his life; the whole Space Agency is in your debt."

"Thank you, but it wasn't like that at all." Changing the subject, Doc said, "Say, you guys need any help? I've got some time until my own equipment gets down here."

The lieutenant said, "No, but thank you for the offer. We are in good shape here. We've already brought everything down. All we have to do now is to get the awards and plaques up on the walls, then set up all the comm electronics."

"Awards? You know back on Earth, no one has even heard of the commander."

"Yes sir, I have heard that, I'm sure glad we don't live there."

Doc said, "What kind of awards does he have?"

In a proud voice, the lieutenant said, "Well sir! He has about every medal and award ever invented in the Space Agency."

"Do you mind if I take a look?"

"Sir, no problem, just don't touch anything labeled with the Big Blue tape and stamped Security Protocol one. Okay? Otherwise, you would probably spend the rest of the day in the brig!"

"Gotcha, no big blue tape boxes; I assure you I won't."

"That's Ok, doctor, we don't have any of those materials on this load anyhow. Here, let me look." The lieutenant glanced down at his comm. "The awards are over there, those top three containers marked 'wall.' You can use the conference table if you like? We already have it in the right location. "

"Thanks, lieutenant, I appreciate it."

Doc made his way over to the containers and picked up the first; it was made out of some lite composite material and the lid was held on with two side latches.

Doc started through the multiple plaques. As he pulled them out one at a time, he would read them and place them in order on the conference table. He was actually kind of amazed, for it seemed that the commander was more of a scientist than a military commander. Doc was struck by the fact that all the plaques and awards he was looking at just named him commander. The Commander's surname was not on any of the awards.

He continued on through the second box with the awards going back more than thirty years. When he got to the third container, he had to stop for a second. Halfway down through the plaques he found an old one with a name on it: "Alexander Kijek"

Doc paused, that name was triggering something, something he had forgotten or been made to forget. Childhood memories flooded into his mind of his grandfather talking to him and explaining that his mom and dad had died. His grandfather would repeatedly remind him that it was all his dad's fault and that his dad was a criminal. He could not remember what had happened, but he knew it happened on the Moon and that he had once lived on the Moon. He remembered as a child that he could not accept what his grandfather was telling him and when he would protest the old man would get so enraged, he would send him away. Doc remembered this now and he was curious as to why that name had triggered these old memories. As he placed the plaque down, he reached in for the next, but instead of a plaque he pulled out a thin object. It was an old drawing on construction paper made by a child and it was sealed in a type of plexiglass with a frame. Doc's hands started to shake and his chest tightened as tears ran down his face. He found it hard to examine the drawing but he knew he didn't have to. Doc was overcome with memories from long ago, when he was but a child of five and being held in his dad's arms. A memory when he presented his dad with the medal he and his mom had made together.

"My Dad Best Hero Ever, Love Tommy"

The emotion was too much for Doc at that point, the memory returning so unexpectedly—the long-buried memory of the last time he had seen his mom and dad. Doc covered his eyes with his hands as he laid his head down on the conference table. The question of why he felt he knew the commander was answered. He should remember his own dad.

After a few moments, he realized the room had gone quiet. He was hoping it was because all the personnel had left. He took a moment, still with his head down, to wipe his eyes and face. Doc slowly lifted his face off the table and used the sleeve of his shirt to wipe the remaining tears from his face.

When he looked across the room, he saw that indeed all the personnel had left the room, but there was still someone standing in the doorway.

Doc rose from his seat and placed the award back into the container. As he walked out from the table toward the door his eyes cleared and he recognized the person standing in the door.

It was Hope.

Doc stopped in front of her. She was standing with the tips of her fingers touching tensely and a slight look of fear on her face as to what would happen next.

Doc was still a little bleary eyed, "Are you my sister?"

Hope, looking up to Doc with eyes that were starting to water, said, "Yes, I am!"

Beginning to tear up, Doc reached out to Hope, "Well then, how about a hug, Sis."

Hope reached out to Doc with a long hug and her head against his shoulder, tears welling up without control and a broad smile on her face, "Oh, Tommy, I'm so happy! Welcome Home."

The End

CPSIA information can be obtained
at www.ICGtesting.com
Printed in the USA
LVHW011309230322
714164LV00003B/570